INTERLOPERS
A Shifters Novel

For Zuri,
Keep reading and never stop searching for new worlds.
Enjoy! L.M. Davis 2019

BY

L. M. DAVIS

A LYNDBERRY BOOK

Text copyright © 2009 by L. M. Davis

All rights reserved. Except as permitted under the U. S. Copyright Act of 1976, no part of this publication may be reproduced, distributed, or transmitted in any form or by any means, electronic, mechanical, photocopying, recording, or otherwise, or stored in a database or retrieval system, without the prior written permission of the publisher. For information regarding permissions, write to Lyndberry Press, Attention: Permissions Department, 736 N. Western Ave., Suite 249, Lake Forest, IL 60045.

First Edition: October 2010

The character and events portrayed in this book are fictitious. Any similarity to real persons, living or dead, is coincidental and not intended by the author.

Davis, L. M. 1978--
Interlopers: A Shifters Novel/ by L. M. Davis.--1st edition.

Summary: At almost 13, Nate Pantera has this whole shifter-in-a-world-full-of-humans thing all figured out. Move like a human: Check. Hide super strength and other powers: Check. Check. Do math homework: Um...Check? He's even gotten used to the idea that he and his family may be the only shape-shifters in the whole wide world. Then, finally, he meets another shifter. And that's when all the trouble begins.

Library of Congress Control Number: 2010909209

ISBN-13: 978-0-9827909-0-8

[1. Shape-shifters-Fiction. 2. Fantasy--Fiction 3. Middle Grades--Fiction. 4. Schools--Fiction. 5. Twins--Fiction.]

10 9 8 7 6 5 4

Printed in the United States of America

For NAS, who inspired me in the first place;

And for TMM, a great friend, who encouraged me every step of the way;

To LDJ, whose counsel during this process was valuable beyond measure;

And to all the family and friends, too numerous to name,

who have always supported me.

CONTENTS

Prologue 1

True Colors 3

Meet the Panteras 11

what happens at the bus stop... 21

P. E. 29

Graduation 39

Promises Made 49

And so it begins 51

Obstacle Elusions 57

The Breaking of PFL #4 69

Captive audience 73

Those carefree summer days 79

BREAKFAST WITH WINDY: PART I   89

BREAKFAST WITH WINDY: PART II   93

ENTER PANTERIA   99

THE KULA   109

THE ROOTS OF THE TREE   117

INTERLOPERS   127

DOMESTIC TRANQUILITY   137

SECRETS TOLD BY MIDNIGHTS   143

JUDGE, JURY, AND RAW MEAT   151

THE WORST KIND OF TRAITOR   167

SAVED BY A TAIL   179

THE PRICE OF WEALTH   185

Grrrll!! 193

Revelations 195

In the beginning 201

Disappointing News 211

Covert operations 215

Down the Hatch 221

Unexpected kin 227

What's wrong with this picture 233

Too little may be too late 247

Homecoming 251

Promises Kept 259

Epilogue 263

Prologue

"Show me the stones!" The command was impatient, almost angry. Even after thirty years, the brusque and gritty tone, somewhere between a growl and a rasp, still made his heart leap in his chest. It still compelled him in a way that he was helpless to explain or resist.

Hastily, the man opened the dark bag that he held and poured the stones onto the tray lined with plush black velvet. The green stones glittered and glinted even in the dim light of the room.

Silence followed the revelation, and the shuffling sounds of his boss's steps echoed through the small room. If the man noticed that the glow of the stones intensified as his boss stepped closer to the desk, his face betrayed nothing. Large and faceted, the stones suddenly seemed to give off light rather than reflect it.

The pair met eyes and smiled. Neither had been sure what would happen once the stones had been transported. The stones were even better than they had hoped for. The cache before them exceeded their wildest dreams. With their sparkle and luster, the gleaming, green gems would easily fetch a healthy sum on the black market. They were not emeralds. They were something so much more.

"This is exactly what we need to begin." The words were followed by a sigh filled with satisfaction and vague relief.

Everything was coming together just as they had planned for all of those years ago. These stones and the crops that would follow would make them wealthy beyond their imaginings. Even glancing around at the tattered curtains and the dank soiled hardwood floors of the room, there was only a sense of freedom. Just this batch of stones would be enough for them to finally bid this squalor goodbye forever.

That, however, was only part of the plan. Theirs was the business of building empires. Empires for both worlds. These stones would help them to resume their rightful place, and they would make sure that they would never lose it again.

"Accelerate the mining of the rough!" The command was still brusque, but now there was a purr of satisfaction beneath. The man turned to go. He stopped in his tracks when his boss spoke again. "And I think that it is time to initiate phase two."

Chapter 1

True Colors

Larissa Pantera stepped daintily down off of the bus, waving goodbye to the chestnut-haired girl she had just been talking to. She shifted her books in her arms and began to stride purposely towards home.

Seconds later, Nate Pantera bounded down the same stairs. Some strange and miraculous grace kept him on his feet even as he struggled with his overloaded book bag and the mp3 player he carried in his other hand. Just as he was about to turn back to the bus he heard it.

Turning around, he saw his best friend Eric leaping from the bottom stair of the bus towards him. Instinctively, he took a step to the side, moving out of Eric's trajectory. Then Nate watched, horrified, as Eric sailed forward and right toward a massive tree trunk. The impulsive boy was nearly horizontal in the air, and now that Nate had moved, there was nothing to stop his momentum. If someone didn't do something, and quick, his friend was going to get really hurt.

Without any further thought, Nate dropped his stuff and raced forward, reaching out to grab Eric around the waist. Wrapping his arms around his friend, he dug his heels into the ground, stopping the boy, who outweighed him by a good fifteen pounds, mid-flight. Ever aware of how strange his actions might look, he took a few unnecessary and stumbling steps, as though

Eric's weight was almost more than he could bear, before gingerly lowering the boy to the ground and setting him on his feet. All of this happened within the space of seconds.

"What are you? Some kind of superhero? How on earth did you do that?" Nate looked quickly over his shoulder to see his other best friend staring in shock and amazement at what had just happened.

Luckily, Ray was the only one staring. The school bus doors had closed, and the yellow vehicle was already chugging away down the street.

Nate met Ray's curious eyes for a moment. "Adrenaline, I guess," he replied, saying the first thing that came to his mind, before turning away. He closed his eyes and took several deep breaths, trying to clear his mind of the scolding voices that suddenly filled his head.

"You must always be careful." This was his father. Along with the warning, an image of his father promptly appeared, his gaze stern and his eyeglasses, which were really just for show, perched at the tip of his nose in typical lecturing fashion.

"No one can know." That voice belonged to his mother. Her voice was soft and vaguely urgent. Her image sprang to his mind even as his father's faded.

I couldn't help it, Nate thought, justifying his actions to the specters, as though his parents actually stood before him. Someone had to help Eric. Shaking his head, he pushed the images of his disappointed parents out of his mind, opened his eyes, and turned sheepishly back towards his friends.

Eric and Ray were still staring at him, and he knew they had been staring the whole time. Nate busied himself with collecting his belongings, which had scattered all over the ground, while studiously avoiding the curious stares of the two boys. When he had picked everything up, he looked again at his friends. The boys now stood together eyeing him with dual suspicion. He was silent for a moment as he tried to figure out how to set their suspicions at ease. Then, like always, Larissa saved him.

"Nate, would you hurry up already!" Nate looked towards his sister, who was already half way down the street. She stood staring at the three of them, her hand on her hip, the picture of impatience. Saved by the glare. He turned back to his friends, giving them a quick wave. "Later!"

The two boys, disbelief still marking their features, waved goodbye to Nate as he broke away from their little pack to turn down the street that led to his house. Nate adjusted his book bag, slinging it over the right shoulder to give his left shoulder a break. There were just a few weeks left of school, which meant more and more homework, more and more studying for finals, and, of course, more and more books. After that, though, was graduation and then, next fall, high school. Nate smothered a groan. He could only begin to imagine how much homework he would have then.

Up ahead of him, Larissa was already disappearing around the bend in the road, moving far more quickly than he did. Of course, she hardly had any books. She never did. But then, why would she? She never needed to study. It was like she remembered everything the first time she read it. That talent came in handy around this time of year.

Nate walked up the street slowly, enjoying the feel of the warm sun on his head and the cool breeze on his face. Spring had to be his favorite time of year. And days like this, when the sun was shining and the sky was this particular shade of blue, were his most favorite of all. He walked slowly, lingering in the dappled sunlight. The lapse of just a few moments ago was all but forgotten already. He couldn't help the hum of satisfaction that escaped him as he strolled down the street. Ahead, Larissa had disappeared from sight, and he knew that within a few minutes she would be at their front door. For a moment, he considered running to catch up with her, but then he shrugged his shoulders. She could wait on the porch if Mom wasn't home.

Once he rounded the bend, he quickened his pace and covered the tree-lined quarter-mile up the hill in impossibly short time. As he reached the top of the hill, the house came into view. It was the only house on the street, resting at the farthest point of the cul-de-sac. His parents had built the house from the ground up almost fifteen years ago.

Their home, which looked like something straight out of an old-fashioned movie, was two-stories with a basement, lots of little nooks, and a big, wide porch. The foundation was made of bricks and the top was yellow painted wood. The entire structure was all but surrounded by trees and the next nearest house had to be more than a mile away. His friends told him that the house was creepy but, for Nate, the feel of sunlight filtered through the leaves of the towering trees was calming and reassuring.

At the driveway, he deliberately slowed his pace again, almost sauntering up the stone path that led to the front door. Larissa sat on the front steps, tapping her foot with impatience. "I don't know why they gave you the key." She hissed, narrowing her eyes at him as he passed by. Curious emerald green eyes, that had unexpected flecks of yellow to them. Cat eyes, their friends called them.

Nate and Larissa had the same eyes. In fact, everything about them was the same. Same curly blue black hair, though Larissa wore hers in spiraling curls down to her shoulders and Nate wore his cut close to his head. Same coppery brown skin, against which their bright green eyes stood out startling and unexpected. Identical faces, with wide set eyes, broad, high cheek bones, round noses, and narrow but stubborn chins. They even had the same oddly shaped birthmark, four little circles grouped in a shape almost like a cat's paw, though weirdly Larissa's was on her right shoulder and his was on his left.

The only other difference besides the hair was their height. At that moment, Larissa was taller than he. Just by an inch or so, because she had had a growth spurt last fall and his had not happened yet. Another little triumph that she loved to crow about.

Nate took his time locating his key, grinning as he heard his sister expel an exasperated sigh. He took such pleasure in tormenting her and, sometimes, she was just so easy to torment.

"Miko is supposed to call me at 3:30," Larissa said, looking pointedly at her watch. "I can hear the phone ringing right now."

Nate tipped his head to the side and listened. He heard it then too. The faint, yet shrill ring coming from Larissa's room on the other side of the house. Relenting, he pulled the key from his bag and unlocked the front door.

Pushing the door open, he stepped into the cool, dark front hall. As he tossed his book-bag on the floor, Larissa rushed by him, flinging a huff in his general direction before climbing the stairs to race for the phone. Smiling slightly, he turned toward the kitchen to find a snack to quiet the sudden rumble in his stomach.

Jeez, he thought as he strolled through the dining room, *is it that serious?*

"Yes. It is that serious," Larissa's voice called down from upstairs and he chuckled. He would never understand his sister and her friends. They had just left each other and already they were so anxious to be back on the phone.

In the kitchen, Nate opened cabinet after cabinet until he found the bag of cheese puffs that he was craving. Opening the bag, he pulled out a handful of puffs and stuffed them in his mouth before going to the refrigerator and pulling out a bottle of the sparkling fruit juice that their mom bought instead of soda. He washed the cheese puffs down with a long drink of juice, before walking back into the hall and kicking his shoes off next to his backpack.

Wandering through the dining room, the living room, and the study, he looked for their mother. Anna Pantera was a freelance writer for a magazine called *Animal Globe*, specializing in stories about leopard behavior and jungle ecosystems. Unless she was working on a project, which could keep her away anywhere from a couple of days to a few weeks, she was typically home when he and Larissa got back from school.

Apparently, however, today was not a typical day. The house was all but silent with the exception of the faint sounds of Larissa's voice drifting down the stairs and his own feet padding softly on the hardwood floors.

When his search turned up nothing on the first floor, he returned to the front hall. Taking another sip of juice, he tilted his head back and called out "Mom." His voice rang out through the empty rooms, echoing off the walls and bouncing back to him. Hearing no response, he began climbing the stairs.

He bypassed his room, which was to the right at the top of the stairs, and headed towards his parents' room, which was down the hall and around the corner. The sound of Larissa's chatter had grown louder and louder as he reached the top of the stairs.

Walking by her room, he heard her giggle, "He didn't," into the phone, in her voice a combination of shock and glee. Nate stopped for moment, holding his body as still as possible and keeping his mind blank, trying to hear who he was and what he had done that had his sister so shocked.

"Mind your own business Nate." Larissa's voice floated through the door. He smiled and rolled his eyes. He had known it wouldn't work, but a guy had to try. He opened the door, sticking his head part of the way inside.

Larissa was on the other side of the room, sitting on the window seat that filled the large bay window that dominated the east wall of her room. As usual, she had immediately changed out of her school clothes into some green velour sweatpants and a white and green t-shirt. Her books were stacked neatly on her desk, and the clothes that she had just removed were in the hamper near the door. Larissa was a girl who liked to have everything in its place, just the opposite of Nate.

Though she tried valiantly to ignore him, Nate kept whispering "Psst," until finally she was forced to acknowledge him.

"Mom?" he questioned when she turned to him. His answer was a well-aimed pillow that shot across the room at lightning speed. It would have hit him in the face had he been just a shade slower.

"Can't you see I am on the phone," she growled, deliberately turning away again. Nate shut the door noisily, grinning at her grumbling response, and headed back down the stairs.

When his search of the basement yielded no mom, Nate went back to the kitchen, dropped the cheese puffs on the counter, threw the bottle in the recycling bin, and went to the back door. Opening one of the sliding glass doors, he stepped out onto the deck, which overlooked a long stretch of green grass that ended abruptly in a forest of trees.

Their house was enclosed on three, actually more like three and a half sides, by trees. Towering trees, with huge, green leaves. The branches crept out over the lawn, creating a dome-like effect and shading a good portion of the grass from the sun, which was still high in the sky.

Nate walked over to the hammock that occupied one side of the large wooden deck and sat down. Unlike his friends who couldn't wait to get home and turn on their video games or get online, the hammock was Nate's favorite place to unwind. Lying there, daydreaming with the warm sun on his face, was Nate's idea of paradise, especially after a long day at school. Homework could wait for a while longer, especially since his mom wasn't around to nag him about getting started. Just as he was about to stretch out, a movement at the edge of the lawn caught his eye.

Nate rose quickly and rushed over the banister at the opposite side of the deck. The movement was coming from the area of the yard that his parents had warned him and his sister not to go near. Mom called it her garden, and he guessed that it could be one, if the hundreds of little colorful, claw-shaped weeds that grew there could be considered flowers. He and Larissa called it "The Forbidden Patch of Doom," and it was a small patch of earth no bigger than a sandbox. Their parents had marked off the area using ropes tied between wooden posts and warned them against entering it ever since he could remember.

The edict was typical Pantera Family Law, just another one of a long list of commandments for which his parents offered no explanation but to which they expected total adherence. As children, both he and Larissa had obeyed this and other PFLs without question, but lately he had begun to wonder not only about this particular PFL, but all the other ones too.

Beyond the garden, he watched the bushes and shrubbery, which covered practically every square inch of the forest floor beneath, rustle back and forth as something big and shadowy moved through them. Nate covered his eyes with his hand and squinted to see better.

At last, the shadows seemed to gather and solidify into a form, and Nate watched with amazement as a huge black cat emerged from the undergrowth and out into the green lawn. At least five feet tall and nine feet long from the tip of its nose to the tip of its tail, this was no mere cat. This was a panther. The animal turned around slowly to face the forest from which it had just emerged. It seemed to be looking for something. It spent long moments like that, and then, nodding its head in a very human-like manner, it turned away from the forest and began padding lazily towards the house. Right towards Nate.

CHAPTER 2

MEET THE PANTERAS

THE CREATURE LOOKED UP at the deck, meeting Nate's eyes after spotting him. There was only the slightest pause in its stride to suggest its surprise at seeing the boy there. Nate's amazement held him in place, and he was helpless to move as the beast crossed the wide green expanse of lawn and placed its paws on the first step leading up to the deck. With great deliberation, the panther settled back onto its haunches and sprang, covering the stairs and half of the deck in a single leap. Then, quickly, the animal loped the last few paces that separated it from Nate, coming to a halt right in front of him.

As Nate watched, wide-eyed and still frozen by shock, the animal leaned back on its hind legs and carefully placed its paws on his shoulders. Nate found himself face to face with green cat eyes, flecked with yellow, remarkably like his own. Then, in the blink of an eye, the panther was gone and before him stood his mother wearing a black body suit that was something like the wet suits that surfers wore, except without the sleeves. A whiff of cinnamon floated away in the breeze as she pulled him into a hug and a kiss on the forehead before he could escape. After a few moments of his squirming, she released him.

"Mom!" Nate exclaimed, shocked. He rubbed his hands over his hair and his face, smoothing it down and wiping away the evidence of her affection. Then he looked at her, feeling a mixture of both confusion and, to his surprise, annoyance at what he had just witnessed.

Shifting or not shifting in public was covered by another cardinal PFL. Nate and Larissa were absolutely forbidden to shift outside of their home, and they were forbidden to leave the house while in panther form. He had always thought that his parents followed the same rules. What he'd just witnessed seemed to suggest otherwise.

"I thought that you told us never to shift in public!"

Without answering him, his mother put her arm around his shoulder and turned him away from the backyard. Casting an anxious glance over her shoulder, she gently guided him back towards the house. Even though he had the distinct feeling that she was trying to distract him, which annoyed him all the more, Nate allowed himself to be maneuvered in the direction of the deck doors.

"I would hardly call our backyard public," she replied finally, with a soft chuckle as she held the door for him. After he walked inside, she swiftly followed, sliding the door shut and locking it. Once inside, she reached over to one of the four hooks next to the doors and pulled down the clothes that hung there. She quickly stepped into the cotton jogging pants and slipped the t-shirt over her head.

"But," Nate sputtered, less than mollified. "What if I had been with one of my friends?" He gently pulled out one of the four wooden stools that lined the countertop, hopped up on it, and turned to his mother expectantly.

She remained silent as she washed her hands, spreading the soap halfway up her forearms before rinsing it off, and then walked over to the refrigerator and began to pull out the ingredients for the family's dinner. The first items she placed next to the stove were two extra large packages of ground beef. Meat was always on the menu. Lots of meat. It had to be for a family full of shape-shifters.

Nate, Larissa, and their parents were all shifters. Were-leopards to be specific, and were-panthers to be the most precise. The difference between the former and the latter was that when the Panteras shifted, their coats were completely black. It was not just that their coats appeared black, as was the case with the regular, non-were panthers. Those, in actuality, only had very dark coats on which their black spots showed faintly. Indeed, the Panteras' fur was a deep, midnight shade of black, and the Panteras had no spots.

To hear his mother tell it, their family came from a long line of were-panthers and that was the reason for the last name, Pantera. Most were-leopards, she said, shifted into creatures that looked like conventional leopards with a tawny coats and black eye spots all over their bodies. Pantera lineage was very special, she reminded them again and again. Even when pressed, she would never explain exactly why. Her reticence was a growing source of irritation and frustration for both of the twins.

Though a voice in the back of his mind, one that grew louder all of the time, told him that there were things that his parents weren't telling them, Anna and Robert Pantera's word on all things shifter continued to be law. Not only because they were his parents, but because they were the only other shifters that he knew.

Nate and Larissa had never even seen another shifter.

They had no aunts or uncles, and neither their mother nor father had ever mentioned their parents. There were no shifters at school, as far as they could tell. Their parents did not seem to have any were-leopard friends. In fact, their parents did not have many friends at all. For all Nate knew, the four of them, his family, were the only shifters on Earth. Unique in all the world.

Of course, though their parents had been telling them all their lives that they were different, it wasn't until he had started at Greendale Middle School, more than two years before, that Nate had begun to believe that what his parents said was true, especially because of Ray and Eric.

True, there were a lot of ways that he was the same as his human friends. They laughed at the same jokes. They would rather spend their days playing soccer than sitting in a boring math class. Lately, all of their voices were starting to change. Ray's was the worst, and Nate and Eric teased him mercilessly whenever his voice cracked. They all had even developed crushes on girls this year. Eric had a crush on Larissa. Of course, Eric had a crush on a new girl every five minutes.

He had discovered that even though he was a shifter, he developed at the same rate as his human friends. As panthers, he and Larissa were basically teenagers, just as they were on the verge of their teens in their human bodies. Regular leopards, not non-weres, reached maturity at around two years of age. The twins, however, were still considered adolescents in both of their forms, and they would reach adulthood at about the same time in each. In fact, he was a little on the small side compared to his friends.

At the same time, the differences had become more and more apparent as the school years passed. It had started last fall, when most of the school had gotten sick with the flu. Nate and Larissa had been two of the few students that had not gotten sick. The more Nate had thought about it, the more he realized that he could not recall ever having been sick. Not a cold. Not a fever. Nothing. He and Larissa had never even had the chicken pox. Then, this year, Eric had broken his wrist. There were no broken bones in Nate or Larissa's pasts either. And that was just the tip of the iceberg.

Though he did not look it, with his slight frame, he was already much stronger than his friends would ever be, even when they were full grown men. He knew that if he wanted to, he could snap and crush bones the same way that Eric or Ray might break a twig between their fingers. He was also faster and more agile.

This was not to mention his other senses, which were like human senses multiplied a hundred times. Along with other heightened physical abilities, all of the Panteras possessed shifter-sight and shifter-hearing, both of which were exponentially better than regular leopards. In panther form, they could hear a phone ring from across the street and the buzz of a conversation from a quarter-mile away. Even in human form, their senses were greatly amplified. Nate had long ago figured out that his parents had chosen the location of the house as much for the buffer that it provided from the noise of the world as for anything else.

With Nate and Larissa, shifter-hearing took an even stranger form, transforming into something that bordered on telepathy. They had been able to communicate to each other without speaking, to hear one another's thoughts, for as long as he could remember. Their parents were certain that the ability had something to do with the fact that they were twins, though they claimed that they had never heard of any shifter with such ability before.

His sense of smell was so acute that he could tell the difference between people, even from a distance, based on that alone. His friends could never sneak up on him, though they tried and tried again. He always knew they were coming, because he could smell them both from a mile away. Eric smelled like oranges, always with a hint of socks that weren't so clean. Ray smelled like the coffee that his mother drank day and night. They could never figure out how he did it, and he could never tell.

Unbidden, the incidents of the afternoon came into his mind. Nate knew that he had to be constantly on guard with Ray and Eric, as Larissa was with her friends. Their parents had drilled that lesson into both him and Larissa before allowing either of them to set a foot near Greendale. What had happened that afternoon had violated all of the PFLs that covered shifter/human interaction. It had been a lapse, but an excusable one he justified once again. Eric could have been seriously hurt. Still, he had to be more careful. He would be lucky if neither Ray nor Eric mentioned it in school tomorrow. And he didn't even want to think about what would happen if his parents found out.

Mrs. Pantera fished a box of pasta and some tomato sauce out of the cabinet to the left of the stove. It looked like they were having spaghetti tonight, which was great because Nate loved his mother's spaghetti. Then she went back to the refrigerator and pulled out lettuce, tomatoes, and carrots. Nate groaned aloud. He didn't know why his mother was always tried to feed a family full of big cats, panthers no less, vegetables. Normally, he would have protested, but at that moment he was still preoccupied by his mother's strange behavior.

"You haven't answered my question," he reminded her,

watching as she dumped the ground beef into a frying pan. Immediately the meat began to sizzle and Nate inhaled the first faint yet delicious smelling wafts of cooking meat. He reopened the bag of cheese puffs and stuffed a few more into his mouth, suddenly ravenous.

His mom pulled a piece of the raw red meat off of the top of the uncooked lump of beef and popped it into her mouth. Nate grimaced. Though he was a panther, the thought of eating raw meat made him squeamish. He was, after all, part human too.

She turned then to look at him, raising her eyebrows very slightly. Like her children, Anna Pantera's eyes were green with the same mildly peculiar yellow flecks. Like Nate and Larissa, her jewel-toned eyes were strangely startling against her burnished copper skin. Her face was surrounded by a riot of jet black curls that tumbled down and around her shoulders. In fact, the twins looked very much like their mother.

"Because it's a silly question," she replied, chewing the meat. "Don't you think that I would have known if you were with one of your friends?"

Nate could not help but smile sheepishly at that. Of course, she would have known. If there had been anyone else there with him, his mother would have seen and heard. She never would have come out of the woods in panther form. In that moment another, more significant, question popped into his mind.

"But what were you doing out there anyway Mom?"

Instantly, the teasing smile dropped from his mother's face and Nate realized that his question had disconcerted her. Her brow furrowed for just the slightest instant before her face became smooth and unreadable again. She looked away from him, glancing outside in the direction of the woods. Then, instead of answering, she reached over and shut the cabinet door with a resounding thump.

Nate slumped in his seat. He recognized the action for what is was. He had unwittingly ventured into a "CKC" zone. Short for curiosity kills the cat, the "CKC" zone was the nickname he and Ris had long ago devised for those topics that they knew those parents would never talk about. The "CKC" zone included anything and everything about who they were, what they were, and where they came from. Both twins knew that if they entered a "CKC" zone, even unknowingly, for all intents and purposes, the conversation was over. None of their questions would be answered.

"Do you have any homework," Mrs. Pantera asked, turning back to the stove to stir the meat. Her not-so-subtle change of subject confirmed his suspicions.

Nate exhaled a disappointed rush of air. He narrowed his eyes, staring at the cheese puff dust that colored the tips of his fingers. Suddenly he felt the weight of his mother's gaze and he looked up to see her expectant eyes on him. Typical. She would not answer his questions, but he dare not ignore hers.

"A little," he grumbled, thinking about the two pages of math problems that his teacher had assigned, much to the collective dismay of the class.

"Then don't you think that you should get started" she asked, dismissing both him and his questions when she turned back towards the stove to stir the meat.

But Nate didn't leave. Instead, he sat there, staring at the back of his mother's head, suddenly fuming. He had gone from annoyed to angry instantaneously. It was so clear that she was hiding something. In fact, she didn't even try to conceal that fact.

It was equally clear that she had no intention of

explaining anything at all. Normally, he would have let it go. But in that moment, his anger made him do something he had never done. Clearing his throat, he asked again.

"So what were you doing out there Mom?" His voice was louder than he had meant it to be, and it shook from the sudden nervousness that he felt because all of his anger left him as soon as he spoke the first words.

His mother froze. Her back stiffened, her hand stopped stirring, and not a muscle twitched. He held his breath, abruptly unable to exhale as he waited for her response. The kitchen was suddenly a million degrees hotter. His face and ears burned, his palms felt sweaty, and his heart pounded so loudly, he was sure that Ris must have heard it in her room. If he had not known better, he would have thought that he was about to shift.

He was afraid. Though whether he was afraid of what his mother might do or what she might say, he did not know. Finally, after what seemed like ages, Anna Pantera spoke.

"Don't you think you should get started?" She asked the question again as though the last awkward minute had never happened.

So that was it? That was the only answer that he was going to get. Nate's shoulders slumped and he pushed back from the counter, wincing as the sound of the stool scraping against the floor tiles pierced his ears. He pushed the stool in and ran out of the kitchen.

Anna gazed worriedly after her son, long after he had disappeared up the stairs. She had known this day would come. A day when both of her children would no longer be appeased by the half truths that she had told them all of their lives. But she hadn't expected it to arrive so soon, and she wasn't prepared. More importantly, they weren't prepared, and that was her fault. She turned back to stove to stir the pan of meat that was starting to burn.

CHAPTER 3

WHAT HAPPENS AT THE BUS STOP...

NATE WALKED OVER TO his locker and fished his Spanish book out of his backpack. He was between periods, and he was dropping off that book and getting another.

As he searched his locker, hoping that he had not forgotten his history book at home, the faint whisper that was always in the back of his mind grew louder, telling him that Larissa was nearby and getting closer.

Their telepathic abilities had a limited range. Though he could always hear her faintly, when she was farther away the sound was more like the faint noise of a distant babbling brook. Just a tickle in his mind. Only when she was within a certain range could he make out thoughts, which were more like impressions of emotion and images, and only when they were both concentrating could they communicate in words. It was getting stronger all the time, though. In the last year, the range had more than doubled. They could carry on conversations at fifty paces now, which definitely made the classes they shared together more entertaining. For Nate anyway.

He looked over and saw Larissa standing with her friends Kayla and Miko. *"Hey Sis,"* he greeted her off-handedly as she turned to open her locker.

"*Bro.*" she acknowledged briefly before turning back to continue chattering with her friends. Nate did his best to block out the conversation. They both did what they could to maintain some boundaries. Still, sometimes a little eavesdropping could not be helped. Like, for instance, when he heard one of the girls say his name.

His head shot back around, and he saw all three girls looking at him. A blush crept up his face as he found Kayla's eyes on him. She smiled shyly, and suddenly his face felt like it was on fire.

He'd had something of crush on Kayla for most of the year but he had never had the guts to say anything about it. Larissa knew, of course. He had never been able to keep secrets from his twin for too long. But she had sworn not to tell. He waved, in what he hoped was a cool way, and the three girls started to giggle.

"*Ris,*" he thought, "*you didn't.*" He turned to his sister who was the picture of innocence. She didn't even have to reply. He could tell that she hadn't said anything, but he certainly was the topic of the conversation.

Abruptly he turned back to his locker, all of a sudden very eager to go to class and to get away from the gaggle of giggling girls. Lifting one text after the other, he searched for his history book.

"Hey Nate!" Nate looked up from his locker to see Ray jogging down the hall toward him. He wasn't surprised. These between period locker runs had become a daily occurrence this year. Because they only had one class together, the only time that they saw each other was between periods and during gym.

Ray skidded to a stop in front of him and Nate grinned. "What's up?"

Instead of answering, Ray grabbed him by the arm and began tugging him down the hall. Larissa gave him a look as Ray pulled him past her locker. He shrugged slightly at Ray's strange behavior but continued along. The boy's pull was insistent, though Nate would have followed him without any resistance. Ray pulled him toward the breezeway that connected the two buildings of the school.

To his surprise, once they were in the breezeway, Nate found himself being dragged outside.

"Ray!" he exclaimed. "What are you doing?" Students of Greendale Middle School were not allowed outside except for gym and a brief recess after lunch. They were never, under any circumstances, allowed outside without supervision. Nate began to struggle against Ray's insistent tug, trying to get back to the door before it closed all of the way.

Ray responded by tightening his grip and pulling Nate harder. Nate looked at Ray's hand on his arm and stumbled forward as Ray wrenched his arm. He could have pulled away, but to do so would have taken a strength that he was not supposed to have.

He turned back to the school, even as Ray dragged him farther away from the building, and watched the doors slowly creak shut.

The doors automatically locked when they closed. Then there would be no way to get back inside without someone inside opening the doors. Well, there were ways, but Nate would rather face the wrath of the teachers than that of his parents.

"Ray! Stop! We are going to get into so much trouble!"

Ray did not reply, instead he tugged that much harder on Nate's arm and pulling him farther away before finally stopping near a clump of trees a little distance from the main building. All of a sudden, Ray stopped pulling. He jerked to a stop and then stood looking at Nate's arm in his hand as though trying to figure out what to do next.

In the silence that followed, the soft click of the locking

door sounded like an explosion in Nate's ears. In that moment, Ray dropped his arm. Immediately, Nate turned, running back towards the building, though it was already too late to stop the door. "Look," Ray called to him, "I didn't think that you would want anyone to overhear our conversation."

His words stopped Nate in his tracks. He looked over his shoulder at Ray and finally saw in his friend's face a seriousness that was completely foreign to the generally easygoing boy. He realized that this wasn't just some joke or prank. Ray was genuinely upset. He glanced worriedly at the now shut doors and then turned back to Ray.

"What is it," he asked, his tone serious now. Instead of answering, Ray said nothing for a long moment. He just stared at Nate as though he were trying to figure him out. But the harder and longer he stared, the more confused he looked. Finally, he spoke.

"It's..." he began and then stopped.

Nate shifted from one foot to the other under the scrutiny of his friend's gaze. He waited for Ray to continue, but his friend looked like he was having trouble putting his thoughts into words.

"It's about..." Ray began again, still searching for the words. The boy turned away and the silence dragged on. Nate huffed, growing simultaneously more concerned, while feeling his patience wearing thin. Upset or not, Ray was about to get them both in some serious trouble.

"Come on Ray. Spit it out," Nate said, impatience winning the battle over concern. "We are really..."

"It's about the other day," Ray blurted out, interrupting him. Once he got the first sentence out, it was like a flood-gate gave way. "How did you do it? I mean, I know you said reflexes. But Nate, I have been thinking about it, and what you did was impossible. No one can move that fast. Not only that, Eric is way bigger than you, and you just caught him like he was a football or something. Like he was nothing. How?"

Nate went still, completely shocked. He had hoped that the incident at the bus stop had been forgotten. In fact, since no one had mentioned it and it had been almost a week, he had begun to breathe a little bit easier because he believed it had been. Now here Ray was, asking him questions that he could not answer. He ran his hand over his hair and chuckled nervously.

"I don't know," he replied, looking away because he could not meet his friend's eyes as he lied to him. "I don't know how I did it."

Ray shook his head in frustration. "I knew you'd say that," he said turning away and walking a few paces. "But I know you're lying too." That accusation was made very softly, but Nate heard each word loud and clear.

"What do you mean," Nate asked quietly, his heart suddenly pounding in his ears.

"I mean," Ray said, pausing for the barest moment as he turned to face Nate once more. "What about soccer tryouts?"

Nate looked at Ray, suddenly completely confused. He tilted his head to the side.

"No one's leg just breaks like that. Not without something happening to the other guy too." The other boy declared, his voice gaining strength.

Nate's jaw dropped open in surprise when he realized what Ray was talking about. It had happened so long ago that he really had forgotten about it. When Nate had first started at Greendale, against his parents' direct commands, he had snuck out to try out for the county-wide league that Ray and Eric both played for. During tryouts, he had collided with another kid when they both ran after the ball. The other guy had to go to the emergency room with a fractured femur, while he had gone home without even a scratch.

"Do you want me to go on," Ray asked, raising his eyebrow and making Nate suddenly wonder what other mistakes he had made in the last three years.

Ray was staring at him, his arms crossed over his chest as he waited for an answer. But Nate couldn't speak, because he didn't have an explanation. At his silence, Ray continued, his voice growing angrier with every word.

"It's all these little things Nate. They all add up to something very strange. You know it. I know it. What do you think? I'm stupid?"

He didn't know what to say. He thought he had been so careful. He turned away from Ray and walked back towards the building, finally stopping to sit on the stoop outside of the breezeway doors. Sitting down, he dropped his head into his hands. After a long moment, he looked up again. Ray hadn't moved.

"What do you want me to say," he asked, shaking his head and shrugging his shoulders at the same time. He looked back at his friend feeling the beginnings of an unfamiliar helplessness. He felt vulnerable and angry at the same time. He felt cornered.

"How about the truth."

Nate shrugged helplessly and watched his friend frown even more angrily. "Look Ray," he said.

"Just tell me the truth," Ray interrupted again with an angry bark. Nate felt his frustration growing as Ray prodded him. It was not that he wanted to lie. He had to lie. The secret wasn't just his. It was Larissa's, and their mom's, and their dad's. They would all be in danger if anyone knew the truth. That was what his parents said anyway, and Nate had seen enough monster movies to know that there was at least some truth to that. Humans didn't react too well to differences.

"Just tell me the truth" Ray urged again, as though through sheer repetition he could get the answers he searched for.

Suddenly Nate couldn't take anymore. Between his parents who wouldn't tell him anything and his friend who wanted him to tell him everything, he was going crazy. Despite his efforts to remain cool, he exploded.

"Look Ray," he yelled, knowing, even as he opened his mouth, that his friend was not going to believe him. "There's nothing to say! I don't know how I did it! I'm sorry that you don't believe me!"

Ray's eyes narrowed into impossibly thin slits and then he threw his hands up. "Fine," he yelled. "If that's how you want to be! Fine!"

To his horror, Nate felt a rumble in the back of his throat and the growl of anger was on his lips before he could stop it. He bit his lip and forced the sound back down his throat, choking on it. He had to get out of there.

Once he had regained control, Nate looked up, met his friend's eyes challengingly, and retorted, "Not how I want to be. How I have to be." He glared at his friend, his eyes glittering with barely contained anger. "And, I don't need any friends who don't get that." With those words, he stood up and brushed past Ray. He didn't stop until he was standing on the other side of the building.

For several minutes he paced back and forth, trying to contain his anger. Though he did not know who he was angrier with, Ray or himself. His own careless actions were the source of all of Ray's questions. He should have been more careful. He took deep breaths, feeling the anger drain away slowly. Finally, he was calm enough to remember that he was supposed to be in History, not pacing out here in front of the school where any teacher might see him just by looking out the window.

He hunched over and started to make his way over to the building. Stepping into the shrubs that surrounded the school, he tried to get as close to the building as he could, so that he would be out of sight. Before he could take another step, he heard a rustling noise.

He froze and looked over his shoulder, in the direction of the sound. Before him spread the pristine manicured lawns of the school which ended abruptly at the equally well-maintained hedge that separated the school grounds from the road on the other side. His eyes scanned back and forth across the hedge, but seeing nothing, he turned away.

Shaking off the creepy feeling that suddenly overwhelmed him, he tried to figure out how he would get back inside. Immediately, it came to him. Larissa. Of course. He moved closer to the building, hustling to get out of sight. Creeping alongside the wall, he reached out to his sister with his mind. Finally, he was close enough for her to hear him.

"I need you to come and let me in," he thought to her as soon as he was within range.

"What?" She sounded confused. *"Where are you? Mrs. Stephens took roll ten minutes ago."*

"I'm outside."

"What?! Nate do you know how much trouble you can get into?"

"Ris," he groaned, not at all in the mood for yet another interrogation. *"Don't ask questions. Just come and get me. I promise I will explain later."* Try as he might, Nate could not help it as some of his frustration slip into his tone.

"Fine," Larissa said. *"Jeez. You don't have to be so snippy,"* she thought back again. Then, in Mrs. Stephen's history class, Larissa raised her hand and asked to go to the bathroom.

Nate crept back along the side of the building to the doors nearest Mrs. Stephen's classroom. As he waited, his mind went to Ray, who was still on the other side of the building. He would need someone to let him in too. Just as quickly, he pushed the thought away. Ray could find his own way back in.

Chapter 4

P. E.

"You have to concentrate Nathanial!" Robert Pantera's words were harsh with an edge of exasperation. His voice was jarring and his use of Nate's full name was the universal sign of parental agitation. Nathanial looked over at his father's tall, slight form pacing anxiously before them.

Though the twins looked mostly like their mother, they had a bit of their father in them too. They were going to be tall, as he was. Mrs. Pantera stood only a couple of inches over five feet, while Mr. Pantera was nearly a foot taller. Nate and Larissa were already taller than their mother. They also had their father's slender build.

It was Saturday morning, almost afternoon, and they were in the basement of the Pantera home. The room was off limits to any guests—though guests were rare —mostly because they would not have easily been able to explain away its oddness to visitors. The room was entirely gray, from the concrete floors to the concrete blocks that made up the walls and support beams that were interspersed throughout the room.

Not only was the room all gray, but every shred of furnishing was the same monotonous shade as well. On one side of the basement, there were huge, gray, foam-rubber mats that covered almost the entire area of the floor. They used the mats for sparring, for meditation, and for whatever other exercises their father conjured up in his mind. On the other side was other fitness equipment as well as dummies for hand to hand exercises. There was not a trace of color to be seen anywhere. This was the P. E. room and they were right in the middle of a marathon P. E. session.

P. E. Panther Education. That's what their father called it, and it was what the twins had done almost every Saturday without fail since they had turned four, learning to control their powers and suppress the panther. They had even undergone intensive six-month training, before their parents had allowed them to enroll in Greendale Middle School for sixth grade. Before that, they had been home-schooled.

During that time, they had learned mind tricks that helped to control their emotions. They took lessons on how to move more like humans and less like shifters, and they learned how to interact with humans without betraying their true nature. Nate's mind flashed back to the many lectures that they had received during that training, about how important it was that they keep the family's secrets and how important it was that their human classmates never suspect what hid beneath the surface. That was probably the reason the session was going so long today. Ris had told their parents about his argument with Ray.

Nate sat cross-legged on one of the mats in the full body suit that they always wore for their training. The suits were pitch-black to match the color of Pantera fur. Though they looked like solid garments, the suits were actually made from thin strips of loosely-connected material that stretched and moved with his body. The garment was designed so that when he shifted, the suit changed to fit his panther form stretching into thin slats through which his fur grew and covered.

He did not know where the suits came from, but they had worn them as far back as he could remember. He had once asked his father about them. In typical fashion, Robert Pantera had side-stepped the question. But every time one suit wore out or got too small, a new one would appear like magic.

They were practicing shifting. Contrary to popular myth, the Panteras were not controlled by the full moon and compelled to shift at its appearance. Though perhaps the lore was correct when it came to werewolves, were-leopards could control the shift, changing when they wanted or needed any time of the day or night. But there was a trick to it, one that could only be learned with a great deal of practice, and one that their parents had never tried to teach them before now.

Mr. Pantera focused his brown eyes on Nate. "You have to learn to control the shift," he continued. "You can't just shift when you are angry or frightened. You have to be able to call your panther when you need it. You have to direct it. You can not let it rule you."

Never before had they been encouraged to call on their animal alter egos. In fact, they had been trained to do the exact opposite. All of their previous lessons had focused on restraining the shift rather than purposely bringing it forth. Looking over at his sister, who was already in panther form and had been that way for at least ten minutes, Nate could not believe that she had mastered it so easily. He was inclined to think that she had been practicing somehow.

Across from him, she sat on her haunches, looking bored. As a panther, Larissa was still on the smaller side, maybe three feet tall and six feet long. Her fur, like the fur of all the Panteras, was pitch-black and spotless. Only her eyes, green and flecked with yellow, hinted at her human form.

Her tail swished, expressing her impatience. Not that Nate needed any physical indication of that fact, as her voice echoed in his mind for the fifth time.

"*Hurry up,*" she thought at him.

"*I am trying.*" He thought back. "*It might help if you

did not keep breaking my train of thought." He frowned with concentration, holding his hands in front of his face. Staring intently at them, he willed them to change into paws and sprout black fur. He stared and stared and stared. Still, nothing happened. Sighing with frustration, he sat back and cast an envious glance at his sister.

"How come this is so easy for you," he mumbled aloud.

"Well girls do mature faster than boys, baby brother," she replied, and if ever a cat looked smug, Larissa did in that moment. Her tail swished indolently now, her eyes narrowed to show only slits of appraising gold-flecked green, and she smiled—as much as a cat could smile.

Technically, she was right. He was the baby brother by all of two minutes. However small the window, it did not stop Larissa from rubbing his nose in that fact every chance that she got, especially when she did something better or faster than he did, which was annoyingly often. It was why he took such joy in the fact that Mom and Dad had given the key to him, not her. It was probably also why their decision continued to bother her so.

Normally their ribbing was good-natured, and he usually took her jabs in stride, but today, for some reason it aggravated him more than usual. Did she always have to be better at everything? He glared at his sister, his concentration completely broken.

"Come on Nate," Larissa's voice echoed in his mind as she exhaled an exasperated sigh. *"The sooner you change, the sooner Dad will end the lesson, and the sooner we can get on with our lives."*

Larissa, though she was more subtle about it, shared his frustrations with their weekly training sessions, especially now that they were getting older. Like Nate, she would have rather spent her Saturdays hanging out with her friends than in this cold gray room beneath their house.

"Well. Maybe if you hadn't run to Dad and Mom about what happened with Ray, we would have been out of here by now," Nate responded, raising an eyebrow at his sister.

Even though he had begged her not to, Larissa had been too worried that Ray was on the verge of discovering their secret not to tell their parents about the fight. Then, despite his insistence that he had deflected Ray's questions and curiosities, his parents had doubled the length of their P. E. this week. It was almost like punishment. For the first portion of their training, they had been treated to an extra long lecture about the importance of being careful around humans. Again. Then it was on to Controlling the Shift: 101.

"You know I had to," she thought to him, looking just slightly vexed. At that, Nate completely stopped what he was doing to meet his sister's panther eyes.

"No," he said simply. *"You really didn't."*

Larissa said nothing. She only narrowed her eyes and stared at him. Finally, Nate relented with an exasperated sigh. He knew his sister. Once she had found out, she really didn't have any other choice then to go to their parents. She had invented the phrase goody two-shoes.

"I guess it was a weird situation," he conceded, still more than a little aggrieved. Before she could gloat entirely, he continued. *"But I told you that I had it under control. It wouldn't hurt you to just trust me sometimes."*

Larissa blinked once. Her panther features were a blank, but he could see that she was mulling over his words. Finally, she responded. *"You're right. I'm sorry."*

"You are going about this the wrong way Nate." Mr. Pantera's voice broke through, interrupting their staring match and drawing Nate's attention back to the task at hand. "You have to visualize the panther in your mind. Call it to you. Call it forth from you. You can not will the change from the outside in.

You must call it from the inside out."

Nate had heard this speech about ten times already that day. However, this time, he looked into his father's insistent brown eyes and something inside him clicked. "Will the change from inside. Will the change from inside." He repeated the words over and over, like a chant. Slowly, his mind went quiet, the basement, his sister, and his father seemed to just melt away, and he focused on the image that appeared quite suddenly in his mind's eye.

At first, he thought that it was just a tree. A huge tree, green with moss, that stretched upward seemingly forever. In his mind, he tilted his head back gazing up into the tree. Searching, he thought, for its top. Then he saw it. A patch of midnight darkness within all of the green and brown. As soon as he saw it, his eyes became like telescopes, focusing on the patch of darkness and then zooming in. It was a panther. Nate concentrated on the image of the panther, which he knew instinctively was more than a conjuring of his imagination. Though, if pressed, he would not have been able to explain what exactly it was or how he understood it.

The panther was nestled in a tree, curled up, sleeping in a space created by the joining of a branch to the tree trunk. Its chest rose slightly with every inhalation and exhalation of breath. *Well*, Nate thought to himself, *no wonder I am having such a hard time. That stupid panther is sleeping.*

At that, the panther's tail swished, and Nate had the distinct feeling that the animal had heard his thoughts and did not enjoy being called stupid.

Sorry, he said, apologizing to the panther. The swishing tail stilled and the panther slowly opened its jewel-green eyes and gazed back at him challengingly, as if to ask "What do you want?"

He willed the animal to come to him. At first, the creature

did not respond. Indeed, the cat ignored him entirely, closing its eyes and repositioning its head, nestling back in for a nap. Its body stilled completely as though it had fallen asleep. The only movement was the rise and fall of its chest.

Come, Nate thought at the creature. Nothing. *Come,* he thought again, his voice sounding stronger in his mind, more commanding. The creature didn't move, but suddenly Nate got the distinct impression that the animal was toying with him. This went on for several long minutes. No matter what Nate did, the stubborn creature refused to raise its head, move, or in any way acknowledge him. At last, when Nate was about to give up in frustration, the beast moved, stretching languorously and confirming for Nate that it was merely feigning sleep. He offered one last call.

Please, he entreated.

It truly was the magic word. The animal lifted its head with just slightly less imperiousness than before and opened its green eyes.

Please come, Nate called to the creature, more humbly this time. Slowly the animal rose to its feet, and Nate felt his frustration drain away and his body relax. Finally. Turning around in a small circle, the animal wheeled about and began walking the length of the branch right towards Nate.

Stubborn creature. The thought formed in his mind before Nate had a chance to quell it. The creature halted in its approach, and Nate was forced to apologize again before it resumed its slow, deliberate pace. Politeness, then, seemed to be the key.

The cat locked eyes with Nate as it approached, gazing at him with an intent and intelligence that would have been both uncanny and unnerving in an actual panther. The closer the animal came, the more his flesh began to tingle. He could feel his bones and muscles elongating and contracting, shifting, to take on their panther size and shape.

But it didn't hurt. Actually, it was just the opposite. It felt good and right. Like scratching a long existing itch. Almost like his body was shedding some ill-fitting costume and assuming its natural state. Nate had forgotten this feeling. He had forgotten how easy it could be and how instinctive it felt.

When he opened his eyes again, the world looked different. Four dimensional. Everything in the room thrummed with a kind of energy. Even the shadows vibrated. Nate looked around him, taking it all in with amazement. He had forgotten about this too. How the world looked through panther eyes. It had been so long since he had shifted. At least three years. Since they had learned to control the emotions, fear and anger, that caused them to shift involuntarily.

"Well done Nate!" his father exclaimed. Nate grinned, as much as his cat form would allow him, and turned back to his sister triumphantly.

"Good job, Nate" she thought. And then, without missing a beat, *"Took you long enough."*

Nate, still celebrating his success, promised himself to get her later for that bit of taunting. They spent the rest of the lesson practicing shifting back and forth between panther and human form. Each time, the shift was easier for Nate. As long as he remembered to be polite to his panther. For that day a least, he and his panther had reached an uneasy truce and had established a working relationship.

By the end of P. E., Nate was able to shift in less than a minute. Never, however, did their father explain the reasons behind the lesson. Why it was suddenly imperative that they learn to call forth the creature that for so many years they had learned to suppress?

"Shouldn't we tell them something? Give them some sort of explanation?" Robert's words were soft, but there was an urgency to them. It was late in the evening. Though the twins had long since gone to bed, Anna and Robert were having this conversation in the backyard under the twinkling starlight to make sure that they were not overheard. "They are both already suspicious because of the changes to their training."

He studied his wife's face, watching as a series of emotions pass over it. Fear, doubt, and resolve chased each other across her face.

They had long ago decided, together, when they would tell the children the full story. He knew Anna had her reasons for wanting to keep the twins in the dark. Most were reasons that he agreed with. At the same time, he knew that he would never fully understand all of her reasons, just as he would never comprehend the weight that she carried on her shoulders each and every day. On the other hand, these extraordinary circumstances called, at least, for a reconsideration of those choices.

Anna exhaled, the breath a noisy rush signaling her frustration not only with the decision that they were making here tonight, but also with the circumstances that prompted the discussion in the first place. So many secrets. Sometimes it felt as if their whole life were a lie. Only she and Robert knew the whole truth.

They had kept these secrets from the twins for so long. Selfish though her choices might have seemed to others, all of this, all of the lies had been for Larissa and Larissa alone. She did not want Larissa to have to make the choice that she'd had to make all those years ago. She didn't want her daughter forced into a life that she had not chosen for herself.

Anna laid her head in her hands and wondered, not for the first time, whether she and Robert had made the right decision.

Maybe things would have been easier.... She let the thought trail off. No time for that tonight.

"No. Not yet." She answered at last, saying the words with a firmness and surety that did not match the uncertainty that still darkened her eyes. "We are getting the situation under control. We are already very close to finding out who is responsible. Besides, there is no threat to them as long as they are here." She nodded her head again, as though working to convince herself as much as to convince him. "We will tell them when they are fifteen, like we planned. They aren't ready yet, and neither are we."

She spoke the last with finality, but looked at her husband for reassurance. Though he was uncertain about the decision, he took her hand and gave it a gentle squeeze.

"We won't tell....yet."

CHAPTER 5

GRADUATION

Nate and Larissa sat next to each other in their white gowns. They were in the auditorium and it was graduation day. On the stage, the assistant principal droned on, entering his fifteenth minute of a speech about commencement meaning new beginnings. Nate rolled his eyes. It seemed like he had heard this speech a thousand times before. As though it were some sort of requirement that they be reminded about the new path that they were about to embark on.

Two rows behind him sat Eric. As Nate turned around, his friend was leaning over to whisper something to Kayla. Nate grinned at him. Eric grinned back and gave him a thumbs up sign. Nate chuckled. Eric was so corny.

Turning back around, he scanned the third row for Ray. They hadn't talked much since their argument, though that had been as much his choice as it had been Ray's. Still, he felt a pang of sadness. Ray had been the first person to befriend him when he had started at Greendale three years ago. They were supposed to be friends for life.

Pushing away the lonely thought of high school without his best friend, Nate turned his attention back to the stage. Mr. Larry finally seemed to be wrapping up, and the principal was walking up to the microphone. All at once, everyone around him began to cheer. Nate and Larissa whooped right along with their classmates. They knew what was coming next.

Within moments, students were marching across the stage. Nate cheered loudly as Ray marched across the stage, though Ray showed no sign that he heard. Frowning, Nate looked over at Larissa who smiled sympathetically. Then, Mrs. Stephens was down at the end of the aisle, motioning for them to stand. Nate heard Larissa's name and then his own. Then it was over, and they were surrounded by friends and parents, who rushed outside from the back of the auditorium following the last of the graduates.

Amid all of the photographs and shouts of congratulations, Nate remembered that he needed to check his locker for his calculator. He hadn't been able to find it at home, and he was hoping that he had just left it in his locker rather than lost it altogether. Breaking away from his parents and sister, he dashed back into the school and jogged down the hall towards his locker.

When he got there, he discovered that he was not alone in his last minute locker clean-up. A few of his classmates, all still in their caps and gowns, stood here and there at their lockers, emptying the contents, ripping down pictures, and throwing trash in the nearby cans. Their loud happy chatter filled his ears, as they excitedly discussed their plans for summer vacation. Nate gave a small sigh of satisfaction. No more homework, no more tests, no more ridiculously heavy book bags for three whole months. Of course, high school would be something else entirely.

At his locker, Nate fumbled with his combination, preoccupied with thought of the festivities planned for that evening. First, there would be dinner with his parents and then Ray was having a huge party to which the whole graduating class was invited. Larissa wanted to go, but Nate was not so sure that he would be welcome.

Determined not to let those thoughts ruin his celebration,

Nate pushed them away, swiveled the knob of his lock first right, then left, then right again and swung the locker door open. A grin spread across Nate's face, when he saw that his calculator was there, all the way in the back. Good thing, since it was an expensive one. He reached in to get it, scanning the locker again for anything else he might have left behind. There was nothing. The locker was empty. Unexpectedly, he was filled with a wave of nostalgia as he realized this was the last time that he would stand at that locker.

He stood up and stepped back, giving his old locker one last glance. Just as he reached under his graduation gown to slip the calculator into the pocket of his slacks, someone bumped him. Hard. Very hard.

Several things happened at once. His calculator flew out of his hand and skittered across the hallway floor. His locker door slammed shut, deafening in the sudden silence of the hallway, and Nate suddenly found himself staring at the Adam's apple of a much taller boy.

Nate was just opening his mouth to say excuse me, when the boy spoke. "Watch yourself, kid." At the venom in his voice, Nate shut his mouth in surprise. He looked up at the boy who towered over him, glaring down at him.

Several things struck Nate immediately. First, he had never seen this boy before. He searched his mind for some sense of recognition. But nothing came to mind that would explain what the strange kid was doing, standing in front of his locker, glaring so fiercely down at him that Nate felt like the boy was trying to bore holes into him.

The next thing that hit him was the fact that this kid was odd looking. He was tall and pale. His skin looked like it had never seen the sun. And there was something else about the boy's face that made it look odd. It took Nate a moment to place, but then he realized the boy had no eyebrows. At least that was what it looked like at first. At second glance, Nate realized that the kid did have eyebrows; they were just so fine and pale that they melted into the background of his alabaster skin. Against that backdrop, his grass-green hair was shocking.

But there was something else about the kid that made Nate feel strange. Woozy, dizzy, and vaguely unsettled, like the shove had knocked the wind out of him or something. Nate braced himself against the locker, suddenly needing to steady himself. All at once, his arms felt weird. He looked down at them, expecting to see tiny creatures traveling up and down his sleeves. But there was nothing there. Still, his skin crawled and the unpleasant sensation grew with each moment that passed. Nate felt a cold shiver travel up his spine as he worked to catch his breath. There was something wrong with this kid, and it was a wrongness that wafted off of the boy in waves.

His feeling of unease tripled as he looked up into the kid's light brown eyes. What he saw there stunned Nate so much that he froze completely. In that moment, the bully struck again.

"What's your problem, dork?" The older boy sneered at Nate, taunting him, shoving him against the now closed locker. Nate's shoulders hit the locker again, hard, and the sound of metal clanging against metal reverberated down the hall.

The entire hall went quiet as the other students turned to watch the altercation. Nate stared up at the tall boy, who glared down at him with so much menace in his eyes that Nate took an involuntary and instinctive step backwards. The boy smiled and took a step closer, pinning Nate in. Instantly it was clear that this was more than just an accidental collision. This boy, Nate realized quite suddenly, was trying to provoke him.

Suddenly, Nate felt a familiar tightening in his chest. Adrenaline began to course through his veins. His temples began to pound and his heart thumped in his chest. Well, if it was a fight the boy wanted, Nate wasn't going to back down.

Despite the boy's size advantage, Nate had the distinct feeling that they would be quite evenly matched. Almost against his will, Nate's lip curled backward and a low, almost inaudible, growl of warning escaped, shocking both Nate and the bully.

"I think that he's at his locker." The sound of Larissa's voice, faint as it was, snapped him back to his senses. She wasn't in the hallway yet, but from the volume of her voice, she was getting closer with every second. Instinct took over, and without thinking about it, he knew he had to warn her, had to keep her out of sight.

"*Stop Ris,*" he thought to her, his voice both wild and urgent in his own mind. He pushed the thought towards her with more force than he had ever used before. Instantly, he felt, heard, and almost saw her come to a dead stop, just beyond eyesight. Then, all at once, he was not seeing the green-haired boy towering over him. Instead he was staring at the trees outside of the window at the end of the hall. The trees outside of the window right in front of where his sister had come to a stop. Nate blinked his eyes, confused and then both the trees and the green-haired bully were there, superimposed, one over the other.

"*What is that?*" His sister's voice whispered fearfully in his mind. He was seeing what she was seeing and by the sound of her voice, she was experiencing the same thing. Any doubt he had was answered as Larissa took another step forward.

He whipped his head around, knowing even as he did it that he was taking a huge risk in turning his back on this kid, even for a second. "*No!*" he shouted silently to her, knowing somehow that it was imperative that this kid, whoever he was, not see her.

Turning back, while silently begging Larissa to stay where she was, he fought to control the fear and anger that were growing inside of him with every passing second. He shook his head, trying to clear away the double vision, and focused on the bully in front of him. All of his movements had been so fast that none of the humans in the hall had been able to detect them.

But the green-haired monster had seen it all.

His eyes peered over Nate's head searching for the object of his attention. Nate's fear shifted instantaneously into full-blown panic. Suddenly he could not think of anything but the fact that he had to stop this kid from seeing his sister. He silently screamed again for Ris to stop, hoping that for once she would listen and not argue. At the same time, he stepped forward and pushed the boy back with all of his strength.

The boy took several huge stumbling steps backward as he tried to catch his footing. Then he fell on his bottom, slid a few more feet down the hall, and banged into a garbage can. The garbage can teetered from one side to the other before toppling over onto the boy, covering him with balled up paper.

A look of surprise blossomed on his face. He gaped up at Nate, momentarily stunned by Nate's sudden aggression. Clearly, he had not expected Nate to fight back, and, normally, Nate wouldn't have. He had never even been in the smallest scuffle. But something instinctive told him to protect his sister at all costs.

Swiftly, the moment passed and the boy recovered from his shock, and his surprise transformed into rage. Like magic, he was on his feet and moving toward Nate again, his intent clear in his eyes. Around him, Nate saw the other students scattering. Whether they were going to find teachers, or just trying to get away from the fight, Nate couldn't tell. All he knew was that he was suddenly alone in the hallway with the green-haired monster coming at him like a freight train.

At the same time, Nate felt the flesh of his palms start to tingle. He swiped them with his thumbs. To his dismay, he felt a raised bumpy pad beginning to take shape, confirming his worst fear. The adrenaline rush had triggered his shift. The rest of his body started to tingle, and Nate felt the beginnings of a thousand other tiny recalibrations taking place. If he did not get himself under control, he would shift right there in the school.

"*Nate! DON'T!*" Larissa fairly shouted the words in his mind. Her voice was filled with horror.

With Larissa's voice echoing in his mind, Nate closed his eyes to block out the fast approaching boy. He took several quick, steadying breaths. Using one of the meditation tricks that he had spent long Saturday hours learning, he did his best to quiet the adrenaline that coursed through his veins threatening to trigger his panther.

Suddenly, he heard the clack of dress shoes on the linoleum floor, and for a moment he thought that Larissa had ignored his pleas and warnings. Then someone was standing in front of him and without even opening his eyes, he knew who it was. He smelled the burnt, nutty, fragrant aroma of coffee and he realized that it was Ray and not Larissa who stood next to him. An odd sort of relief washed over him and, immediately, Nate felt the tingling in his flesh subside. His face felt tight, like a strange mask, but when he checked his palms, to his relief, the raised pads had disappeared.

When he opened his eyes, the strange boy stood just a few feet front of him, fists raised. Between them stood Ray, his own fists tightly balled. But when Nate met his eyes, the boy stopped in his tracks and his fists dropped to his sides. For the first time since he had appeared in the hallway, the boy looked uncertain, and suddenly he did not seem to be quite the threat that he had been just moments before.

Nate reached out and moved Ray aside. This was his fight. He quietly considered the other boy and it was clear that somehow the ground had shifted and suddenly Nate was in the position of power. When he spoke, Nate said only one word. "Leave." The word was all but lost in the deep growl that made his voice almost unrecognizable to his own ears.

Then, just as he began to feel in control, a smile of triumph appeared on the older boy's face. The smile bloomed into a full-blown grin that was almost mocking. Then, without another word, the older boy turned away. He did not know if he had imagined it, but Nate thought he heard the faint sound of a hiss, and then the boy was gone.

Confused, frustrated, disgusted, and suddenly exhausted, Nate turned and began walking down the hall to retrieve his calculator. He had only gone a few steps when he realized that Ray was not following him.

Nate turned to his friend, gesturing for Ray to follow him, but Ray did not move. He just stared at Nate, his eyes wide with fear.

"Come on Ray," Nate said. The other boy shook his head in shock and amazement but said nothing. After a few moments of silence, Ray turned and ran in the other direction. Just then, Larissa came to his side. In her hand, she held his calculator. He turned from away from the spot where Ray had just stood and reached to take it from her. As he turned, Larissa inhaled sharply, her face dropping into a mask of astonishment that mirrored the look that had covered Ray's face.

"Your eyes," she hissed to him when he looked at her confused. Immediately and unbidden, Nate raised his hand to his eyes. Hastily, Larissa reached into the dainty little purse that she carried and pulled out her compact. Nate took it from her and opened it curiously. He tilted the mirror upward and found himself staring into eyes that were not human.

This time, it was not just the color that made them curious. Now the shape had changed too. Gone were the human shaped irises with round pupils. It was as though his irises had bled outward, covering all of the whites of his eyes. The yellow-flecked green color was broken only by the thin slits of black that were his pupils. They were cat's eyes in every sense of the phrase. It seemed he had not been as successful at controlling his panther as he thought. Ray's actions suddenly made a lot more sense.

Closing his eyes and concentrating once again, Nate willed the panther away. In his mind's eye, the panther were standing behind him, looking through his eyes right out at the world. He didn't know how he hadn't recognized it before, and the creature did not want to relinquish its view.

Nate fought the creature for several moments before he forced it to retreat and felt the corresponding change in his eyes. When he opened them, familiar and human irises and pupils greeted him in his sister's compact. He breathed a sigh of relief.

"What was that about," Larissa whispered, motioning in the direction of his locker, her eyes wide with fear and concern. She took the compact back from him and stuffed it in her purse.

"I don't know," Nate said, shaking his head, still trying to make sense of what had just happened. He had a sneaking suspicion that the boy had been trying to get him to shift, though he could not figure out why. Or, for that matter, how the boy had known who he was and what he could do. And then Ray had seen his eyes. He looked sharply over at Ris.

"What was Ray doing here," he asked.

"He wanted to talk to you," she answered. "I think he wanted to apologize or something." Nate shook his head at the lousy timing of it all.

"Listen," he said, grabbing her wrist firmly. "You can't tell Mom and Dad what Ray saw."

"But Nate," she said softly. "What if he tells? Mom and Dad have to know. What if he tells?" she asked again.

"He won't tell, Ris." He met his sister's eyes imploringly. "Ris. Trust me. Just give me a chance to talk to him."

Larissa looked down the hall, doubt written on every feature of her face. After several moments, she looked back towards him. Huffing, she grumbled, "Fine, I won't tell. But you have to talk to him."

"I will." He had no idea what he would say, but he would figure it out. One thing was clear. Ray would have to wait. He needed to talk to his parents immediately. Because what he saw in the eyes of the baffling green-haired bully was something that he had never seen before in another human being. The boy's eyes, which were the color of weak tea, had curious flecks of yellow throughout, a trait that he had only seen in members of his family. A trait he had only seen in shifters. Maybe it meant nothing and maybe it meant everything. Only his parents would know.

"It's been confirmed. The Pantera boy was identified at the graduation ceremony."

The report was delivered by a man in the same dingy room as before. The room, however, was increasingly barren. They were preparing for a move, only the location had yet to be determined. From the sound of this news, they had found their new home.

"How can you be sure?" The response was excited, yet skeptical.

The man chuckled. "The child is so poorly trained that he can barely control his beast."

The news was excellent. Finally, the Panteras had been found. Even better, Anna Pantera had apparently been remiss in her heir's training. It seemed as if the forces were aligning in their favor.

Moving on to the next item, the boss asked, "And how goes the other part of phase two."

"Well," was the confident response. "We should have our results in a few days. A week at the most."

"Excellent. Carry on."

Chapter 6

Promises Made

"You can't tell anyone what you saw."

Ray was finally on the phone, but getting him there hadn't been easy. It had taken two days and about twenty calls. A long silence followed his words, but Nate could hear the sound of Ray's soft breathing.

"Ray! Did you hear me?" Nate's agitation had grown as the silence went on. "You can't tell anyone. This is important. You have to promise."

"How can I make that promise?" Ray asked when he finally spoke. "To be honest, I don't even know what I saw," he said, his voice wary. "Your eyes. You looked like an alien or something. What was that Nate?"

Nate was silent. He should have known that it would not be as easy as asking Ray not to tell. His friend already had too many questions. They would not go away so easily, and he did not have any simple answers. It seemed like all that was left was the truth.

"Look. I promise I will explain when I can. But right now I can't. Do you get it? Until then, you have to trust me. You can't tell anyone what you saw. Just give me a chance to explain first. Can you do that?"

Nate could almost hear the gears turning in Ray's mind, as the other boy considered his words. Finally, he said, "Okay," and Nate expelled the breath that he did not know he had been holding.

"Thanks Ray," he said gratefully. "I knew I could count on you."

CHAPTER 7

AND SO IT BEGINS...

THE PANTHER CREPT STEALTHILY along the jungle floor towards the dull echoing roar ahead. Though she could not see them, she knew that the roar came from the motors of machines. They were basic machines, but they were machines that until recently had been foreign to the landscape of Panteria.

She swallowed a growl. There was nothing that she wanted more than to tear down into the mine and take down as many of their enemies as she could. But, she could not let her anger get the better of her. She had to be wary here. She rose for a moment from her low crouched position and surveyed the ground around her. Seeing no reason to pause, she moved forward a few more paces on huge, padded feet.

Finally, when she was close enough, she chose a tree and quickly climbed it to get a better view of what was happening. Hidden among the leaves, she watched the scene below with growing rage.

The land beneath the tree had once been a gently sloping hill covered with the same trees that populated the jungle in which she now hid. Now, however, it had been all but scraped clean of the vegetation that had once grown in abundance there. All that remained was a barren patch of land that looked like the beginnings of a disease intent on ravaging the jungle around it. A large hole had been ripped into the side of the hill and a steady stream of people moved in and out of the opening, pushing large wheelbarrows full of stone. Though most of the rough was shapeless and brown, a few pieces showed slivers of green, signs of the sparkling green material that lay beneath the dirt, dust, and stone.

Some of the bandits were were-leopards. She could tell by the way that they moved and the ease with which they carried their undoubtedly heavy loads. But others, more it seemed than the last time, were humans. How humans were getting into Panteria was another mystery. The portals had been carefully calibrated so that they could only be accessed in leopard form.

The site before her was just one of several such sites that were cropping up with alarming frequency around Panteria. All were mining sites, where miners went greedily after the green crystal material that existed so abundantly beneath Panteria's green jungles.

The crystal was very much like what those in the human world would call emerald, but it was so much more precious than that. The green material was the very life blood of Panteria. Taking it from the earth weakened not only that small patch of land, but the whole of their world. And every leopard knew this fact. It was a lesson that they learned while still anakula, which made what was happening all the more disturbing.

Each time she sent regiments in to shut down one mine, another popped up. Each mine left gaping holes in the ground. There were months-old mines that were still barren and decimated. She did not know if those places would ever be green again.

The trees surrounding this mine were already starting to reflect the catastrophic damages that the mining wreaked. Dull and brown, their once evergreen leaves fell from the branches to the land below, suffocating the plants that grew at their bases.

She dug her claws into the tree, ripping the branches to shreds as her anger threatened to overwhelm her. There had been other smugglers in Panteria's past, lured by the promise of the luxury that Panteria's resources might afford them in the human world. After all, even one stone from Panteria's core would fetch a very pretty penny in the human world, and there had been and would always be leopards unable to resist that siren call. But there had been none who had operated so openly, on such a large scale, with such blatant disregard for Panteria's rules or the damage they wrought.

Four months ago, the Dowager Bastion had first mentioned her concern that something wrong was happening in their world. Within two weeks, Anna had discovered the location of the first mine. Immediately, she had rallied forces to shut down the mine and capture the thieves. That had begun the pattern. Each time she shut down one mine, another appeared, and she had yet to discover who was behind this horrific breach of Panterian laws.

After the last one, she had begun to believe that at last the problem was solved. Then, this new mine had appeared almost overnight. Where the other mines had been smaller and in the outer reaches of Panteria, this mine was huge. Bigger than all the others combined. Their enemy was becoming more brazen, which could only mean one of two things. Either they were deliberately flaunting their crimes and challenging her, or they did not care about, or worse did not fear, being caught.

Since discovering this new mine, she had kept silent, telling no one but the Dowager about it. Her hope was that, in the seeming absence of surveillance, the svengalis behind the mining would grow lax and reveal themselves. Only then she could finally put an end to this plot that was destroying Panteria.

For a brief moment, the guilt that had plagued her since she had discovered the first mine paralyzed Anna. Maybe if she had been a better Bastion, more committed. Maybe if she had made different choices. Maybe, then, this never would have happened.

She had scouted the mine for several days trying to gather some bit of information that would lead her to the identity of their enemy. But there was nothing, only person after person bearing the life's blood of Panteria out from deep beneath the surface of the earth.

Her tail twitched, and she had to fight to remain still in the branches. She itched to get closer. Even with shifter-sight, she could only vaguely make out forms, and she could see no faces. She couldn't risk getting closer though. She was too easy to identify, both in panther and in human form.

Then, there was the *fuerza*. Because of it, she dare not step for too long on the dying land. Even being this close, for this long, was making her sick. The *fuerza* took in all the energy of the land. Both the good and the bad. She would have to leave, soon.

Like a flash of lightning, the idea struck. What they needed was a spy. Someone to infiltrate the ranks of this band of despoilers to find out who was in charge. Though she could send more forces and this mine would be shut down as well, the only way to stop this once and for all would be to cut off the head. The only way to find out who that was would be to send one of their people in.

She descended the tree, eager to return to the Kula and put her new plan into action. The closer she got to the ground, the more nauseous she became. All during her surveillance, the *fuerza* had been affecting her, drawing in both the strength and the weakness of the land without filtering. She was beginning to feel light-headed.

Looking at the sun overhead, Anna figured that she had a few more hours before nightfall, just enough time to return to the Kula, share her findings with the Dowager, and get home. She wanted very much to be back at home with her family. It had been almost a week since she had seen them.

Reaching the jungle floor, Anna sniffed the ground around her before moving forward. A quick sniff was all she needed to find out whether others, were-leopard or human, had been nearby recently. Finding it clear, she set off hastily in the direction of the Kula. She had only traveled a few feet when it happened. As soon as she set her foot down, she heard the click, and before she knew it, she was thirty feet in the air, surrounded by netting. The criss-cross pattern of rope bit into her fur and her skin, and Anna realized, to her horror, that this was no regular netting.

Another moment's examination confirmed her worst suspicions. Interwoven into the strands of the rope were links of silver chain. Anna sheathed her claws, knowing they would be useless. This trap had been set by some who was very familiar with shifters in general and with her in particular.

Whoever had set this trap had known that in order to disable a shifter, silver was a must. However, this person also knew that for silver to be effective against the Anna, she must be separated from the earth, the source of her strength. The *fuerza* was one of the most closely guarded Pantera secrets and this netting sparked a revelation that Anna would never have imagined. Among the traitors was someone very close to the Pantera family.

Anna tilted her head back and let out a roar of frustration, anger, and betrayal. The cry reverberated through the jungle and echoed across the landscape of Panteria.

Miles away, in her library, the Dowager heard the cry.

Signaling for her lieutenant, a man with a round face and kind blue eyes, she ordered an immediate search of the eastern quadrant, certain that the cry had arisen from there. The man nodded his compliance and dashed from the room to gather his forces.

CHAPTER 8

OBSTACLE ELUSIONS

"Pay attention you two." The twins were back in the basement, but this time it was a Wednesday night. Like them, their father had his summers off. He was a historian and a lecturer at the local college, so he had plenty of time to torture them between semesters. Since the last day of school, they had been training at least three days a week; and Nate was sure that it was because of the near fight with the green hulk at school, though neither of their parents would confirm that fact.

He had told them the story that very same night over dinner, minus the part where Ray had seen his half-shifted face. As he related the incident, his parents had not been able to conceal their reactions. Their emotions were written across their faces. First, anger when he told them that the boy had shoved him. Then, relief when they learned that it had not gone much further than a pushing match. Finally, worry when he told them about the boy's eyes.

The last of the three responses had been the source of many hours of conversation, spoken and unspoken, between the twins. Even though, typically, neither of their parents had responded in any way to their questions, it was clear that something about the incident had bothered them.

Nate still could not banish his mother's look of concern from his mind, nor could he forget the several whispered conversations that he had happened upon in the days right after graduation. Whispered conversations that immediately stopped whenever he entered the room.

It seemed, too, that his parents had grown increasingly agitated over the last few weeks. He and Larissa had both noted that their parents were looking more and more worn. And now, here they were, with P. E. three times a week. Actually, this week it was more like every day and all night too. Their mother had been gone since last week on a research trip and their father had had them training every night.

Again, the training had changed drastically. Before, any sort of physical training was only supplemental. Now, their father was training them in martial art and combat forms, both as humans and as panthers. They were being trained to defend themselves.

He was surprised at how easily both he and Larissa were able to learn the complex aikido and judo techniques that their father presented with each lesson. He had known that as shifters, they were stronger and more agile. But did being shifters also make them natural fighters?

"Nate!" His father said sharply, with the urgency that seemed to be ever present these days. Nate reined in his wandering thoughts and turned to his father. When Mr. Pantera had his son's attention, he continued. "Today, I am going to take you outside for a bit, so that we can practice some of what we have been learning in a 'real world' setting."

Nate couldn't believe his ears. He looked quizzically at Larissa, whose expression was equally shocked. She clearly had no clue what was going on either. Their father was about to break another cardinal PFL. They had never, ever, been allowed outside in their panther form. In fact, one of the reasons that they had been home-schooled for so long was that their parents had been afraid that they would shift in public and betray the family secret.

For young shifters, any intense emotion, fear, anger, embarrassment, happiness, was enough to trigger the change. At home, there had been little to startle them and trigger a shift. Besides, their mother wouldn't have batted an eyelash if a panther cub suddenly took the place of the child sitting before her.

Nate wondered if this had anything to do with the project their father had been working on for the last few nights. For several days, they had heard hammering and sawing from the backyard, but their father had kept his projects scrupulously covered with a tarp and neither of them had been daring enough to peek.

Nate's mind flickered back to the day when his mother had stalked out of the woods in panther form. First that, then the green-haired monster, and now their father was taking them outside in panther form. It was all too strange to be coincidence.

Now was not the right time for questions. Though it seemed that there was never a right time. Not that he could have asked any questions in his current state. His father was already marching up the stairs, and Larissa turned to pad quickly behind him. Nate gathered his wits, squashed his curiosity yet again, and rushed up the stairs behind them.

After leading them up the stairs and into the kitchen, Mr. Pantera stopped at the doors to the deck. Larissa and Nate came silently to a halt. Nate could barely contain himself. Around him the kitchen vibrated, humming in his shifter-sight. He itched to see the outdoor world through his panther's eyes. His nose quivered, his whiskers shook, and his tail whipped anxiously back and forth. His body quaked with excitement, despite the vague sense of unease that filled him when he thought about what they were about to do and the possible reasons behind it.

Their father turned back to them, a grave and increasingly familiar look on his face.

"It is very important that you two do exactly as I tell you once we leave this house," he said. "When we are outside," Mr. Pantera continued. "You must stay close to me at all times, and you must never enter the woods. Not one paw, not one whisker. Do you understand?" The worry in his voice and the strain on his face quelled Nate's excitement like cold water on a fire.

He looked past his father and out of the kitchen window at the familiar treetops of the forest that had been his playground for as long as he could remember. He couldn't count the times that he and Larissa had explored the depths of those very woods when they were younger. There was even a makeshift fort in one corner, the product of a long summer day a few years back.

Back then, the woods had seemed so much bigger and more enigmatic. Like a jungle. As he had gotten older, they had lost much of their mystery. They were as familiar as a teddy bear or a favorite blanket. In fact, they weren't even proper woods, just a few acres of trees on the other side of which was an expressway.

Those happy memories wavered and vanished under the weight of their father's somber gaze. Somehow, suddenly, the woods looked ominous, the tops of the trees swaying gently in the breeze. Suddenly, he did not want to see the outdoors. Suddenly, he did not want to do anything that reminded him of all the strange happenings in the past few months. He just wanted to be a normal kid, in his room watching television or at the park with his friends, looking forward to the next soccer game, not imagining the dangers that lurked in his own backyard. Of course, normal wasn't really an option. For the twins, it never had been. He sat back on his haunches and looked intently at his father.

"You must do whatever I tell you. Do you understand?" he repeated again.

Sitting on the hardwood kitchen floors, the two panther cubs nodded their obedience with all due seriousness. With that, Mr. Pantera opened the deck doors. Motioning for them to stay put, he shifted and walked outside.

Mr. Pantera made a rather large panther, much larger than a non-were. Nine to ten feet long, from nose to tail, he dwarfed both Nate and Larissa. His massive paws were almost as large as his head, and his claws, when he flexed them, were razor sharp.

Though he was a panther, Robert was not like Nate and Larissa. His fur was black as night, but it was not spotless. The dark spots that speckled his coat were practically invisible against his black fur, but they were there. His eyes, unlike his children's and his wife's, were entirely golden yellow.

Nate watched as his father walked to the edge of the deck and scanned the yard and the woods beyond. Satisfied, Robert Pantera walked back to the door and growled, signaling for the twins to follow him outside. Nate, still anxious, hesitated only for a second before striding out the door with more confidence than he felt. What he saw as he crossed the threshold brought him to a stop so sudden that Larissa bumped into him on her way out the door.

"Move it," she said, and Nate, still spellbound walked forward just a few more feet.

Before him, the sun was just beginning to set and the sky was the color of twilight. In shifter-vision though, the blues and purples of the early evening sky were completely changed. The sky, instead, shimmered with every color of the spectrum. Whites, yellows, oranges, reds, greens, purples, blues, and even blacks danced across the sky, blending and separating before his eyes.

In this strange, intense light, every color, every texture

seemed one hundred times more vibrant. The grass was even greener, the deck furniture more red, and everything practically hummed with energy.

More than that, Nate felt like he had x-ray vision or something. The woods, which would have been dense and impenetrable in the dusk light if he were in human form, spread before him like an open book. Every rustling bush, every leaf fluttering to the earth, was as clear as if were six feet in front of him rather than sixty yards away.

Their father growled again. When he had their attention, he turned, walked over to the edge of the deck, claws clicking against the wood with every step, leaped on to the banister and down to the yard below. Larissa and Nate glanced at each another with a little trepidation, and then hastened to follow suit. They leaped up to the banister, and it was then that they saw the project that their father had been working on.

It was like an obstacle course, similar to the obstacle courses that their school set up for Field Day, a sort of mini-Olympics that Greendale Middle had every spring, but with some weird additions. There were wooden hurdles that were two times taller and ten times broader than the small plastic ones that were used at school. There was a climbing wall, also made of wood, with irregularly spaced hand and toe holds and no ropes. There were platforms that rested about twenty feet apart and also, curiously, a high jump pole, beneath which lay one of the thick gray mats from the basement.

Their father roared up at them expectantly. He wanted them down on the lawn now, and it was clear that the stairs were not an option today. Standing atop the banister, Nate looked down at the lawn. It was so far below, at least thirty feet. He had never jumped that far. Next to him, Ris stood so close that he wondered if she could feel his trembling. Then, he heard her voice. *"On the count of three okay."*

"Okay" his voice was a breathless whisper in his mind. She counted to three and then she was sailing through the air. Nate, however, had not moved. He watched Larissa land gracefully on the ground, and then walk nonchalantly to their father's side as though she had not just leapt from nearly thirty feet in the air. Now he was alone on the banister, while his father and his sister stared up at him, waiting for him to jump, which for some reason he could not.

He felt an abrupt wave of dizziness and something like fear made his heart flutter. Immediately, he felt silly. Who had ever heard of a cat that was afraid of heights? Besides, he had never been afraid of heights before. Of course, he had never had to jump from this high before.

Ris and his father were still staring up at him, and he could tell that his father was growing more impatient. He wanted to jump. He imagined himself leaping from the banister and landing as gracefully as Larissa had. But instead of jumping, he found himself digging his claws more firmly into the wood.

"Come on Nate," Larissa encouraged him. *"Once you're in the air, it's not that scary at all. In fact, it was kind of cool."*

Nate glowered down at his sister. He knew that she was trying to be encouraging, but it was sometimes so irritating that she always seemed to be just a step ahead of him. If he got an A- on the math test, she got an A+. If it took him two minutes to shift, it took her a minute and a half. And here she was again, beating him to the punch.

"Remember Nate," she called out to him again. *"Cats always land on their feet."*

Nate closed his eyes and tuned out everything around him, including his sister's encouraging, if irritating, words. Determined not to give Larissa anything more to crow about later, he gathered his courage, took a deep breath, and launched himself off of the banister. Then there was nothing between him and the earth but air. Unable to stop himself, he flailed his limbs uselessly as he fell to the ground. He tried to grab at the banister, at the deck, anything to stop the freefall.

Then, just as quickly, he landed and amazingly, as Ris had predicted, he was on his feet. He was so busy being grateful that he had not broken all of his bones that for several moments he missed the fact that Ris was laughing at him. He paused in his mental assessment of his limbs to glare daggers at her.

"What," she chuckled, leaning back on her haunches to mimic his flailing with her front legs. *"It was funny."* Nate reared back and prepared to pounce on her to wipe the grin off of her face. But their father stopped all of that by stepping between them. He growled; a low, threatening, and thoroughly intimidating rumble from deep in his chest. Though in leopard form, their communication was less exact, they did have a language of sorts, which both Larissa and Nate understood intuitively. Their father had grown exasperated by their silliness and he was reminding them of their promise.

With that, their father took off towards the far edge of the lawn, directing them to follow him. Nate promised himself that he would get his sister later, and took off after their father. He would beat Larissa at something tonight, if he killed himself to do it. Mr. Pantera stopped just short of the woods, shifted back, and produced a stop watch.

"First," he explained, "You will run the circumference of the yard. That is a distance of about two hundred yards. You should be able to complete the loop in less than five seconds. You will both run it until you do."

Nate's eyes widened. Two hundred yards in five seconds. That had to be impossible. Nothing, not even a were-leopard, should be able to move that fast.

"On your mark," his father said, and there was no further discussion. Two seconds later, he blew a whistle, and they were off. The first time around, neither of the twins came anywhere close to that time. So their father blew the whistle again, and they ran on, even as both of them still huffed from the previous race.

With each circuit, Nate felt his muscles warm and settle into panther form. His movements became instinctive, and he found himself moving faster and faster. His body seemed to do this of its own accord. He did not have to think about it at all or even try that hard. It was like his body was made to run like this and reveled in it. Like it had done this so many times before, and it was designed for this sort of challenge. He was shocked when after only five times around the track, he heard his father blow the whistle again, for longer this time. He skidded to a halt, the soft green grass like a cushion beneath his paws, and looked back at his father.

"Well done," was all the man said, as the twins came huffing to his side.

But it did not stop there. Their father moved the hurdles into place at different distances, added two seconds to their completion time. By then, the sun had completely set, and though the sky was not pitch dark, the ground was full of inky shadows cast by the trees that arched overhead. As Nate tried to mark the position of the hurdles that melted into the shadows, his father blew the whistle again.

This time it took them only four times around the course before their father stopped them again. That included the extra lap they had to run because he had knocked down one of the hurdles as he raced around the makeshift track.

Then it was on to the wall and more seemingly impossible tasks. As he climbed, Nate actually had to leap from toehold to handhold, because they were too far apart to reach otherwise. This, too, came naturally. He launched himself up the climbing wall, unbothered by the height now that he was climbing up, rather than falling down. He was amazed that his body could do things that he would never have imagined. It would have been scary, if it were not so exciting.

Their father cycled them through the rest of the apparatuses and then started them at the beginning and led them through the course again. Finally, just as Nate felt like he could not run another sprint or climb another wall, his father shifted again, growled low, and then trotted across the lawn. The exhausted twins followed. When he reached the deck, Mr. Pantera stopped, crouched low, and leapt onto the banister, landing lightly, gracefully, as if he had only hopped a foot and as though the banister were three feet, rather than three inches, wide.

The twins looked at each other doubtfully. He had to be kidding. There was no way they could jump that high. His low growl immediately signaled that he was not. This was their last test of the day, and there would be no rest until they accomplished this feat.

Their father growled again, more insistently this time. He might have been encouraging them; he might have been angry. It was sometimes hard to tell. The growling was not an exact science.

Determined to be first at something, Nate looked at Larissa, who was still contemplating the banister and then at their dad, who sat atop the banister. He crouched and, without giving himself any more time to think, launched himself into the air.

As it turned out, he could jump that high. It was the landing part that was tricky. He sailed up through the air, over the banister, and down onto the patio. Digging his paws in, he skidded to a halt mere inches before smashing into the glass doors that lead into the kitchen. He winced as the dead wood entered into the delicate pads on his feet.

Turning around, he walked gingerly back over to his father, carefully avoiding his left front paw, which had sustained the most damage. Putting his front paws on the banister, he peered over the side. Larissa was still down on the ground, looking no closer to making the leap than she was when he was on the ground beside her. It was his turn to be encouraging.

"*Come on Ris, you can do it.*" Their eyes locked and he realized that she was utterly terrified. The day kept getting odder and odder. He couldn't recall the last time that Ris had been afraid of anything.

Without asking, Nate shifted back. "Don't make her do this Dad."

For a moment his father just stared at him, his unnerving golden eyes completely devoid of sympathy. Then, in the blink of an eye, his father shifted to human form. He jumped nimbly down from the banister. Leaning over the banister, he called down to Larissa. "Come on up, I have something to talk to you two about."

Mr. Pantera walked away from the banister and took a seat in one of the four plastic red chairs that surrounded the red plastic patio table. Nate joined him. As the two waited in silence for Larissa to come up the stairs, Nate concentrated on picking the splinters out of his hands that had not been ejected by the shift.

When Larissa's head peeked over the steps, she was still in panther form. Nate could tell by the way that she was walking, slowly, with her head hung low and her eyes on the ground, that she was ashamed. She shifted as she walked towards them, saying nothing as she reached the table and took a seat in her chair.

Nate tried to think of a way to cheer her up. He was proud of his accomplishment, but not if they made his sister feel like a failure. He knew this was hard for her, that Larissa was not used to failing. "At least you don't have splinters," he said aloud. At last, she smiled, just a little.

"I brought you out here for a reason," Robert said, capturing their attention. The twins turned to him wide-eyed, with anticipation. "You both need to begin to truly understand the depth of your gifts and your powers," he went on. "The time is fast approaching when you might need them."

CHAPTER 9

THE BREAKING OF PFL #4

Long, noiseless moments passed as Nate and Larissa gaped at their father. The feeling of unease, which had been building in Nate's stomach all evening, blossomed into a full grown dread.

"What do you mean?" Nate finally blurted out. Mr. Pantera remained silent for several more long, to Nate eternal, seconds. He closed his eyes and his forehead scrunched up as though he were thinking about a particularly difficult problem. When he spoke again, his voice had a far off tone.

"What I mean is that….We have kept you safe for as long as we could….But things are changing."

In the distance, a bird's song, chirpy, happy, echoed across the lawn. Robert's eyes shot open and his gaze darted in the direction of the bird's call. He closed his mouth abruptly with a queer shake of his head, as though realizing that he had said something that he should not have. He peered off into the distance, his head cocked as though looking for something. The twins watched him, confused, and waited for him to continue.

When he began to speak again, he was facing them. "What I mean is that you need to master your abilities at this stage before we can move on to the next level of training."

The twins, who had been leaning eagerly forward, hoping at last to find some answers to all of their questions, slumped back into their seats. Nate felt an odd sense of disappointment. It was clear as the moon in the sky that something was happening. Something had changed in all of their lives. Something that quite possibly put them all in danger. Yet, for some reason, neither of their parents would tell them what was going on.

His disappointment quickly morphed into anger. Every time they were on the verge of learning some bit of information that might make sense of this series of mysterious events, their parents inevitably clammed up.

Nate opened his mouth to prod his father, but then he snapped it shut. To argue would be pointless, and the next thing his father said confirmed that fact.

"Well, I guess that is as good as any place to end the lesson. You two get washed up and I'll go make dinner." He rose and walked to the house ignoring the looks of confusion and frustration worn by Larissa and Nate respectively. Before either of the twins could say a word, he slipped through the door and was gone, leaving them to ponder his perplexing words and actions.

When they finally spoke, it was at the same time.

"Do you think...?" Larissa said.

"Wasn't that weird when," Nate begin.

Both trailed off with grim laughter.

"It was weird," Larissa agreed, finishing Nate's thought.

"Clearly something is up. Why won't they just tell us what it is?" He glanced at her out of the corner of his eye. This time, Larissa's face was scrunched up and her eyes narrowed. She looked quite like their father when she was contemplating a problem.

Nate stood up and walked over to the banister, waiting for her to answer. He peered down at the obstacle course, which cast long monster-like shadows on the grass, even in the darkness. As he scanned the yard, his eyes fell on the roped off section of the yard and without thinking about it, he backed away from the banister. He took the stairs two at a time, and before he knew it, he was down the stairs and marching across the grass. Larissa was right behind him.

"Nate," she hissed. "What are you doing? Where are you going?"

He didn't answer. He just kept marching forward. The only thing that he could think of was that he was going to get some answers tonight; one way or another. He marched right up to the rope and stepped over it.

"Nate," Larissa's voice was still in his ear, but she was farther away this time. He turned back to see that she had stopped about ten feet from the garden. "If Dad sees you,…" she warned, but her voice had a hint of curiosity in it as well. He turned away and took another step forward.

As he carefully picked his way through the weed-like flowers, they moved against his bare arms, scratching at him as though alive. He brushed them aside, stepping out of the garden and into the woods. With each step, he cautiously toed the ground before putting his full weight down. With each step, he expected to crash down through the cover of a buried well, or some such danger that would justify his parents in forbidding them to lay foot on this part of their land. And with each step, there was nothing but the firmest ground beneath his feet.

He walked deeper and deeper into the woods, not knowing what he was searching for, but knowing that the woods must hold some answers. Finally, he stopped. He was about fifteen feet in, surrounded by pines, with an occasional oak or maple, and there was nothing as far as he could see but more of the same. Turning around, he could see Larissa, just faintly, her copper skin glowing in the moonlight, her black P. E. suit blending with the shadows so that she appeared to be just a floating head.

He began to make his way out of the woods, taking no care in where his feet fell this time. With each step, he grew more and more confused and more and more angry. By the time he stepped out of the woods, he was seething.

"Did you see anything," Larissa asked, as soon as he emerged from the trees. He stepped over the rope and started back across the lawn.

"Nothing," he grunted at his sister, sweeping past her and back up to the house. "Nothing at all."

Mr. Pantera slid the glass door open and stepped out onto the deck. The yard was dark in the pale light cast by the crescent moon, but he had no trouble seeing the messenger.

"The Bastion is missing. Presumed captured." The messenger offered this pronouncement without ceremony, and Robert's heart dropped in his chest. Not Anna.

"What is being done," he asked, when he could finally speak again.

"The Dowager has ordered a search. She expects to have the Bastion recovered soon." Though the messenger sounded confident, Robert was not reassured. He knew that he would never be able to sit here and wait for news of his wife's rescue. He had to find her.

As soon as he had the thought, his mind turned to the twins. His first instinct was to take them with him, but then it occurred to him that they would be safer if he did not. There had not been any further threat here, and he might not be able to protect them there. He could leave in the morning and be back by night. They would be safe.

CHAPTER 10

CAPTIVE AUDIENCE

Anna paced the area of the small cage that held her. It was so tiny that she could traverse it in three steps. The cage was suspended off of the ground, hanging by two long silver-infused ropes from the thick, strong, tree branch. She had looked again and again for a weakness that would allow her to escape. But the cage was well-made, just as the net that had originally caught her had been.

The bars of her prison looked like stainless steel. But she could tell from the sting that she felt whenever she accidentally brushed against them, that the metal had been infused with silver as well. Though not deadly to were-leopards, silver could wound them, and too much exposure to it drained them of their supernatural strength. Plus, it was painful to touch. The top and the bottom of the cage were also infused with the metal. Only the wooden slats that lined the bottom of the cage prevented every step that she took from being agony were .

Down below was another cage. Though it was empty, it worried her. Clearly, she was not the only quarry her captors had set their sights on. She could not help but wonder who else they were after.

Growling, she turned away from the puzzling cage and her eyes fell on the rotten food that sat in one corner of her prison. The hunks of unidentifiable meat were growing green around the edges, and flies buzzed lazily above the dish. She grimaced in disgust. She had not touched the food since she had been captured, fearing what was in it. Instead she chewed on the leaves and branches that she could reach from the cage. That supply was growing preciously thin though.

She was being held in a small clearing, no more than ten yards from end to end. Besides the second cage, there were also two tents in the clearing, for her guards. There were four of them. All men. All human. There was one with curly blond hair and blue eyes, whose name was Peter. The other, Eddie, had very straight black hair and almond-shaped eyes. She didn't know anything about the other two. They came and went frequently, spending only short hours there, sleeping in the tents.

She had been there, by her count, three days, though it was difficult to keep track. They had come for her immediately, lowering her into the cage that she now occupied which was always kept elevated from the ground. Clearly, they had been well-trained. She did not know whether she would have been able to draw the *terra fuerza* through the silver reinforced bottom of the cage, and they made certain that she never had even one opportunity to try.

Surprisingly, the men were frequently unarmed. This was either a complete lapse in judgment, because there was no way that an unarmed human could hope to best a were-leopard, or supreme confidence. Given how careful all other aspects of their preparation had been, Anna was willing to bet it was the latter. Obviously, they did not expect to be found, and that worried her more than anything else.

She was in panther form and had been that way since she had been captured. That was beginning to worry her too. She did not know how long she could remain a panther without consequences.

All anakulan, the children of the leopard clan, were warned, practically from birth, that if they stayed leopards for too long, they would get stuck like that. Indeed, Panteria was filled with people who had lived too long as leopards, some by accident and some by choice, and could not shift back fully, if at all. In fact, the jungles and plains of their world were filled with leopards that had once been human that had chosen or been condemned to abandon that form forever. She had never tested the limits, herself. There was always too much at stake. And, now, against her will, she was being forced to take this risk.

She couldn't shift because her captors were human. Another lesson, ingrained practically from birth, was never to shift before a human. Anakula were schooled to stay in leopard form if they ever encountered a human. At least, until they could escape.

All of these lessons were to protect the secret of their existence. Certainly, there were humans that speculated about the existence of were-creatures, but were-leopards did their best to make sure that it remained just that. Speculation. Anakula were warned never to give humans any proof because that proof would endanger not only them but all of Panteria.

Of course, given the construction of the cage and the net, and all of the precautions that the humans took, Anna knew that their secret was exposed. And when one of the human captors spoke, he confirmed it.

"You might as well go ahead and shift back kitty." The voice came from below. "We know who you are already, your Eminence," his words were mocking. "Pitch black fur, green eyes, you are just as she described you."

Anna's ears perked up and the light of new discovery lit her eyes.

"Be quiet Eddie," the human's partner yelled at him from across the little clearing, throwing something at the man. "You talk too much."

Eddie immediately clammed up, but it was too late. He had already revealed something very important.

Anna had not known whether she was looking for a man or a woman. From the sound of it, the mastermind behind this plot was a woman. She turned in her cage and began pacing again. If it was a woman that she was after, then the list of suspects narrowed considerably. Eddie's little slip-up would come in handy, if she ever got out of this cage.

At the thought of freedom, her mind turned to the twins. She could only hope that they were safe, and their father was watching over them.

Thinking of them, her anger rose again. She paced the length of the cage, swishing her tail back and forth. Whoever this woman was, she better not have dared to touch her children. She would be very sorry if she had.

A sudden noise distracted Anna. She turned towards the source of the commotion and her heart dropped.

Out of the trees emerged two men, one of whom she had not see before, at least not in the camp. He was a leopard, and the other one was a human. The human was one of the two captors that came and went. A tall, bald, mahogany-skinned man, he rarely spoke and she had yet to learn his name.

The leopard, with his pale blond hair and fine features, was familiar. He was, she realized with a sinking heart, a part of the Imperial Bastion's Guard, which meant that their adversary was still one step ahead of them and already had someone on the inside.

Between them, the two men carried a net, much like the one that had captured her. In the net struggled another panther. Ignoring his thrashing, the two men carried him across the clearing and dumped him unceremoniously into the cage that the other men had opened for them. Once the leopard was locked inside, the men reached through the bars, cutting just enough of the netting to allow the panther to free itself.

The panther fought for a few moments more to escape the stinging netting. Finally free, the cat turned around. When Anna saw the golden brown eyes of the cat, she could not stop the growl of rage that escaped her.

Robert. They had captured her husband. Now, the twins were completely alone.

The Dowager turned to the pale-haired man who stood next to Marcus with a fearful look in his eyes. "Is this true?"

"Yes, Guardian. I am afraid it is. They came out of nowhere, I barely escaped." The man twisted his hands together in nervousness. "I am sorry. I have failed you."

The Dowager stared down at the man from her seat. There was something about him that she did not like, that she had never liked. Something about his words and his manner rang false, but she could not put her finger on it.

She looked over at Marcus, her raised eyebrow communicating her suspicion. The lieutenant gave the slightest of nods in return. He would watch the man more closely from now on. If he had anything to do with these disappearances, Marcus would find out. With that, she dismissed the two men, waiting until they were gone to rise from her chair.

Stepping off of the dais, she walked behind it and exited the chamber through a smaller door. The small room she entered was empty and cold, but the chill did not bother her at all. Shifter blood ran hot.

Striding across the room, while trying to ignore the fear that gripped her heart like a vise, she rang the bell that summoned Joffre for the second time in as many days. The worst had happened, and it could be delayed no longer. Someone must retrieve the child.

CHAPTER 11

THOSE CAREFREE, SUMMER DAYS

"ARE YOU SURE THERE is someone there?" Ms. Zhang, Eric's mom, asked the question as Nate and Larissa busily gathered their bags, mostly Larissa's, from their day at the mall. Nate turned and looked at Larissa, suppressing the smile that was trying to bloom on his face. If they were lucky, the answer to her question was no.

They had awakened earlier that morning to a note from their father. He had gone over to the campus to do some work and expected to be there all day....

Nate read the note after his sister, letting it flutter the short distance to the table when he finished it. Before the paper had settled, he was looking at his sister with a mischievous grin. "Let's go to a movie," he said, his grin widening with his words.

Larissa's first response was a dubious glance. "I don't know if that's a good idea," she said after a moment of thought.

"Not a good idea. It's the best idea I've heard in weeks." Nate exclaimed, letting out a huff of breath. "Come on Ris. Stop being a goody two-shoes. We have been cooped up in this house all summer. We didn't even get to do anything for our birthday. Don't you think we deserve at least some sort of summer vacation?"

"That's just it," Larissa replied, always the voice of reason. "They haven't been keeping us here for nothing. You and I both know that something strange is happening. What if it's not safe? What if that's why they've been keeping us at home?"

Nate shrugged. "They haven't said anything to me about us being in danger," he said pointedly, crossing his arms over his chest. "Why? Did they mention something to you?"

Nate could not help the smirk that spread across his face as his sister tried to think of a response. She knew as well as he did that their parents were keeping them in the dark about something important. It was getting harder and harder for her to justify their behavior too.

"Either way, I don't care," he concluded, saving her the trouble of responding. "This house is driving me crazy. I have to get out of here." His voice changed then, becoming coaxing. At times, he could muster a bit of her talent for persuasion. "It'll be easy. We'll go to an early movie and be back before Dad gets home. They'll never know."

He watched his sister's resolve begin to melt away. "So are you coming or what?" The last was said almost as a dare, and it was the final straw. Larissa caved.

Though she was reluctant at first, even Larissa started to get excited as they planned their adventure. They had been virtually under house arrest since the graduation. At last, their summer vacation was starting.

It was her idea to call their friends. Larissa invited Miko and Kayla, Nate invited Eric. He did not called Ray, though. In fact, he had not spoken to Ray since the call a few days after the graduation. Mostly because he did not know exactly what he would say to him when he did. Still, he knew that the conversation would have to happen sooner or later. For right now, until he figured something out, he was okay with later.

As far as he could tell though, Ray was keeping his end of the bargain. At the very least, no mob of angry villagers, or the Greendale County equivalent, had arrived at their door. So Nate guessed that Ray was keeping his word and their secret was safe for now.

Despite Ray's absence, the afternoon had been great. It was like a dream to have a normal day for the first time in a good long while. Though the twins had been worried about the time, it hadn't taken much for their friends to convince them to stay out longer than they originally planned.

After the movie, Larissa went shopping with her friends and Nate and Eric spent an hour in the arcade. By the time that they left the mall, it was already late afternoon. Luckily, Eric's mom had insisted on giving them a ride home. Still, both of the twins had been more than a little worried as Ms. Zhang turned onto their street....

Nate looked again at the dark house. "Dad is probably in the back of the house," he answered, breathing a sigh of relief that their father wasn't home yet.

"Here, Nate. Why don't you call and check. I don't want to leave you kids here, if there is no one home." She pulled out her cell phone and reached back to Nate. Nate looked at the phone and quickly shook his head.

"If he's not here yet, he's probably on his way. Dad sometimes loses track of time when he's over on campus, right Ris." He looked at his sister for support. Larissa nodded and smiled at Eric's mom.

"Nate's right, Ms. Zhang. Don't worry."

"Are you sure?" Ms. Zhang was a little over-protective.

"Mom, they'll be okay," Eric groaned, his embarrassment evident in his voice. So Ms. Zhang relented, but she still looked concerned as the twins finished gathering their things and got out of the car.

The twins walked into the house, aware that Ms. Zhang was watching them from the driveway. Larissa closed the door, locking it behind her. Then she went over to the window, lifted the curtain, and waved at Ms. Zhang. Only then did the black car back down out of the driveway.

When she was gone, Larissa turned to face Nate, and wide grins spread simultaneously across their faces. It had been obvious as soon as they walked in the door that no one was home. They stared at each other for a few breathless moments, and then they began to giggle. Nate slumped against the wall, feeling not a little triumphant. They had gotten away with their little adventure. Still giggling, the twins went upstairs to hide the evidence in their rooms.

When Nate came back downstairs, Larissa was lounging in a chair watching a show about witches and wizards that played on one of the kid's networks. She looked like she had been in the same spot all night. Smiling, Nate leapt onto the couch and together they watched the show and waited for their father.

An hour later, their father still had not arrived. By then, the sun was beginning to set. Nate glanced at Larissa, got up, and walked to the front door. Looking out of one of the windows, he scanned the fast-settling darkness for any sign of their father. The driveway remained empty and there were no tell-tale headlights moving up the road. He closed the shade, turned around, and almost bumped into Larissa who was standing right behind him, a worried frown on her face.

Stepping around her, he led the way to the garage, which was connected to the house through a door that led into the kitchen. He threw open the door, turned on the light, and his stomach sank as he realized that the car was still parked in the garage. For a moment, there was nothing but confusion, then Nate realized that maybe their dad had taken his bike. The campus was a good ten miles away, but their father sometimes rode there and back. Scanning the rack that hung from the ceiling, Nate saw that all four of the family bikes were undisturbed. Turning to Larissa, who had gone through the same deductive process, he shrugged confused, trying to think of what to do next.

The office. "We can try Dad's office," Nate said, speaking his thoughts aloud. He went to the phone and dialed the number. It rang three times, and then, unexpectedly, someone picked up. For a second, all he heard was soft slightly labored breathing at the other end of the line and then a woman's voice spoke.

"Good evening." It was the weathered voice of his father's office mate, Professor Hansen.

"Professor Hansen, this is Nate Pantera. Is my Dad still there?"

"Oh, hello dear. Robert? No, he's not here. He hasn't been here all day."

For a second, Nate wasn't sure that he understood her. "Did you say that he wasn't there," he asked, his voice sounding strangely breathless to his own ears.

"No dear. I haven't seen him all day, and I have been here since ten this morning."

Nate did not know how to respond. He managed to mumble some sort of goodbye to Professor Hansen before hanging up the phone. He did not need to repeat the conversation to Larissa. She had heard the whole thing. She turned and walked into the dining room, picking up the note. She read it over again, catching this time the postscript at the bottom of the page.

> *"If I am not home by dinner, there is lasagna in the fridge.*
> *Dad."*

She handed the note to Nate. "There's lasagna." Nate peered at the writing for long moments. It was his father's writing, at least. Squashing the knots of worry that were forming with alarming speed in his belly, Nate went, pulled the pan out of the refrigerator, and turned on the oven.

While the lasagna warmed, the twins wandered into the den. This time, noises blared forth from the television and colorful images danced across the screen unnoticed. Neither of them could pay much attention to the screen at all. Both were too caught up in their worries over their father's continued absence.

They ate their dinner in similar silence, not tasting at all the lasagna that they consumed. With every noise, with every little creak, they turned toward the front door, hoping to see their father walking through it.

As they ate, it occurred to Nate that they knew next to nothing about the business trip their mother was on. Though occasionally there wouldn't be any contact information—because of the remote locations she had to travel to for research—normally, there would at least be hotel information on the refrigerator, a phone number, something. He shared his realization with Larissa, whose eyes widened first with recognition and then even more as fear settled in.

When they finished the meal, both glanced nervously at the clock. It was already after nine. Together, they cleared the dishes. As they finished putting everything away, the clock on the microwave clicked 10:00 p.m.

"Should we call the police," Larissa asked.

"What can the police do?" Nate responded harshly, fear and frustration making his voice gruff. Larissa stepped back as though stung by his words. Nate immediately apologized.

His question was a valid one though. If what was happening had anything to do with their being shifters, the police wouldn't be able to do anything. They would only come asking questions that the twins would not be able to answer.

"If he's not here in the morning, we'll call," he said. "Maybe he just lost track of time in the library." Nate's voice was hopeful, but they both knew that wasn't the case.

After several more long moments of silence, Larissa suggested that they bring their sleeping bags downstairs. They could pop some popcorn and watch a movie. Nate agreed, and by silent understanding neither of them mentioned the true reasons for their vigil, afraid to even speak aloud their fears. With all of the other strange things that had happened in the past couple of months, neither of them would be able to sleep until their father came home. Nate went upstairs to grab their sleeping bags, while Larissa made the popcorn.

By the time Larissa was walking into the living room with the popcorn, Nate had spread out their sleeping bags and was flipping through the on-screen guide. He selected one of their favorites. It had started just a few minutes earlier, and he turned just in time for them to watch the wizard slay the creature from deep beneath the earth.

The twins settled in, wrapping themselves in their sleeping bags, though it was not cold. Listlessly, they ate the popcorn and watched the movie, each struggling to keep fear at bay.

Only hours later did they drift off into a troubled and restless sleep.

Tap. Tap. Tap.

Nate awoke to the sound. A persistent tap, tap, tap that invaded his dreams, finally breaking through his light slumber.

Tap. Tap. Tap.

He raised his head and looked around, confused, at first, when he saw that he was not in his own bed in his own room. Next to him, Larissa lay curled up in a little ball. At once, the events of the previous evening flooded into his mind. He bolted up off the floor anxiously.

Tap. Tap. Tap.

The sound grew more insistent. Nate quickly rose to his feet. The living room was still dark, but the first pale rays of dawn sunlight peeked through beneath the drapery.

Tap. Tap. Tap.

Nate stepped softly over his sister, moving toward the sound, which seemed to be coming from the kitchen. As he entered the room the sound grew louder.

Tap. Tap. Tap.

Nate's suspicions were confirmed. It was definitely coming from the deck, near the door. The curtains were drawn, so he could not see what stood beyond them. His heart started to pound in his chest as he stared at the sliding doors.

Tap. Tap. Tap.

He walked quickly over to the deck doors, standing off to one side. Reaching an arm out, he slowly pushed aside the curtain, peeking through the opening he made.

There was nothing there.

Nate let the curtain fall, exhaling a long breath in relief. It was nothing. Probably just a branch tapping against the window or something.

Tap. Tap. Tap.

Tap. Tap. Tap.

The tapping came again, growing louder by the moment.

Tap. Tap. Tap.

Nate looked around, completely confused and not a little afraid. It couldn't be just a branch, but there was nothing on the deck that could be making that noise. Screwing up all of his courage, he drew the curtain completely aside, only to find himself staring at nothing but the gray morning mists. Just as he was about to turn away, by chance he glanced down.

To his surprise, there stood a tiny but rather colorful bird, the likes of which he had never seen before. The bird was silvery, with a shock of yellow feathers on its forehead and beneath its throat that faded into a pure white belly. It had a pinkish-brown beak, pinkish feet, and its wings were grey and yellow. It stared up at him inquisitively. Then, as Nate watched, the bird leaned forward and tapped again at the door three times.

Nate felt all of the tension drain from his body. It was a bird. A bird! Probably after some worm or something. Nate's shoulder shook in silent mirth at his now evaporated fear. What a scaredy-cat he was!

He bent over, waving his hand rapidly to shoo the bird away. The bird looked up at him for the barest second with an oddly irritated look on its face. Just as quickly, it spread its wings and was airborne. Nate's shoulders shook some more, and he dropped the curtain back into place.

He turned away from the door and walked quietly back across the room. Just as he was about to leave the kitchen, he heard it again.

Tap. Tap. Tap.

He whirled around. This time the bird was at the window

over the kitchen sink, and it was staring directly at him.

CHAPTER 12

Breakfast with Windy: Part I

Nate could not believe his eyes. This was no fluke. The way that it was staring at him was uncanny. That bird wanted more than just some hard to reach worm.

Nate walked hesitantly over to the deck door, and, this time, he turned the knob. When the door had opened little more than an inch, the bird flew into the kitchen and landed unceremoniously on the granite counter-top of the center island.

As he watched, the creature proceeded to fussily smooth the feathers of its wings with its beak before turning to gaze directly into his eyes. The tiny animal's eyes contained a disconcertingly human-like intelligence.

Then, as Nate watched, the creature did the oddest thing. It bowed. Well as much as a bird might be said to bow, the bird did. Bobbing its head downward in a most serious and decorous way, the bird held it there for a long moment before raising it again. There could be no confusing the act.

It was at that moment that Nate noticed the medallion that the creature wore around its neck. Though it was tiny, Nate could detect the form of a panther with a miniscule, sparkling, green eye on the medallion that was fashioned out of some metal that looked like gold.

His mother sometimes wore a necklace like that, and he, Larissa and his father all had their own versions as well, though his mom kept them locked away most of the time. Then, when Nate thought things could not get any stranger, the animal chirped a couple of times—as if to clear it's throat—opened its beak and began to speak.

But the language it spoke was not one that Nate could understand. It was very clearly more than some birdish chirping, he could make out just enough of it to recognize that. Yet he just could not understand a word of what was being said, even as there was something so familiar about the cadence and the words.

The creature paused, blinking intensely up at him, seemingly waiting for some sort of response, which Nate could not give. After a moment, the bird cocked his head to the side, studying Nate for a moment. Then, when it spoke again, Nate understood.

"Your Eminence," it said in English, and Nate's head spun. The rest of the little creature's speech was lost on him, as he tried to make sense of what was happening. Here, before him, was a talking bird. And this was no parrot, able to mimic a few choice phrases. No, this creature had a full and well-developed vocabulary, which it was using to convey a message that was all but lost on a very flustered Nate.

Reaching up, Nate pinched himself. Hard. Surely, he must be dreaming. Certainly, he must still be lying in the living room, having crazy dreams about talking birds, brought on by too much late night television and too much stress.

"I assure you, Eminence, this is no dream." The bird looked pointedly at Nate's arm, on which his hand still rested. There was something of an English butler's formality to the bird. Each word was precise and spoken in clipped tones. Nate shook his head slightly as though coming out of a daze, and then focused in on the small quivering creature before him.

"What?....Where?....What's going on?" The question finally came out after several failed tries. "Why are you calling me your eminence?"

"Your questions will have to wait." The bird said, fluttering its wings as though they possessed the ability to push the questions away. He, and Nate only assumed it was a he because it wasn't really clear from the bird's high pitched voice, stepped across the counter to stand closer to Nate. Nate had to stop himself from stepping back as the creature moved closer. It was, after all, only a bird, he reminded himself, and he was a panther.

"Right now," the bird continued urgently, "Your parents, you, and all of Panteria for that matter, are in grave danger. You must come with me immediately."

Satisfied that it had delivered its message and its command would be obeyed, the bird launched itself off of the table towards the door. But Nate refused to open it.

"Wait!" He practically yelled the words, lowering his voice at the end when he remembered that Larissa was still asleep in the other room. A hundred different emotions and thoughts coursed through him.

"What do you mean my parents are in danger? What is Panteria? What are you talking about?"

Nate's voice took on a frantic edge as he struggled to understand everything that the bird had revealed in those few short sentences. It was not that he did not believe it. The bird's words made an odd, if unsettling, sense. But he could not go dashing off, willy nilly, on such limited information.

The bird dropped to the counter next to the door, its face a picture of birdish shock. "Worse than we thought," it mumbled, almost to itself. "Completely unprepared." The bird seemed to take a moment to regroup, fluttering its wings and chirruping to itself. Finally, it seemed ready to continue.

"Panteria," it said, "is the land over which your family rules. Well, your mother to be more exact, who is Imperial Bastion to her people. You are the heir apparent to that throne. Though if something is not done very soon, there will be no title left to claim and no Panteria to defend."

Nate shook his head, utterly confused. His parents were royalty? His mother, Imperial Bastion? And he was some kind of prince? He rubbed his hands over his face and through his hair.

"Where is this place? This Panteria?" he asked.

"That," the bird replied, anxiously hopping from one foot to the other, "I can not tell you. I will have to show you, and you will need to come with me immediately. I must insist."

Nate's mind scrambled, finally coming to rest on the most important thing that he had learned from the bird. His parents were in danger. If his parents were in trouble, he had to help them. He did not know exactly what he could do, but he would do whatever he could. He would go.

He looked down at the bird resolutely. "Fine," he said. "I'm coming. I just need to get dressed. And, I'm bringing my sister."

At that, the bird's beak dropped open. In a moment, it changed from looking completely pleased with itself to looking completely taken aback.

"You have a sister?" It croaked, sounding more like a frog than a bird.

"Sure, she's my twin....Why?"

Chapter 13

Breakfast with Windy: Part II

THE BIRD HOPPED UP and down, his demeanor of calm formality momentarily and completely shaken. The little creature was so excited that Nate thought he might have a fit.

"A sister! A sister! There is a girl! Well that changes everything!" The small feathered animal was so excited, that Nate could not help but be suspicious.

"Why?" he demanded.

"No time for that now!" The bird's voice took on an excited, high-pitched sound, so quick and chirpy that Nate could barely understand. "Of course, you must bring your sister! The Dowager said nothing about a girl! She only mentioned the boy! This will be exactly the thing!" The bird went on and on, almost as though he had forgotten Nate was in the room.

The bird's words fell away into an excited chirruping sound, and just in that moment, Larissa appeared in the kitchen doorway.

Her hair was still disheveled from sleep, errant curls sticking out at odd angels all over her head. She wore her pink cotton pajama set with the green frogs on it, and she was rubbing the sleep out of her eyes.

"Why does that change everything?" Nate demanded again. But the little bird all but ignored him now that his sister had entered the room. The creature had turned from Nate to face Larissa still chirping excitedly, while Larissa's eyes flew back and forth between Nate and their tiny visitor.

"What's going on?" she asked. "Is Dad back?" At the sound of her voice, the bird fell absolutely silent and its beak dropped open, the image of birdlike surprise. After a few moments of looking flabbergasted, the creature recovered, visibly collecting its wits and then swept a deep bow, unfurling its wings in front of it.

"Your Imperial Eminence, it is my deepest honor." Larissa looked at Nate, her face reflecting the same confusion and shock that he had experienced just a few moments earlier.

"I will explain what I can later," he said, answering the questions that formed on her face and in her mind. "Right now, Mom and Dad are in trouble, and we have to go with…" he trailed off. Turning to the bird, he asked, "What did you say your name was again?"

"Joffre Ignatius Windington the III," was the quick and proud reply. "Most trusted messenger of the Dowager Bastion of Panteria." The bird's chest puffed with pride at each word, while Nate and Larissa stared at him in amazement. That was a lot of name for such a small bird.

Nate turned back to Larissa. "And we have to go with Windy here to help them." The bird instantly deflated, bristling at the shortened version of his name, but he said nothing as they both waited for Larissa to respond.

The girl offered no words, but her actions spoke louder than any words ever could. In the blink of an eye, she disappeared from the kitchen doorway, and Nate saw her on the stairs. He followed suit, and less than a minute later, both children were back in the kitchen fully, and almost identically, clothed.

Both wore jeans, comfortable gym shoes, and green shirts,

though Larissa's was a soft mint green and Nate's was a darker grass green shirt with a collar. Underneath, Nate had put on his P. E. suit. He didn't know why, but his gut told him that he might need it before the day was done. The strap of Larissa's suit peeked out from underneath the collar of her shirt as well. Apparently, they had the same thought.

Hastily, Nate took the book bag that Larissa had brought and filled it with bottled drinks from the fridge. He took out two plastic containers and scooped hearty portions of leftover lasagna into each and passed them to his sister. Sealing them tightly, Larissa put those in the bag too. The snacks had been Larissa's idea. Ever practical, she had pointed out that they did not know where they were going or how long it would take to get there.

Just as Larissa was closing the book bag, Nate tossed her a bag of bread that had about two slices left in it. The girl looked knowingly at the small bird that was waiting impatiently for them, and put the bread in the bag too.

After only five minutes, the twins were ready. They walked over to the bird, who paced the floor next to the sliding doors. Nate slid the door open and, immediately, Windy was airborne, flying out the door and then making several giant circles over the house. The twins walked outside and Larissa closed the door behind them. The click of the lock echoed with a kind of finality in Nate's head. He knew, without a doubt, that from that moment forward their lives would never be the same.

Abruptly, Windy stopped circling the patio and flew off towards the trees, directly for the dead zone. Nate and Larissa followed, running down the stairs after him, hesitating only a moment before crossing over the rope that sectioned it off. When he reached the woods, Windy flew forward into the trees. Then, quite suddenly, he was gone.

Nate and Larissa stopped short. They looked quickly at each

other and then turned to peer at the spot where the bird had disappeared from sight.

"Where do you suppose he went?" Larissa asked.

"He has to be in there somewhere," Nate replied, squinting harder. "Maybe he's hidden by the leaves." They waited for the bird to reappear. Suddenly they saw movement in the trees, and Windy was flying back towards them at top speed.

Landing on Nate's shoulder with a military precision that would have been astonishing had the circumstances not been so serious, the bird turned to Larissa and said, "I had forgotten to tell you. You must be in leopard, erh, panther form to enter Panteria from this world."

Quite suddenly, the twins were very unsure. Here they were, following this creature, a talking bird no less, out to who knew where.

Larissa spoke first. *"Nate are you sure we can trust this bird? What if he is not who he says he is."*

"I'm not sure," the boy admitted, sighing with frustration. *"But he says that Mom and Dad are in trouble. We know that Dad didn't come home last night, and we haven't heard from Mom in more than a week. How else would he know that they weren't here?"*

"You can shift back once you are on the other side," Windy informed them, sensing the reason for their hesitation. "Of course, that will make our travel slightly more difficult and a good deal longer." The twins' eyes shifted momentarily to the bird and then back to each other.

"If Mom and Dad are in trouble, how do we know that he is not the reason why?"

At that, a grim chuckle escaped Nate. *"Him? Really Ris?"*

Larissa narrowed her eyes. *"You know full well what I mean. How do we know he's not leading us into some sort of trap?"*

"Well," Nate thought for a moment, his brow deeply

furrowed. *"What about his medallion?"* Larissa's eyes flickered to the medal around the bird's neck. *"It's kind of like Mom's and ours. Maybe that's a sign we can trust him. Besides Mom and Dad are in trouble, Ris! What else are we going to do?"*

Larissa considered his words for a long moment and then nodded. Nate breathed a sigh of relief. At least she didn't argue with him about it; not for that long anyway. They had to go, even if Windy turned out to be foe rather than friend. And, of course, if he were foe, well, they could just eat him or something.

Quickly, Nate and Larissa took off their t-shirts and jeans and stuffed them into the book bag. Luckily, there was plenty of room. Suddenly, putting on their P. E. suits seemed like a really smart idea. Nate shifted, as Windy launched himself from the boy's shoulder into the air.

"A little warning next time would be nice," the bird huffed as Larissa secured their provisions on his back.

As Nate adjusted to shifter-sight, he focused on the woods before him, realizing that they too had changed. Is this what their woods looked like in shifter-sight? How was it that he had never noticed it before?

It was no subtle difference. Gone were the familiar pines, maples, and oaks. In their place were massive trees with huge roots, green with moss, that burst forth from the ground growing skyward before plunging precariously back down into the earth. The effect created an obstacle course of raised root hurdles, underneath which grew impenetrable bush.

The trees rose hundreds of feet in the air, with huge branches, almost the size of tree trunks themselves, that burst randomly forth from the massive trunks. From the resulting web of branches grew huge, umbrella-like leaves. Some were shaped like hearts; other like fans. Others still had branches with hundreds of tiny feather-like leaves. All were so thick that the sunlight was practically blocked from reaching the ground below. Instead of the bright yellow light that was beginning to color the sky over their heads, the jungle before them—because this was a jungle and not just some backyard woods—was bathed in a cool green light, under which everything looked almost normal to Nate and Larissa's shifter-sight.

"*What is that?*" The question was voiced with quiet awe.

"*It's amazing,*" was the equally awed response.

"That is Panteria." Windy's words came as though in answer to the twin's unspoken question, though the twins knew that he could not have heard their thoughts.

The bird fluttered into the jungle ahead of them, and the twins, after a moment of hesitation, took their first steps into Panteria.

CHAPTER 14

Enter Panteria

As they entered the jungle, the house behind them all but disappeared. When Nate turned back, all that he could see was the faint, ghostly image of the backyard and the house, superimposed like a mirage over trees that extended as far as he could see into the distance. And he could only make out that much if he squinted.

He walked back toward the place where the backyard should have been and reached towards it. To his amazement, he watched his paw fade until it was a mere ghostly outline of itself. A mirage, like the house and the backyard. Oddly, he could still feel the full weight of it, wiggling on the other side, but he could see right through it to the plants that darkened the jungle floor beneath. He turned to Windy, his panther features twisted in confusion. Again, anticipating the question, Windy offered an explanation.

"It is both a mirage and not a mirage," he came to rest on an upturned root near Nate. "To any other creature who passes this way, the path continues unbroken. Which is fortunate. Otherwise, you would routinely end up with a yard full of Panterian creatures. Only you and your family have access to the portal through to your yard. Oh, and those given a special pass." He puffed out his chest to display the panther medallion tied around his neck on a cord. "Now we must go. The Dowager Bastion awaits and we have at least several hours of travel before us. More, if you want to shift back into human form."

Nate and Larissa agreed silently that it was best to stay in panther form. What did it matter at this point? They had already broken the rule. They might as well make their travel easier.

As Nate turned to follow, he abruptly noticed the curious feeling in his paws. They were tingling as though they had fallen asleep. He stamped his paws, trying to rid them of the strange and irritating tingling sensation. It worked. Temporarily. Each time he lifted a paw from the ground, the tingling feeling disappeared instantly, like magic. But the feeling returned just as soon as he placed his paw back on the ground. What was worse was that the tingling seemed to be spreading, traveling up his legs and into the rest of his body, so that in mere moments his entire body felt as though it were being pricked by millions of little pins. Not exactly painful, but definitely uncomfortable.

He looked curiously over at Larissa, trying to figure out whether she could feel it too. She was gazing around at their surroundings with a look of awe on her face. What she was not doing was the strange dance that he now performed, trying to rid himself of the sensation that was rapidly becoming unpleasant.

In that moment, the feeling changed. Suddenly rather than a million tiny, irritating pin pricks, his body felt like it was being washed over by wave after wave of hot, almost scalding, water, traveling up from the pads of his feet to the tips of his ears. The energy made him feel both alive and energized but also vaguely frazzled, as though he were losing control of his body.

"Nate." His sister's voice hissed in his mind. *"Nate."* The

call was louder this time. He looked over at her. He had no idea how many times she had called his name.

"*What?*" He replied, lifting first one paw and then the other, testing the curious effects of the sensation that he was experiencing.

"*Windy has asked twice if we were ready to leave.*" Larissa eyes were narrowed as she contemplated his strange activity. Her face was a mask of confusion. "*Are you okay?*" She asked, tilting her head to the side.

"*Can't you feel that,*" he asked. Larissa thought about it for a moment.

"*Well, I did feel the ground shake a little just a second ago.*" She replied.

"*No, no. That's not what I'm talking about. Don't you feel that tingling?*" She shook her graceful feline head once, and he realized that she had no idea what he was talking about. Meanwhile, glancing up, he saw Windy staring impatiently down at them both.

"*Never mind,*" he said finally. "*Let's go.*" Both of the twins looked back to their guide, and Windy, taking his cue, launched himself skyward, flying south. This time the bird stayed low beneath the branches of the trees so that the twins could follow.

The twins trailed after the creature running, at times, through the undergrowth, at other times leaping from root to root, because that seemed easier than trying to pick their way through the thick brush that grew beneath. With each stride, Nate felt waves of energy entering his body. Energy that both unsettled him and simultaneously invigorated him.

Even as they traveled at their urgent pace, the twins could not help but gaze around them at the wondrous landscape over which they journeyed. While it had seemed like a wall of green when first they stepped into Panteria, the twins soon discovered that the jungle was filled with unexpected color. Everywhere there were gigantic blooms of pink, orange, purple, and red around which fluttered butterflies of the most vibrant sapphire blue and sunshine yellow. Large, brightly colored birds, some red, some green, some yellow flitted in and out of the tree branches overhead. Nate wondered if they could talk too, like Windy.

As he leapt from root to root, Nate watched closely for the bright green frogs with glowing red eyes that seemed to be everywhere. Their skin was poisonous, or so Windy warned. The poison wouldn't harm the twins too badly, but it would sting like a jellyfish. Salamanders and chameleons ran up and down tree trunks, the latter half green, half brown, changing color as they moved. To Nate it was all so utterly foreign, and yet there was a nagging familiarity about it at the same time.

There were other creatures too. Creatures that he could not see but that he could smell. Their scents were varied, pungent and sharp and, to Nate's growing horror, appetizing. He was shocked that his mouth began to water and he had a sudden urge to veer off course and find the source of those smells.

After traveling for a couple of hours, Nate could tell that Larissa needed to rest. She was falling behind as he and Windy raced through the jungle. All of the leaping and running was exhausting, especially after a night when neither of them had gotten much rest. Logically, he knew that he should be fatigued too. His night had been just as restless as Larissa's had. Instead, his body coursed with energy and he felt like he could run all day. Even so he signaled to Larissa that they should stop for a while, knowing that she would never be the first to admit that she was tired. Besides, he was suddenly starving.

Larissa nodded at him and let out a short roar, signaling to Windy, who was high above, that they would stop. As the bird came fluttering down from the sky, she shifted and then helped Nate remove the book bag that held their snacks.

The jungle around them chattered with the noise of unseen creatures. Birds called to one another. Insects hummed and trilled, though they stayed, thankfully, far away from the twins. There were other sounds. Sounds that neither Nate nor Larissa could identify. Sounds that were vaguely haunting in this place that was lit only by a cool green light.

They chose trees that were close to each other and used the upturned roots as chairs, leaning their backs against the tree trunks as they scarfed down the cold lasagna and drank lukewarm water. To Nate, who had never been so hungry in his life, it was the most wonderful meal that he had ever eaten, and the double layers of meat in the lasagna did much to replenish Larissa's flagging energy. Nate quickly downed his first bottle of water in seconds but only sipped at the second, though he was still parched. Not knowing how much further they would travel, he thought that maybe he should try to conserve.

"Windy," Nate asked, resealing his now empty lasagna container. "Where are we going anyhow? Where does this Dowager live?"

The bird took a few more pecks at the crusts of bread that the children had thoughtfully packed. He was grateful for the meal, as he had flown all the way to their home without stopping and was actually quite famished. He swallowed the mouthful, took several sips from the water that Larissa had poured into the bottle cap for him, and finally spoke.

"We are going to the Kula," he replied. "That is where the Dowager Bastion awaits."

"The Kula," Larissa said slowly as though testing the weight of the word on her tongue, confusion awash on both her and Nate's faces.

"It is the home of the Kulan," Windy said, which did not really help the twins. They had never heard that word before either. "The leopard people," the bird explained further, and then with a little more exasperation, "Your people."

Understanding lit the twins eyes, and he continued. "In a way, the Kula is like a keep. All Kulan can live there, when they choose or need. All can find home and sanctuary there. It is also the home of the Bastion, the leader of the Kulan. The Dowager Bastion lives there and has been its steward since your mother left."

Nate's mind spun for what must have been the hundredth time that day. He could not believe that his mother used to live here, and yet she had never mentioned this place at all. With each word that Windy spoke, his world seemed to unravel a little bit more. He was beginning to feel like nothing that he thought he knew was true.

The bird opened his mouth to speak again, clearly warming to his subject matter. Then, abruptly, a loud angry growl echoed through the forest. The roar was filled with rage. The twins turned to each other fearfully. The noise echoed around them, raising the hairs on Nate's arms, and Windy suddenly became noticeably anxious.

At once, he was in the air, moving so fast that even the twins had trouble following his flight. Then he was back on the ground, next to Nate.

"Hide," he squeaked, trying to lower his high-pitched voice to a whisper.

Nate looked over at Larissa. She was already in a flurry of frantic motion. Quickly, he gathered his things, stuffing them haphazardly back into the bag. Then, following

Larissa's lead, he dove beneath the root that he had just been sitting atop. The bushes beneath the trees provided plenty of cover, and he pressed himself as far into the nook as he could.

"Can you see anything," he thought to Larissa, who was completely hidden from his view.

"Nothing," she replied, her voice sounding faint and breathless in his mind.

Long moments of silence followed, and then he felt it. The cold shiver traveled violently up his back, and the hairs on the back of his neck stood at attention. The shock of it was so sudden that it was actually painful. His skin felt like there were thousands of tiny little vermin marching across it. He wanted to swipe his hands across his arms, but he held himself still as the unpleasant sensation slithered over him.

He recognized the feeling. It was the same thing that he had felt on graduation day, when he had first encountered the still mysterious green-haired bully. Swallowing the growl that was crawling up his throat, he pulled himself more tightly into a ball, held his breath, and waited for the feeling to pass. Slowly, it did. Seconds later, he heard Windy's voice again.

"Quickly children," he said. "We have rested here for too long. You will not be truly safe until you are inside the walls of the Kula. Until we get you to the Dowager." Larissa handed Nate the plastic container that had held her lunch, which he hastily packed in the bag with his own. They both swallowed the last of their drinks, and then shoved those bottles into the bag as well. After Nate shifted, at once feeling the tingling energy surge back into his body, Larissa helped with the bag before shifting herself. Then they were off again, traveling south once more.

Soon the trees began to thin out, and they were able to travel even faster. Then, all at once, they left the jungle behind completely, and they were traveling across a wide plain grown tall with lush grasses, just a few shades lighter than the dense jungle growth. The blades were so tall that they nearly reached the top of the twins' heads and tickled their underbellies as they passed over the plain.

Out of the corner of his eye, Nate saw a flutter of movement. Across the grassland leapt dense herds of gazelle, and their pungent, heady aroma reached Nate from across the distance. It was the scent that he had smelled earlier in the jungle. Nate slowed for a moment, captivated at once by their beauty, but also amazed because they looked, quite suddenly, like food. He unexpectedly ached to chase after them, to try his skills as a hunter. It was a conscious effort to stay the course behind their flying leader, rather than to veer off after that delectable prey. Just beyond the gazelle, a turquoise-green lake, so huge it looked like an ocean, glimmered in the now yellowy sunlight.

"The Lake of Falcons," Windy told them, circling back to fly between the twins who ran exhaustedly side by side. As he spoke, Nate noticed the dark shadows that whirled and dipped in the sky above the lake. "It's just a bit further now." The bird continued and then he was aloft again, flying with seemingly greater speed toward the dark jungle that loomed ahead. Hearing his words, the twins quickened their pace, eager both to end their journey and to discover the mysteries behind it. Never for a moment, even in encountering this fantastical new place, had the twins forgotten that somewhere, somehow, their parents needed them.

Beyond the trees just ahead, they could see the tall green peaks of what looked like mountains in the distance. *"I hope we don't have to climb that,"* Larissa thought.

"I know," Nate huffed, even his energy starting to flag. *"I feel like my paws are about to fall off."*

They plunged ahead into the shadows beneath the trees,

and as they moved deeper into this patch of jungle, Nate felt the earth beneath his feet change. The difference was subtle, but Nate felt it in the energy that entered his body now. Before, it had been tingly, electrifying, now there was an almost soothing quality to it. Nate's muscles, tense from the long journey, seemed to immediately relax. The nervous energy that he had collected over the course of their travels, quieted, no longer racing through his body, looking for a way out. He felt, quite suddenly, refreshed, like he could run for another half day, or even more.

It was so strong that even Larissa felt it this time. *"What is that,"* she thought at him, shivering from the sensation that filled the air around them.

Without knowing how he knew, Nate said to her, *"I think that we are getting closer."*

Ahead, Windy alighted on a tree branch and Nate and Larissa realized that the path they traveled fell off to an abrupt end. Directly in front of them was a huge chasm that seemed to stretch on for miles. Out of the chasm rose the tall mountain they had spied when entering this last patch of jungle. The mountain was covered with trees, so that it almost blended with the jungle that was its backdrop. The two stopped and glanced up at Windy expectantly.

"There it is," the bird said with pomp and an almost proprietary pride. "The Kula." The twins looked around. The only thing that they saw was a huge mountain rising out of the chasm.

"Look more closely," Windy advised. "It's right in front of you."

The twins turned to each other. *"Silly bird,"* Larissa thought training her eyes back on the mountain, *"the only thing here is that....OMG!"*

"What?" Nate questioned looking frantically around,

trying to figure out what he missed.

"*Nate,*" Larissa's voice was an awed whisper echoing inside of his mind. "*It's the mountain. The mountain is the Kula.*"

CHAPTER 15

THE KULA

It was like something out of a movie, and yet like nothing they had ever or could have ever imagined. What had appeared from the distance to be the peaks of a mountain, were actually the highest turrets in what would have more aptly been called a city. Even more spectacular, the city seemed to be made entirely of trees. Not simply wood or logs, but living trees that had somehow naturally sprouted into a city.

Massive trunks and branches, green with leaves, intertwined to form a wall that opened into a massive, elaborately-wrought front gate. The same sort of trees formed all of the buildings that the twins could make out. Nate and Larissa could make out the vague lines of the turreted towers and terraced levels that all seemed to lead upward to the highest tower of the Kula. At every level, the buildings were covered with leaves and vines that intertwined with the tree trunks and branches.

The cliff that they stood on was not really a cliff but a steeply sloping hill that descended down into the wide valley below, which extended as far as the eye could see in either direction. The valley was blanketed in lush grass, though, here and there, clumps of trees burst forth from the tall green blades.

In the grass, the twins saw leopards, dozens of leopards, of all sizes. Some were resting, some were playing, and some seemed to just be out for a stroll.

Throughout the valley, paths of cleared land cut swaths through the grass creating walkways. There were paths that went both east and west, splitting in the distance in either direction. Another path began at the bottom of the very hill that they stood atop. It traveled in a straight line toward the gates of the Kula, intersecting with the other paths to create a huge crossroads. At the point where the path intersected with all of the others, there was a lavish fountain carved with all sorts of leopard images and made with some sort of burnished metal that gleamed warmly in the sunlight. The path continued on the other side of the fountain and led right up to the ornate front gates.

The twins' astounded reverie was interrupted as Windy quite suddenly opened his beak and let out several loud shrill chirps. Nate and Larissa both turned to the bird, amazed that such a tiny creature could summon such a sound from inside. The sound trumpeted out across the valley, seeming to reverberate endlessly. All of the leopards below stopped and turned towards the hill. Instinctively, the twins crouched low, hiding themselves among the shrubs.

Windy glanced down at them. "We have traveled this far alone by necessity," he explained. "With just the three of us, we were safer, less conspicuous. The Dowager has arranged an escort for the rest of the journey. It would not do for you to meet with harm when you are so near."

As the twins watched from their hiding place, single leopards began to break away from smaller groups scattered across the plan, as though they had been waiting for the call. In moments, a battalion of ten leopards had gathered near the fountain. Then, at once, the ten were loping down the path coming to a halt at the base of the cliff. As the leopards fell into position, Windy spoke again.

"The Dowager awaits," he said briskly. Importantly. Without another word, he was aloft and making his way down into the valley and towards the waiting group.

The twins followed, though with caution. It was much easier for him to fly than it was for them to pick their way down the steep hill. To their surprise and relief, their panther bodies seemed to be made for just this sort of climbing, and they were able to manage the hill in quick order even though Nate struggled a bit with the bag strapped across his back.

As they reached the bottom, the leopards moved toward them. They were a rainbow of creatures, their fur ranging in color from the palest gold to a burnished orange that was almost red. This surprised Nate. For some reason, he had believed that, aside from panthers, all leopards had the same golden fur and yellow eyes. But these leopards were as distinctly shaded as he and Larissa, though all of them had the same amber eyes.

As the strange creatures approached, Nate once again felt the violent shiver up his back, amplified by ten this time. His fur felt like there were thousands of tiny, invisible insects scuttling through it. He realized, then, that the feeling must have something to do with being around other shifters. It was weird though, because he had never had that feeling around his family.

As he considered this, the waiting leopards flanked them on all sides. Three to the left, three to the right, and two in both the front and the back. Once the cats had positioned themselves, Windy was aloft again leading them down the path towards the Kula, and slowly the company moved forward, trailing behind the bird.

As they approached the fountain, the twins began to

notice that something strange was happening. Everywhere around them, the leopards that they had seen walking, resting, and playing from above, were staring. Games stopped. Walks halted. Even the sleeping cats seemed to sense something and began to raise their heads. The children felt the weight of hundreds of appraising golden eyes upon them as they moved forward.

Gradually, leopards left the grass and others descended from the trees. All of them walked over to gather along the path the twins now traveled. By the time the twins reached the fountain, the gathering leopards had formed a phalanx of sorts, silently watching their progression. Nate quite suddenly felt less like a panther and more like a fish in a bowl, and the feeling made his hackles rise. Added to that, the skin-crawling, shiver-inducing feeling of shifter power had intensified exponentially.

He could feel the fur on his back standing on end, even as he fought against the feeling that was fast overwhelming him. He wanted to break away and run, but the leopards that flanked them maintained their stately pace. It was almost like the display was deliberate.

"This is creepy," he thought to his sister, wishing that all of these strange cats would stop staring.

"I know," his sister thought back. *"But I don't think they mean us any harm. I think they are just…curious."*

Indeed, they had much to be curious about. The spectacle of the leopard battalion would have been enough by itself. However, Nate quickly realized that it was more than their escort that made the twins a curiosity for those who watched them pass. Something else about him and Larissa made them stand out among all of the other cats that gathered there. For of all the leopards that gathered, and there must have been almost a hundred there, none shared the twins' unique coloring. There were other dark-coated leopards, but none with coats quite so midnight black. All had spots and none possessed the Pantera clan's green eyes.

"Don't be nervous," Larissa instructed, sounding like her usual bossy self, which was oddly comforting to Nate in that moment. *"Just keep walking."*

As they approached the Kula, the gates began to open, spreading wide before them. They walked inside and quickly discovered that they were in a little vestibule of sorts at the other end of which was another set of gates. Nate, relieved to be away from the hundreds of silent watching eyes, exhaled a deep breath.

Beyond this second set of gates, the twins could see an inner courtyard covered by a layer of short green grass. In the center of the courtyard was another octagonal fountain very much like the one that they had just passed. Behind the fountain, a large domed building came into view. Abruptly their escort came to a halt. Still completely surrounded, the twins were helpless to do anything but follow suit. Windy fluttered down out of the sky and landed in front of them.

"It is customary," he explained, "to enter the Kula in human form." As he said the words, the leopards around them began to shift. In seconds, they were encircled by humans of varying sizes, shapes, and colors. All of them wore a version of the P. E. suit, except that theirs were lighter in color, tawny to match their fur. Nate could tell, just from the looks on their faces, that they were not average leopards. They looked hardened, military, their glances scanning even the empty vestibule for signs of danger.

There was one exception, a young girl with hair that was shockingly red. Not strawberry blond, not carrot red, but some shade of scarlet that did not appear in nature. She appeared to be only a few years older than the twins, probably about sixteen, and , like the twins, the girl's brown eyes were flecked with yellow. Her eyes were as watchful as the rest of the troop, but her face, despite her attempts to make it hard, was still soft and girlish.

As the twins watched, the girl walked over to the wall near the inner gate. She gave a tug and slid open a door of a compartment that had been invisible until that moment. She proceeded to pull some garments out of the chamber, tossing one to each member of the company. Within seconds, all of the members of their guard were dressed in the weird, flowing clothing.

The twins eyed the bird that had become their trusted guide. "For purposes of identification," he continued as explanation. "Though it is true that no two leopards have the same spots, it is sometimes rather difficult to identify friend or foe when in leopard form. Of course, identification has never been a Pantera problem." The bird paused for a moment, appraising the twins' pitch black fur. "It is a very old custom, dating back to darker times in Panterian history. It is mostly just tradition now. It is, however, protocol," he finished, moving his little wings in a gesture like a shrug.

The twins did not need any further urging. Nate felt an odd sort of relief at the idea of seeing his human hands again. This was the longest either of them had spent as panthers in years, if not in their entire lives. Quickly, Larissa shifted and removed the bag from Nate's back so that he could do the same.

Only, suddenly, he couldn't do the same. In his mind, just as he had done many times over the last several weeks, he urged the panther to depart, but this time, the creature wouldn't budge. Nate grew frustrated. He thought that he had reached a tentative truce with his beast, yet it struggled with him now as he tried to will it away. The panther seemed to revel too much in the feel of this land. It did not want to relinquish its hold.

All at once, Nate was aware of the creature that seemed to be both a part of him and yet separate from him inside of the panther shell. As before, the image appeared in his mind's eye. He saw that it was his panther half that inhabited and animated his body, infusing every part of the panther, from the paws to the tail to the tips of the ears. His human half, on the other hand, was wrapped neatly inside the panther, tucked away from contact with his own bones and skin.

Several long moments passed as Larissa and the others waited expectantly.

"What's wrong?" Larissa thought to him.

"I don't know," Nate replied as he waged a power struggle with his creature. *"I can't seem to shift."*

Larissa turned to the others in the group who watched curiously. "I think he's tired," she explained. Several of the escort nodded in understanding, but the redhead only looked on quietly, a sneer of disgust curling on her lips. The look of anger in the girl's eyes almost made Larissa physically recoil.

Still, her explanation bought Nate a few more moments. He used that time to plead silently with his panther, which, just as it had before, gave no indication that it heard him at all. Fed up, Nate gave up on trying to negotiate with the stubborn beast. Turning back to the image in his mind, he focused on his human half instead, willing it to move. It took some doing, but finally he was able to get his human side to move. Reaching his phantom human hand down into his front paw, he pierced through the panther form and touched his fingers to the ground, which was suddenly quite real beneath their tips. That seemed to do it.

At last, he began to feel the shift taking place as bones changed size and fur and tail receded. Seconds later, he was kneeling on the grass in human form. He stood and, together, the twins put on the clothes that they had packed.

Finally, when all stood human and clothed, the inner gate swung inward and away from them. Together, the band entered the Kula.

CHAPTER 16

THE ROOTS OF THE TREE

INSIDE THE GATES, THE courtyard bustled with activity. Everywhere, there were people, all different kinds of people, moving about. Everyone wore the long, flowing, tunic-like clothing that the guards had donned before entering the gates. The tunics were fitted with v-necks and flared out slightly from the hip. They seemed to be made of a linen-like material and, without exception, all were sleeveless.

The men and boys wore pants beneath their tunics, and some of the women and girls did too. Some of the women wore them without. On others, the tell-tale, textured leg of a P. E. suit peeked out from beneath their flowing clothes. Some wore belts made from the same light weight material. Others wore no accessories. A few of the people wore light colored sandals on their feet, but most were barefoot.

Nate and Larissa quickly surmised that while it was customary to shift when entering the Kula, it was apparently not customary to remain in human form once inside. Among the people padded leopards of all different sizes. Some walked side by side with humans, clearly their companions. Others moved alone through the vast courtyard. Both people and leopards meandered through the plaza, which, like a town square, was filled with various shops, going about their daily business. However, with the twins' arrival, all of that came to a halt. Everywhere, shifters stopped what they were doing to stare at the small band. Their chatter, in that same familiar yet indecipherable language, quieted as they curiously considered the twins.

As they moved slowly through the crowd, Nate noticed three things that struck him as odd. First, almost all of the people were wearing some shade of green. There were a few white, grey, black, and even tawny tunics among them. But without question, green was the color of choice among the people of Panteria. Even their guards wore the same color tunic, which was the palest shade of green, so pale that it was almost white.

Nate looked down at his own green shirt in wonder. In it, he seemed to blend, at least a little, with the strange leopards that surrounded him, though the cut of the shirt and the jeans that he wore still marked him as an outsider. Larissa, too, seemed to fit, in her mint-green shirt. For him, the choice had been automatic, instinctive, even though he rarely wore the color; green was his sister's thing. It was as though somehow they had known.

The second thing that Nate noticed was the way that the people around him moved. All of them, from the youngest toddlers walking with their mothers, to the gray-haired men and women, moved with a mesmerizing and fluid grace. But it was more than just a sinewy grace that characterized their movements. They moved faster, rushing here and there, at a pace that would have been difficult for a human to maintain, but that seemed natural and even leisurely for these creatures.

Again, there was something that was simultaneously alien and familiar in their movements. Then he remembered. It was the way that he and Larissa used to move, unconsciously graceful and supernaturally agile, until their father had trained it out of them. It had been so long since he had moved that way, because no human, which is what he was supposed to be, could move that way.

The last thing didn't so much strike him as odd, as it was just plain odd. At first, he thought that his eyes were playing tricks on him when he saw a spotted tail peeking out from beneath the green tunic of one woman who had stopped to gawk as the group passed by. He turned to get a better look but was hustled forward by the shifters that still flanked him and Larissa.

Then he began to notice other oddities sprinkled throughout the crowd, shifters that seemed to be caught between human and leopard form. Some had cat ears rising out of the sides of their faces. Others had paws and claws instead of hands. One was completely human, in form, but was covered with fine spotted fur from head to toe. He could not help but gape. It was as though someone had loosed a circus into their midst.

"Did you see that," he thought to his sister as they were hustled through the crowd. Her answer was an imperceptible nod. Just when they had thought that this day could not get any more strange.

Windy, who had momentarily disappeared, fluttered down, perching on the redhead's shoulder for a minute and whispering to her. Grimacing, she turned back to the group. Again, Larissa was struck, almost physically, by the cold anger that filled the girl's eyes as her eyes fell on them. When the older girl spoke, her tones were clipped and harsh.

"Follow me. The Dowager has ordered that we bring you to her immediately." Taking the lead, she moved the band through the maze of people and buildings. The girl led them around the large domed building towards the part of the Kula farthest from the gate. Windy flew ahead, above the crowds, into the archway of one of the tallest towers in the Kula. As they reached the tower, the redhead turned to the others.

"I will take them from here." Hearing her words, the rest of the group turned and immediately left the entrance, dispersing into the crowd. It was clear that the girl carried much more authority than her years would suggest.

As the twins entered into the building, they realized that the tower enclosed a staircase that spiraled up, up, up, disappearing into the darkness.

"You have got to be kidding." Nate whispered the words aloud. After their journey, he did not know if he had it in him to make it up those stairs.

"There has to be an elevator." Larissa huffed almost at the same time.

"Elevator?" Windy questioned, continuing on without waiting for their explanation. "These stairs will take you to the Bastion's Chamber. Bailey will guide you the rest of the way."

At the sound of her name, the girl swept into the tower and with a brusque, "Follow me," began to climb the stairs.

The children paused, turning back to Windy, who rested on the floor. As he had done when they had first met, which though it was only that morning seemed so long ago, the bird did a birdly little bow. "Until next we meet, descendants of the Kulan."

His goodbye was very formal. The bird seemed to wait for some sort of response, and Nate sensed that there was some proscribed way to reply. But not knowing it, he simply raised his hand and waved good-bye.

"Thanks Windy," the twins cried as the bird flew off, waving until he disappeared from sight. Then with a quick glance at each other, they turned and began the long climb up the stairs.

Unlike the bustling courtyard, the stairs inside the turreted building were strangely silent. The twins passed not one other person as they trudged towards the top. At regular intervals, the walls were hung with funny little lamps that dimly lit the dark recesses of the tower. Where the power of the lighting stopped, the twin's amplified vision kicked in, so that they were able to see their way pretty easily despite the low light.

Bailey was waiting at the top for them, her face impatient, her crimson hair dimmed to a much more reasonable deep burgundy in the faint light of the tower. As soon as they reach the last stair, she turned away, motioning for them to follow her with a curt nod of her head.

"What's her problem," Nate asked, finally noticing the older girl's attitude.

Larissa shrugged as they fell into step behind her.

The girl led them out of the tower and across a bridge of thick, interwoven tree branches. At the end of the bridge, they walked under another octagonal archway and into a large, enclosed, octagon-shaped room. The twins followed her silently, though they were very aware of each other's growing anxiety.

The twins figured at once that this must be the Bastion's Chamber that Windy had spoken of. Different from the tower, the only other building they had seen the from the inside, the interior walls of this great room were made of some sort of stone, so pale gray that it was almost white. The walls climbed upward, more than thirty feet. There, the tree branches reemerged, arching overhead to create a great dome. At regular intervals, there were openings in the dome covered with what looked like leaves. Through the thin layer of material, light—tinted green— drifted down.

The walls were carved at eye-level with images that looked

ancient to Nate's eyes. The carvings were of running leopards, intricately detailed right down to the spots. Starting at the door that they had just entered, the carvings circled around to come together behind the only pieces of furniture in the room, three chairs on an elevated platform. The last two leopards were not carved in a running stance, as the others had been, but rather, reared back on their hind legs, facing each other, with their front paws touching. The arch of the paws connected right over the center chair.

All three of the chairs were intricately carved and made from some material that shone gold in the soft green light. The largest of the three chairs, the center one, was decorated with green stones that glowed softly with a light of their own. Inexplicably, Nate felt drawn to the stones. He wanted to go and touch them, but he stayed behind the girl, who was leading them quickly forward, around the dais, to another door that was all but hidden behind the large, center chair. They followed the girl through a short tunnel into an antechamber, constructed of the same pale gray stone of the great room, but with a far more comfortable and cozy air than the room they had just left.

The room was octagonal, just like the Bastion's Chamber and the fountain. Like the great room, it had a miniature dome, slated with something that looked like leaves to let in the light. Rather than ornate carvings, however, the walls of this room were lined with floor to ceiling bookcases that covered almost every bit of the wall space, with the exceptions of the spaces where the windows, eight of them around the chamber, were.

The shelves of the bookcases were lined with ancient looking volumes bound in something that looked like leather. In one corner of the room was a weathered octagonal table, surrounded by eight chairs, all made of dark brown, ornately carved wood. A plush looking forest green rug covered most of the floor, and everywhere there were chaises and benches, made of the same dark wood and covered with pillows in shades of green, silver gray, and white.

The girl led them a few steps into the room, and then motioned for them to wait. She did all of this silently, seemingly intent on not speaking to them one bit more than was absolutely necessary. Leaving them, she walked deeper into the room, coming to a stop in front of one of the chaises.

On the chaise lounged a woman. She was much older, if her hair, which was the color of the stone walls that surrounded them, was any indication. For a moment, that was all that they could see, as the woman was facing Bailey, listening to her give a soft-voiced report on the twins' arrival. As the girl finished her report, the woman stood, patted the girl's shoulder fondly, and began to walk towards the twins.

She moved with the same fluid grace and speed that marked all of the leopards that they had seen so far. Her hair stood in a little halo of soft spiraling curls around her head, framing a chestnut colored face that could only be described as feline. She had high, broad cheekbones. Her nose was wider at the top than at the bottom, and all of her features drew together at a point just above her pert, narrow chin.

"Her eyes," Nate thought to his twin. As she came closer, he noted with wonder that the woman had eyes like their mother's and their own. Though hers were perhaps a shade or two darker, they were the Pantera eyes, green and flecked with yellow.

She wore what the twins were beginning to recognize as the customary Panterian attire. However, her tunic was noticeably different from the many examples they had seen below, not only because of the dark, emerald-green color, but also because of the golden thread that was woven into the collar and at the hem. She was barefoot, and Nate noticed that she stood daintily on the balls of her feet and yet seemed perfectly balanced. Encircling her forehead was a thin golden diadem that met in a v-shape over her nose. Set into the v-shape were five green stones, growing large in size and darker in color as they moved towards the center. All of the stones glowed more brightly as the woman's eyes fell on Larissa.

She came to a stop before them, and then turned to speak to the girl who had led them there. "Thank you Bailey. I will call you when they are ready." Her voice was low and melodious, like a purr. It both made the twins shiver and raised the hairs on the back of their arms. The girl, whose eyes had softened—if only minutely—since they had entered the room, gestured in something of a salute and then turned and silently left the room.

Larissa opened her mouth, full of questions that wanted to tumble out, all at once. But the woman waved away her questions with a gesture.

Turning, the woman walked back to the chaise where she had been sitting and resettled herself. Shrugging, the twins turned to follow her, taking a seat on one of the benches near the woman. Her pose was catlike as she leaned against the arm of the chaise, drawing her feet up to tuck them beneath her tunic. For long moments, none of the three spoke but silent questions buzzed back and forth between the twins like rapid fire. Who is this? Why does she have eyes like ours? Where are our parents? What is going on? Finally the woman spoke.

"I was not expecting you," she said focusing her gaze on Larissa. Her voice, still very much like a purr, held a tinge of exasperation and something else. "Anna never told me that she had twins. Though I suppose I can understand why." This last she murmured to herself, her gaze leaving the twins to contemplate the blue sky that shone through the window behind them.

More moments of silence followed that declaration. Nate waited, his mind racing and his nerves absolutely fried. Still the woman said nothing, she just stared appraisingly at him and his sister. With each silent moment, Nate's agitation grew. He tried to be patient though, waiting for the woman to do something, anything, really, that might begin to explain what they had been through, not only that morning but for the last few months. He knew, without a doubt, that it was all related. But the woman only gazed, a faint, bittersweet smile on her face. Finally, Nate couldn't hold his tongue any longer.

"Look. Miss," he said breaking the silence and startling both the woman and his sister in the process. "Where are our parents? Why did you bring us here?"

"Miss," she said, raising an ironic eyebrow and chuckling. The sound, a low rumble in her chest, was like chocolate, sweet, deep, rich, and dark all at the same time. "I am no miss. I am Marisol Larosa Pantera, Dowager Bastion of Panteria. Besides that, I am your grandmother."

Outside the Bastion's Chamber, the Kula was abuzz with chatter about the twin anakulan that had just arrived. Twins who bore the distinctive coloring of the Pantera clan, right up to the green eyes. Could they be the children of the Imperial Bastion? Could the girl-child be the Bastion Imminent?

The news and details of the arrival flew like wildfire through the Kula. The entire Pantera family, so long absent from Panteria, had finally returned. But only in the most dire of circumstances.

Among the crowds, the traitor watched and listened, his yellow-brown eyes gleaming with interest. So the Pantera offspring had emerged from hiding. And there was a girl child, an heir. His mistress would be most eager for this news. With a studied nonchalance, he turned and walked towards the castle gates. Moments later, a large, pale, golden leopard dashed across the grass plains towards the jungle.

Chapter 17

Interlopers

THE TWINS STARED AT the woman, their grandmother, shocked but not completely taken aback by the revelation. They had figured that the woman was some relation to them because of her eyes. Larissa was willing to bet that, like the rest of them, this woman's eyes stayed green when she shifted too.

Still, they were amazed. The woman before them was a real, live relative; one their parents had never mentioned. In fact, as Nate searched his mind, he could not remember either of his parents ever talking about their family. They had never before met any of their other family members, let alone their grandparents. No mention of a grandmother at all.

Of course, the day had been full of many surprising firsts. It was the first time they had heard of Panteria, been to Panteria, met another were-leopard, and, for that matter, a talking bird. Adding a long-lost grandmother to the list only seemed to make sense.

At that thought, Nate found himself growing angrier and angrier. With each passing moment, it seemed like he knew less and less about who he was; as though his whole life had been some sort of elaborately constructed lie.

The night before he had gone to sleep Nathanial Pantera, average thirteen year-old boy. Well, except that he could shift into a panther at will and his parents were mysteriously absent. This morning, he had awakened to discover that not only were his parents missing, but he and his sister were heirs to some sort of crown, and now this woman was telling them that she was their grandmother. What was he supposed to make of all of this? Why had their parents never told them? He felt betrayed, but before he could open his mouth, his sister spoke.

"Why have we never met you?" Larissa asked, voicing their mutual suspicion. Nate had to hand it to her. She sounded much calmer than he felt. But that was his sister, ever the diplomat.

"That," the Dowager sighed, "is a long and complicated story. One that your mother really must tell you, as I don't quite understand the reasons myself. I have wanted to see you—well Nathanial anyway, since Anna only told me of his birth—but your mother would not allow me to visit, and she would never bring you here."

"Then why does this place seem so familiar?" Nate mumbled these words to himself, missing the Dowager's sharp glance in his direction.

"But what I say to you is true," she swept on, a mite imperiously. "I am your grandmother and I have brought you here because your parents are missing, and I feared that you were in grave danger as well." She paused then, and the twins tried to absorb what she had said.

Attempting to stay calm, Nate finally spoke. "None of this makes sense," he said. "Nothing has made any sense all day!" He felt the anger that he had worked hard to control rising again.

"Nate," Larissa said softly, laying her hand on his arm. Nate shook it off. He wasn't going to be quiet this time.

"No," he said. "It's true! First some freaky talking bird shows up at our door calling me your eminence and her," he glanced towards his sister, "your Imperial Eminence, and saying that our mother is Imperial Bastion, whatever that means, of some place that we have never heard of. And we followed him! And now, here were are, in this place that we have never heard of with a lady that we have never met claiming that she is the grandmother we never knew we had. Really? And then she tells us that our parents are missing, but for some reason she would rather sit here staring at us than tell us the reason why! Why are they missing? Why can't you find them? What's up with all of the secrecy? Why won't someone just tell us what is going on?"

Nate broke off, huffing as he fought to control his anger. All of a sudden, he wasn't just yelling at the woman sitting in front of him, he was yelling at his absent parents too. Venting his frustration about the constant silence and secrets. And he was just getting started. He took a deep breath, ready to start another tirade.

The only thing that stopped him was the vise grip that Larissa clamped down on his hand. He tried to shake her off again, but this time she would not let him. His fists were balled up in frustration at his sides. The silence that followed his outburst was deafening and prolonged.

Then, abruptly, the Dowager sat up, abandoning her feline pose, leaning forward with a new compassion and understanding marking all of her features. "Forgive me," she said softly, to both of them. "I wasn't thinking about how strange this must be for you both." She seemed to recompose herself in front of them, becoming less and less feline and more and more human before their eyes.

Literally, her face changed. Her eyes became less almond shaped, her face a bit more round, until gone was the otherworldly creature that had greeted them and before them sat a woman who was much more matronly. The room filled with the scent of cinnamon; the flavor spicing the air with warmth, sweetness, and just an undercurrent of bitterness. It was a familiar smell. It was the scent of the Panteras, the scent of family, and Nate found himself being calmed by it, despite his desire to stay angry.

The Dowager watched as the change registered on the boy's face. When he was totally calm, she moved to the front of the chaise and looked the children in the eye. "You must be hungry," she said, giving each of the twins a once over as if noticing for the first time their slightly disheveled appearance. "Would you like something to eat?"

Nate, despite his anger and lingering questions, found himself nodding eagerly. It seemed like it had been hours since they stopped for lunch. The Dowager leaned over to the table that sat next to the chaise. She lifted a large wooden bowl with a wooden lid from it. She held the dish out to the twins, using one hand to support its weight effortlessly and the other to lift the lid from the container.

In the bowl were chunks of raw meat that looked like steak, so fresh that it was bright pink and still slightly bloody. The Dowager offered the meat nonchalantly, as though it were trail mix or popcorn. Nate grimaced before he could stop himself, casting a sidelong glance at Larissa, who was suddenly struck by a coughing fit that sounded mysteriously like a laugh. Then he shook his head, not at all attempting to conceal is his distaste.

"Never mind," he said.

The Dowager gave a sigh that was both exasperated and good-natured at the same time. She replaced the dish on the table, placing the lid back on top. Not, however, before taking a chunk of meat and popping it into her mouth. "I will start at the beginning," she said, once she finished chewing.

She rose from the chaise and walked to one of the windows, signaling for the twins to follow. The three of them stood together at the large window that overlooked part of the Panterian terrain.

The twins were immediately spellbound by what they saw. Traveling across the plains and through the jungle had not prepared them for the grandeur of Panteria seen from this perspective.

On one side, spread out before them were an infinite number of green topped trees, vibrant against the azure-blue of the mid-afternoon sky. On the other side was the plain that they had crossed to reach the Kula gates, an ocean of lush green grass. In the distance, a river meandered, bisecting the plain, which continued on the other side for quite some distance before it, too, ended in a jumble of jungle.

"This," the Dowager said, breaking the awed silence, "is Panteria. It is the land of the Kulan and the land of all of our ancestors." She spoke with great pride but also some small bit of quiet reverence. "It is the place that I devoted my life to protecting and defending when I was Imperial Bastion. It is the world that your mother has protected as the Imperial Bastion for the last thirty years, and that is the duty that you, Larissa, will inherit one day as well."

The children looked up at her in question. There was that term again, Imperial Bastion.

"Does that mean that we are royalty," Larissa ventured.

"No. Not really," came the Dowager's soft but grave reply. The name itself hinted at what they truly were to their people. Defenders. Protectors. Not rulers. "We are more like guardians. Leaders and defenders of all Kulan." At their mutual looks of confusion, she added, "It has many meanings: community, family, tribe. We are all of those things and more to each other. We are Kulan." As the twins nodded in understanding, she continued.

"We Panteras have held the position for generations, but only because the people have been satisfied with our leadership. If they ever become dissatisfied with us, they can easily choose another, just as they did six generations ago, when your great,

great, great grandmother became the first of the Panteras to become Bastion."

The children nodded, and satisfied that they understood, the Dowager continued. "Panteria, along with the three other Great Cat Realms, exists alongside the human world, a part of it, and yet separate, and that it is the way that it has been for all of Panteria's recorded history."

The twins turned to one another, feeling shocked, awed, and confused all at the same time. Did she mean that there were three other worlds like this one? Were there other types of shifters? But their questions would have to wait, because their grandmother continued speaking without pause.

"Panteria has always been a shelter for our people. A place of refuge and respite. Here, our people can find whatever they need, food, shelter, clothing, and people who are just like them and understand them. Many, like your mother and father, choose to live in the human world, but Panteria is always home."

"We have always been an open society too, allowing people to travel between the worlds as they please. There are four portals around Panteria that lead out into the human world. Portals that can only be accessed by were-leopards. Or so we thought. Until very recently. Until the interlopers."

At the Dowager's use of the word, the air in the room changed. The warm, comforting, cinnamon disappeared all at once, leaving the room feeling suddenly colder and more dismal. Nate looked over at the woman and saw that her face was twisted in disgust, as though she had just seen something that was repellent to her. Her fingers gripped the edge of the windowsill, and he realized that she was trying to control her anger too. Something compelled him to reach out to her, to try to offer her some comfort, but another, equally strong impulse held him motionless. At last, when the Dowager regained control, she went on.

"There are humans in Panteria for the first time in recorded history. We don't know how they found this place or how they are getting in. Panterians all know better than to reveal themselves or the existence of this world to humans. History has taught us those lessons well. We have checked all of the portals. We have them guarded day and night, but still somehow, more and more humans are slipping through." She was grim and cryptic, explaining herself no further.

"Someone has found a way to open our world to the humans. That traitor has allowed them in, and they have been taking Panteria's most precious resources from our world back into theirs."

"You see, our land is rich in a material that is highly valued in the human world. Buried beneath the land, we have deposits of rare metals which the human world deems precious and places great value on. Those deposits are largely untapped because Panterians do not live or believe in the same way as humans. We also have this." She turned towards the twins, tapping the green stones on her crown.

"Emeralds?" Larissa guessed, peering at the dark green, clear, glowing stones.

"No, not emeralds," the Dowager said. "Though they would appear to be emeralds to humans and would fetch a high sum because of their fine color and their clarity. This is panterite, the life-blood of Panteria. It is the source from which all that you see before you flows. This is why the land stays ever-green and the jungles grow so lush and thick. Without it, Panteria would wither away, unable to sustain itself or our people any longer." The twins took deep, simultaneous breaths, trying to comprehend the gravity of the tale the Dowager told.

"And someone is mining it. Stripping away huge quantities of it and taking it, we believe, into the human world because it would have no value here. You see, our life is simple. We use what we need, nothing more and nothing less. We do not hoard these materials or strip the land barren to acquire them. We know that the health of our people relies on the health of Panterian land. We would not sacrifice the health of the empire for our own individual desires. Or, at least, that is the way that it used to be." Her words were grim and angry now.

"Someone has forgotten that lesson. And the land is ailing as a result. Dying in places, but infected and ailing all over. Someone is allowing Panteria to die to serve their own greed." Her voice shook and her fist came down heavily on the window sill.

"That is what your mother has been investigating for the last few months. That was what she was doing when she went missing three days ago. And your father was searching for her when he went missing yesterday."

With those words, something clicked in Nate's mind. He looked at Larissa and realized that she was thinking the same thing. Quite suddenly, it all made sense. Their dad's anxious behavior, their mom's mysterious business trip. Again, Nate felt himself growing angry. "Why didn't they tell us?" He fairly shouted the words. "Why didn't she tell us?"

The Dowager continued once more as though he had not spoken. "Since news of your father's disappearance reached us yesterday, there has been an increasing unrest among the people. People are talking of leaving Panteria and going into the human world or to one of the other cat realms, for good. The people are afraid. Your mother is the Imperial Bastion and they are sworn to protect her as she is sworn to protect them. If she can be taken and her family threatened, who here is safe?"

The Dowager stopped speaking and the twins were quiet, digesting everything that she had just told them. Slowly, as the older woman watched, questions seemed to bubble up on their faces, even as she raised her hand to silence them. "No more questions for now," she said. "You are exhausted and already have much to think about. You must rest, and save your questions for later. There will be plenty of time, since you must remain here until your parents are found."

Immediately, both twins realized that she was right. Adrenaline had held their exhaustion at bay, but now it came rushing back full strength. The Dowager left them then and walked across the room. She reached up and pulled on a delicate greenish cord that hung from the wall. Moments later, the same angry young woman appeared in the doorway.

"Bailey will show you to your rooms," the Dowager announced, turning to look at the twins once more. The young girl nodded her head with characteristically brisk affirmation. "You can show Larissa to her room now, and then come back for Nathanial." The girl nodded.

Larissa, though, had frozen. She glanced at Nate with a question in her eyes. He nodded once, gesturing that it was okay for her to go. He still didn't completely trust the Dowager, but he was pretty sure that he would be safe alone with her. Larissa stood then and followed the other girl out of the room.

As the two girls left, Nate and the Dowager considered each other for several minutes. Nate still felt vaguely defiant, despite all that the woman had shared. He crossed his arms over his chest and waited. The Dowager smiled to herself, recognizing the boy's bravado, and gestured towards the chaises where they had been sitting before.

As they sat, the Dowager perked her ears up to listen to the two sets of footsteps, which echoed and grew more faint as the two girls crossed the Bastion's Chamber, fade away. When she was sure that they were alone, the Dowager spoke.

"I wanted to ask you something Nathanial. Something that is very important. That is why I held you back." Nate looked at the woman both wary and expectant.

"You said before that this place seemed familiar," the Dowager continued, noting the emotions that warred on his face. "What did you mean by that?" She tilted her head slightly to the side as she spoke, her face alive with curiosity. Nate thought for a moment, as he tried to put the feelings and sensations into words.

"It's like I can feel the land," he said, his words slow and halting, "and it feels different in different places. It shoots these little darts of energy into me that make me feel…something. Stronger, I guess. And the land around the Kula, it feels like…" His voice trailed off as he searched for the right word to describe it and finally he settled on the only one that seemed to work. "It feels like home."

The Dowager nodded, a different light in her eyes now. At that moment, Bailey reappeared. The Dowager waved Nate away, seemingly deep in thought. He realized that she was not going to tell him why that question had been so important, at least not now. Nate rose from the chaise, picked up his book bag, and followed the girl out of the chamber.

CHAPTER 18

DOMESTIC TRANQUILITY

ALONE IN THE LIBRARY, the Dowager considered Nate's revelation with growing concern. It was odd that the boy should express such a connection to the land. If what he said was true, then it was he and not Larissa, not the girl, who possessed the *fuerza*. And if that were the case then all, quite possibly, was lost.

The *fuerza*, or *terra fuerza*, was unique to their family. None of the other leopard families possessed it, as far as she, or any of her ancestors, knew. Because it was such a rare power, the Panteras guarded their secret vigorously.

The *fuerza* enabled the one Pantera in each generation that wielded it to draw strength from the earth. The strength made that panther all but invincible as long as she stood on Panterian land. It was what made them such ideal Bastions, this heightened awareness of the land and connection to it. It was a power that could be wielded with devastating effect given the proper training.

In the past, for as long as the family had kept written record, that Pantera had always been a she. None of the family knew why it was that only the female members of the Pantera clan that could wield the power. But for as long as she had been alive, that had always been the case. Her mother had possessed the *fuerza*, training her to use the power, as her mother had before her.

On the other hand, the Panteras were a very small clan, generally with only one anakulan born each generation. And, for the last six generations that cub had been a girl. Maybe what they had believed for so long was wrong.

The Dowager returned to the window where she had stood just moments earlier with the twins. She wondered whether Nathanial alone possessed the gift, or whether Larissa felt it as well. If the girl did not carry the *terra fuerza*, that could mean the end of Pantera stewardship of Panteria.

The position of Imperial Bastion was the highest honor that the Kulan could bestow. To be elected Bastion was to be entrusted to lead and defend all of the leopards both in Panteria and in the human world. And there were significant dangers. More at certain times than at others. So, it was not a duty that was given or taken lightly.

For all of Panteria's recorded history, the Imperial Bastion had always been a woman. It was a position that, once bestowed, could be passed, always before from mother to daughter, so long as the people were pleased with the leadership of the family. If that faith wavered, the people would select a new Bastion and a new family to lead them.

She wrung her hands.

There were already rumblings about replacing Anna. The talk had begun several years ago, when it became clear that Anna and Robert would not return to Panteria to live permanently. Never before had an Imperial Bastion chosen to live outside of Panteria.

Of course, all of the Bastions had some experience with the human world. It had been that way as long as they could remember. Generally, that experience came before the Bastion

Imminent ascended to the Seat.

Some went there to be educated, returning to Panteria with new knowledge that helped to make their world a better place. Some traveled through the human world to the other Great Empires. The experience was, in a sense, necessary, so that they could better know how to protect Panteria and serve all of their citizens, many of whom chose to live in the human world.

Even she had spent her time in the human world, some sixty years earlier. And while she marveled at aspects of that world and its inhabitants, there were too many things about both that did not sit well with her. Too many unfamiliar tensions and prejudices. She had never felt safe among the humans. She had quickly and happily returned to Panteria, where she was loved and respected by all, only too happy to assume her role as Imperial Bastion and never return to the human world.

Anna had been different, though. She had never wanted to be Bastion. When she left Panteria before her Ascension, it was almost as though she were running away. As though she expected to find something so much better in the human world. To the Dowager's best knowledge, she had found it. When she met Robert, a leopard that had been raised almost entirely in the human world, the Dowager had been afraid that she might never come back.

Anna hadn't wanted to return. She even went so far as to initiate the Battle, an open competition for potential Bastion candidates. It was only after she had seen the pool of applicants, women from families, whose ancestors' reigns had fueled nothing but discord among the Kulan, that the girl had entered and won the Battle herself. Her status as Bastion was cemented with the victory, and Anna had grudgingly been Installed. Still, she had always kept one foot in the human world.

Robert stayed there, and Anna visited when she could. It was not an unusual relationship, not by Bastion standards. In fact, it was rare that a Bastion had what humans might call a traditional marriage. In some ways, it was too difficult to manage, precisely because of the duties of the Bastion. She, herself, had never taken a husband.

Then, right before the child—children—were born, Anna had done the unthinkable. She had moved into the human world entirely. She had said she wanted to give Nathanial a chance at a normal life, as much as a were-leopard might have a normal life in the human world. The Dowager realized now that she must have been talking about Larissa too. Had the girl grown up here, in the Kula, she would have known all along that she was expected to be the next Imperial Bastion, and Anna had never dealt well with that pressure.

Her daughter had done her best for the past fourteen years to live her life both in the human world and Panteria. She returned once or twice a week, more often since the children had started school, to attend to the business of the Bastion. It was an arrangement that worked, though it was not ideal. The people of Panteria had tenuously accepted it.

However, that had all changed with the discovery of the interlopers. People were beginning to suggest that this had only happened because of Anna's absence. That no one would have dared so brazen an act had the Bastion and her family actually lived in Panteria full time. The Kulan were scared, and they were directing their fear and anger towards Anna and the rest of the Panteras, the Dowager included.

"Eh hem," the clearing throat caught the Dowager's attention and she turned in the direction of the noise. Windy had flown into the room while she had been lost in her thoughts and was now perched on the chaise the children had so recently vacated.

"Guardian," the bird said, bowing deeply. "The scouts have returned. Marcus is on his way to the Bastion's Chamber as we speak. He should be here in a few moments."

The Dowager nodded, crossing the library with shifter speed and heading to the door that led to the Bastion's Chamber. By the time Marcus entered the room, the Dowager was seated in the chair to the left of the panterite-studded center chair. Perched on the back of her chair was Windy.

At one time, the center throne, the Seat of the Bastion, had been her chair. When her daughter had assumed the role of Imperial Bastion at the age of twenty-one, the Dowager had stepped aside, but not too far. She still sat at her daughter's left hand, offering advice and guidance on the leading of the people.

"Yes Marcus," she said to the round-faced, blue-eyed man who stood before her. Marcus was the leopard that she had sent the day before to scour the eastern region of Panteria in search of her daughter and son-in-law. He was unassuming in human form. Stout with curly brown hair and a mild-mannered, even jovial, face. But he was a formidable leopard and had been a trusted leader within the leopard ranks for years.

"The eastern region has been thoroughly searched Guardian, and there is no sign of the Imperial Bastion or her husband."

At Marcus's words, the Dowager's concerns doubled. She had been certain of the source of that cry. She had sent forces out immediately, as soon as she had received confirmation of Robert's capture. How could they have moved them so quickly? Where were they concealing them now? Gathering her thoughts, she spoke urgently to the man who stood before her. "I want you to gather every able-bodied man or woman who is willing to help. I want every inch of Panteria searched. I want my daughter and Robert found!" The last of her command was almost lost in a growl. Her voice shook with anger and panic.

"Yes Guardian" Marcus said, bowing low, before quickly departing.

CHAPTER 19

SECRETS TOLD BY MIDNIGHTS

Nate sat bolt upright, the haze of sleep leaving him almost immediately. He was surrounded by an inky blackness, and, for a moment, he could not see anything. After a couple of seconds, shifter-sight kicked in and he was able to make out the grey and black shapes in his surroundings. Even then he still felt out of sorts.

It was the room that Bailey had shown him to earlier that day or yesterday. The chamber was clearly intended only for sleeping, as the only piece of furniture in the whole room was a big circular bed. The room, like all of the rooms that he had seen in the Kula thus far, was shaped like an octagon with eight equal-length sides. He was beginning to wonder if there was some sort of significance to the shape. The walls were made of wood, with no windows. Against one wall rested his book bag and clothes, where he had discarded them before lying down on the bed for what he thought would be a quick nap.

He was not quite sure how long he had been asleep. However, when he had laid down for his nap, the room had been bathed in light from the weird leaf shaped lamps that sprang from the wall. Though Nate could see the little lamps extended from the walls all around the room, they were all dark now.

He got out of bed and slipped on his jeans, skipping the shirt because he still had on his P. E. suit, the top of which was like a tank-top, even if it was a little snug. Walking as softly as he could manage, aware that he was in a building full of shifters, he crossed the room and stepped out into the hallway. He knew Larissa's room was somewhere nearby, but he wasn't sure exactly where.

Out in the hall, which was also pitch black, he struggled to remember which door Bailey had pointed out to him as they made their way to the room he had just exited. Had they come from the right or the left? He could not remember.

Memories flashed in his mind of the walk from the Bastion's Chamber to the bedroom. Bailey in front of him, crimson ponytail bobbing, shot rapid fire information in his general direction, never looking back to make sure that he understood.

He could not recall a word of what she had said. His mind had been so overwhelmed at that point that he had hardly heard anything that the older girl had told him about this place, called the Inner Kula. Though he vaguely recalled some mention of a kitchen. With that thought, his stomach growled. Larissa and then food, he thought.

Abandoning his spotty memory, he turned instead to his shifter senses. He sniffed the air around him, concentrating on picking up Larissa's scent. Just like his friends had unique scents, his family had a special scent too. They were all distinct, but at their core all shared a hint of spicy cinnamon-like warmth. Larissa's, to him, seemed to smell a bit like vanilla, which mingled soothingly with the cinnamon.

After a couple of seconds, he picked up on the strong aroma of cinnamon intertwined with a multitude of other smells. This scent, however, had an undertone of green things—freshly cut grass, newly turned earth—that mixed and somehow did not clash with the cinnamon. Definitely not Larissa. It was the Dowager, he decided. She had stood near this place not long ago. Cautiously, he scanned the hallway again. It was clear, even though the scent lingered.

He sniffed some more, moving forward in one direction then another, trying to pick up any hint of Larissa's scent. Finally, after a few moments and a change in direction, he caught the faintest whiff of his sister to the left of the door. He followed the smell, which grew stronger with each step he took, and without thinking about it, he reached silently out to Larissa with his mind.

She was standing at the door waiting for him when he reached her room. She looked like she had fallen asleep in her cloths. Her curls were a mess, and she had a criss-cross of lines on her face from where she had laid her head while sleeping.

"I guess we both missed dinner," Nate joked softly as Larissa hustled him into her room, which was identical to the one that he had just left.

Larissa giggled. "And I am starving too," she replied. "Though, come to think of it, I don't know if I could have eaten what was on the menu." Remembering the Dowager's bloody offerings, they both laughed a little more. Abruptly their mirth died off, and they were silent for a long moment.

"So what are we going to do?" Nate finally asked as they flopped back down on the bed in the dark room. Neither he nor Larissa could figure out how to work the lamps that sprouted intermittently from the walls.

"I don't know," said Larissa. She chewed her lip as she thought about the situation, scrunching her face up as was her habit. "I mean, it's pretty clear that she did not bring us here to help find Mom and Dad. She brought us here so that we wouldn't be taken too."

"But we can't just sit here and do nothing while Mom and Dad are out there somewhere." Nate broke in. "We have to find them!"

"How, Nate?" Larissa asked staring at her brother. He was so impatient and impetuous sometimes. He did not always think things through. Sometimes, she had to do it for him. "Where would we even begin to look? We don't know anything about this place."

Nate shrugged. She was right. They knew next to nothing about Panteria. Even as much as the Dowager had told them that afternoon, he still felt like there were huge, gaping holes in the picture.

If, for instance, his mother were so valuable, how was it even possible that she had been taken in the first place? More importantly, who would want to take her? If the people of Panteria were as loyal as the Dowager claimed, then who was behind his parent's disappearance? He could not believe that the humans were acting alone. There was still so much that did not add up.

"I have a feeling that the Dowager isn't going to let us out of her sight, if she can help it," he mused aloud, unable to bring himself to call the woman grandmother. Besides, even if they could escape the Dowager, it was not as though they would be able to just walk out of the Kula gates. "Still, we have to do something, don't we? Come on Larissa, you're the brains of this operation. How are we going to do this?"

Larissa looked back at him, her face a mixture of helplessness and annoyance. "I don't know, I'll think of something," she said. They were quiet again for a long time. Nate could sense his sister's frustration with herself, as she searched for a plan and came up empty handed.

"Do you want to try to find something to eat," he suggested softly, trying to take his mind off this problem, which seemed to have no solution. She looked at him and nodded her agreement. Together, they left the chamber in search of food.

This was no easy task. The Inner Kula was like a maze, full of long corridors that were all connected to one another. The twins walked quickly and quietly, opening doors here and there, looking for a kitchen.

They were very careful, first listening at the door to make sure that no one rested behind it before opening it slowly and softly. Finally, after about ten doors, Nate opened another and a gust of cool evening air blew into the hall carrying with it the heady scent of jungle blooms. Curious, he and Larissa slipped through the door.

Into the room, the soft blue-white light of the crescent moon shone, almost blindingly bright after the utter darkness of the hall. The room was another bedchamber, just like theirs with the exception that one of the walls had a large open archway that led out onto a huge wide terrace. In the middle of the room was a large circular bed, and underneath the fragrance of the jungle air, Nate could detect the faint spicy scent of cinnamon. Someone in their family had slept here recently, though the scent was just old enough that Nate could not tell who.

They walked past the bed and out onto the terrace, all the way to the edge. In unison, they leaned against the banister and gazed in wonder at the sight before them.

The terrace seemed to overlook the whole of the Kula. Beneath them, they could see turrets and similar terraces descending downward like stair steps, all the way down to the huge domed building, which they had passed earlier, the courtyard, and the fountain. Nothing stirred beneath them. There were not even guards at the gates. Perhaps it would not be as difficult to leave the Kula as Nate had imagined. Perhaps they would be able to just walk out after all.

Out beyond the gates, Panteria spread before them, bathed in the cool blue-white light of the moon. Stars twinkled in the night sky, rivaling the moon in their brightness. In the distance, beyond the plain where the grasses waved gently in the soft breeze, an ocean of trees, black with only faint hints of their daytime green, stretched out to the horizon. Nate's eyes flitted over the tree tops, inexplicably certain that his parents were somewhere out there among those trees.

"What's that," Larissa asked breathlessly, breaking his train of thought.

"What," he whispered. She pointed and he followed the line of her finger gazing out into the distance. It was hard to see at first. In the darkness, the line of trees seemed to continue unbroken to the horizon. But as he peered a bit more closely, he saw what Larissa was pointing at.

There, among the trees, was a gap. A stretch of darkness, unbroken by the faintly discernible pattern of light-flecked leaves that marked the other areas of the forest. It was just empty, and its emptiness filled Nate with a sense of dread that made his stomach turn.

"I think," he said, his dread growing with every moment that he gazed upon the dark, empty, space. "I think that is where we need to look for Mom and Dad."

Larissa's head whipped around and she looked at him strangely. Seeing the look on his face, however, she bit her tongue.

Both of them turned again to stare at the empty space with a growing sense of foreboding. They tried to commit to memory its location with relation to the Kula, recording the path that they would have to take from the gates to find it. Nate had a sinking suspicion that he would be able to locate the spot without much trouble once they were close enough, just based on the feeling of the land. He knew that just like the land around the Kula, that land would feel different—but not in a good way.

The twins were so intently focused on the darkness before them, that they almost missed the shadowy creature slinking up to the Kula gates. Out of the corner of his eye, Nate saw the paradoxically pale and shadowy creature, a leopard most certainly, running up to the gates.

Briefly the leopard disappeared, and then Nate spotted it again. This time, it was atop the gate, walking across the wall that bordered the vestibule that they had entered the day before. He pointed out the creature to Larissa and both of them watched as it leaped down into the courtyard. The creature hurried across the courtyard, shifting as it slinked into the shadows.

Nate was unable to discern much about the person the creature became as it melted into the shadows, except that it was a man, he was huge and, in the moonlight, his pale hair gleamed almost white.

The twins looked at each other, their mutual suspicions written across their faces. It was an odd time to be slinking around. The man disappeared into the darkness, and just as fast, the twins forgot him as they turned back to the night, their eyes finding the spot of emptiness once more.

"If they are not found by tomorrow night, we start our search," Nate said quietly and with great determination.

Beside him, Larissa nodded once.

CHAPTER 20

JUDGE, JURY, AND RAW MEAT

EARLY THE NEXT MORNING, after lying awake for most of the night, Nate slipped from Larissa's room and made his way back to his own, which was much easier to find in the now lit halls. After their discovery, the twins had continued their hunt for food, finding nothing. They had ended up back in Larissa's room, hungry, exhausted, and unable to sleep.

Upon entering his chamber he found an emerald green tunic, the exact same shade as the Dowager's, and a pair of loose fitting white pants in the same lightweight material laid out on his bed.

His stomach grumbled as he crossed the room, picked up the tunic, and held it in front of him to examine it. The garment was lightweight and felt no heavier than a bit of tissue paper in his hands. At the same time, it was strong, as he discovered when he tugged it over his head. The threads stretched as he pulled the tunic down, but sprang right back into shape as the garment settled over his chest.

He rubbed his hand over his shoulder, marveling at the soft feel of the material, which was so different from anything that he would ever wear in the human world. He could barely feel the weight of the thin material. It was like a second skin.

Almost eagerly, he slipped off his jeans and pulled on the pants. By the time he heard the knock at the door, he was completely dressed and looked, at least, like a life-long Panterian. That was, until, he glanced at his feet. The gym shoes, which he had chosen to wear instead of the brown-colored sandals that were placed at the foot of the bed, almost ruined the effect. Almost, but not quite.

He opened the door, and there stood Larissa with Bailey. Larissa was dressed in Panterian garb as well, her outfit almost identical to Nate's. She wore the same emerald green tunic with white pants, but on her feet she wore the sandals.

On her face, on the other hand, she wore an expression that was somewhere between confusion and exasperation. Nate looked at her quizzically as they fell into step behind Bailey, who had barely paused as he opened the door before continuing down the hallway.

"I was trying to get her to tell me more about Panteria," Larissa thought in response to his look. *"Trying being the operative word."*

It was a good idea. The older girl might be able to tell them something that would be useful to them later, because Nate had a sneaking suspicion that the Dowager was not going to be helpful at all in this matter. However, while Larissa's plan to pump the girl for information was admirable in theory, it wasn't working so well in practice. Not with G. I. Bailey, anyway. Though if anyone could wheedle information out of someone, it would be his sister with her patented combination of diplomacy and charm. Neither of which, at that moment, seemed to be at all effective on the older girl, judging from Larissa's dejected expression.

"She's still giving attitude, hunh," he asked, though he didn't really need Larissa's reply. The answer was as clear as the scowl on the older girl's face.

"*Attitude,*" Larissa scoffed. "*If that isn't an understatement. It's like she hates us.*"

It was true. The girl barely looked at them as she marched them down the hall. And whenever she was forced to turn back, there was a look of cold anger in her eyes that the twins just could not understand.

Bailey kept an almost complete and absolutely icy silence as she marched them through the maze of corridors to a large dining room for breakfast. She spoke only to point out the location of different facilities in the Inner Kula. All of Larissa's questions were met with pointed glares tossed over her shoulder. Nate had to admire his sister though. She just kept plugging away.

The dining room, for which the twins had searched so long the night before, turned out to be right down the hall from Nate's room. Bailey pushed open the double doors, entering the room, as the twins trailed nervously behind her. There were a few other people in the hall, here and there, eating their breakfasts. Nate immediately recognized that they must have been a part of the Dowager's staff, because all of them wore the same mint green tunics that were bordered in emerald green.

He was beginning to discern a pattern in the way that these people dressed. The color of the tunics seemed to indicate rank or at least the position of the wearer within the society. Like the day before, Nate suddenly felt many pairs of eyes on him as he stood with Larissa and waited for instruction.

If it were possible, Bailey scowled harder at the unsolicited attention that the twins attracted, exhaling an audible huff as she maneuvered through the tables and clusters of gawkers towards the elaborately arrayed buffet table in the back.

From a distance, the buffet looked cheery, with its pink and red serving trays. As they drew closer, however, Nate realized that what he was looking at was actually tray after tray of pink and red meats. He scanned the table, beginning to panic. It was raw. It was all raw.

On the first tray, there was what looked like salmon, so pink and fresh that it must have been caught that morning. It was laid out in huge, heavy, pink chunks on the platter. On down the line, there were other trays with chunks of steak, raw and bloody. On the next, there was something that smelled like pig, only wilder and gamier.

Each of the trays had on it a small sprig of greenery as a garnish. Other than that, all that was in sight was raw meat taken from various species in the animal kingdom. On the last tray were long, red, bloody strips of something that Nate could not identify. It was not lamb, or any other meat that he recognized.

Nate's stomach churned as he stared at the strips, which looked like a cross between uncooked bacon and uncooked chicken. He took a deep sniff and still it remained a mystery.

"Gazelle," Bailey said curtly.

Nate looked at her in confusion.

"It's gazelle," she said again, turning away and picking up a plate which she proceeded to load down with bits from each tray. Nate watched as she scooped portion after portion onto her plate using her fingers—there were no utensils—until there was not an uncovered inch to be found. Then she started on the next layer.

"The girl likes her protein," Nate thought to his sister, as Bailey made her way quickly down the line. Larissa snickered.

Nate went over to the table and picked up a plate. He scanned the food again, trying to figure out where to begin. It all looked so…unappetizing. What he wouldn't give for some of his mom's vegetables now.

At that moment, Bailey glanced back at him as if to question what was taking so long. Seeing his still empty plate, she sneered and chuckled, muttering something about "cooked meat" and "soft" as she grabbed a glass of water and went to sit with some other members of the guard.

Nate looked back at Larissa and the two frowned at the older girl's meanness before Nate turned back to the buffet. Determined not to be outdone by the wicked witch of the Kula, Nate loaded his plate down with samples from each of the platters. Larissa followed suit, and soon the twins were maneuvering through tables with plates and water in their hands. They chose a table in the corner and sat down together, contemplating their plates for a long moment.

Nate examined the contents of his plate, trying not to let his face register the disgust that was growing inside. He had never understood his mother's habit of eating raw meat and the fare on his plate did nothing but make his stomach churn rather than growl. Still, he knew without even looking that he was being watched. He could feel the weight of multiple pairs of eyes on him. Oddly, he felt in that moment that not only was he being watched, he was also being judged. He knew that somehow, he would not be considered a proper leopard if he couldn't eat like one.

Grimacing just a bit, he picked up a piece of salmon, the least offending thing on the plate, as there were no bloody juices dripping from it. The fish felt cool and soft in his hand. Trying not to give too much thought to what he was about to do, he popped the fish in his mouth.

For a moment, it lay there on his tongue, dense and heavy. He could taste the faint and fishy flavor and his stomach began to protest even more. He wanted nothing more than to spit the fish back out, but when he turned and confirmed that Bailey was watching, spiteful humor having replaced the cold anger in her eyes, he knew that was not an option.

So, instead, he started to chew, squirming inside at the rubbery density of the fish, which he couldn't help but think was so much more delicious when it was cooked with a little lemon and butter. His eyes watered as pieces of the fish slid down his throat, but he fought to keep chewing. Finally, he swallowed, much to the displeasure of his gurgling stomach, and swiftly picked up his glass of water and drank the whole thing. Stomach still churning, he looked down at his plate and wondered if there was any way that he could manage another piece.

Glancing over at Larissa, he was surprised to find that she was plowing through the meat on her plate. His mouth dropped open in astonishment.

"What," she thought to him as she popped another bleeding chunk of beef into her mouth. *"I'm starving and it's not that bad."*

Nate smiled wanly and looked back at his plate. He tried to force himself to pick up another piece of meat, but that was it. He was done.

A few minutes later, Bailey came over to their table. She looked scathingly at Nate's still full plate, with an expression that held just a bit of cruelty.

"I wasn't that hungry," he muttered defensively, feeling a little ashamed of himself. All the more so, when he saw the glimmer of grudging approval in the girl's eyes as she noticed Larissa's now empty plate. Then again when she was distinctly nicer to Larissa as she told them where to put their plates. It was as though breakfast had been some sort of test that Larissa had passed and he had not.

Larissa gave Nate a significant glance as they followed Bailey into the hall. She too had caught Bailey's response to her appetite. Her hopeful look told him that she would try again to get Bailey to talk to them. No sooner had they exited the dining room than Larissa began to press her advantage by resuming her questioning. However, before the first question was out of Larissa's mouth, the girl hardened again, reverting once more to barking out information about the halls they traveled.

Bailey led them back through the maze towards the Bastion's Chamber. There, she informed them, the Dowager was waiting for them. Just ahead, they could see the doors of the room. The time for them to find out anything useful was fast running out. Never one to admit defeat, Larissa made one last ditch effort.

By then, they were standing in front of the entrance to the Bastion's Chamber. The great wooden doors that led into the room were shut, and Bailey had paused in front of them. She turned to look at the twins, as though preparing to give them some instruction. She looked distinctly relieved to be there, a fact that she did not bother to try and conceal from the twins.

"Do you know where my mother was going when she went missing?"

At Larissa's question, a look of deep hurt passed over the girl's face. Indeed, for a fleeting moment she looked as though she might cry, though Nate would have said just seconds before that such a thing would have been impossible. Just as quickly, the look was gone and the girl's face was once again a cold, angry mask. She opened her mouth to speak, but Larissa interrupted.

"Why do you hate us," she blurted out. Then she covered her mouth with her hand, her eyes wide as though not even she had expected for that question to pop out.

Bailey's eyes widened in shock and then, just as quickly, narrowed with flashing anger. Her eyes darted back and forth between Nate and Larissa as though she were measuring them. This continued for so long that Nate began to believe that they weren't going to get an answer to this question either. When she finally spoke, her voice was soft.

"I don't hate you," she said. The tone of her voice was both weary and dismissive, as though it would be a waste of time to hate them. Before the twins could reconcile that pronouncement with her odd behavior, she continued. "What I hate is that I am being forced to baby-sit two silly little anakulan, when I should be out looking for my Bastion." She said the word so fiercely, so protectively, so possessively, that recognition began to dawn for Larissa. "What I hate is that I am being pumped for information by the same silly anakulan, like I am some sort of amateur."

"What, did you think I didn't know what you were doing," she asked as Larissa's cheeks turned red with embarrassment. "I didn't train for all of these years to become a nursemaid to some soft little human wannabes." She spat the last word with more disgust than Nate ever imagined could be injected into one word.

He recoiled physically. Soft. Is that what she thought of them, that they were soft. Just because they lived in the human world. Bailey didn't even give them a chance to respond. She whirled around and pressed open the door, leaving the twins in the hall too shocked to move. After a long moment of strained silence, Nate reacted first.

"I'm not soft," he thought to his twin, his voice hot with indignation. He glared after Bailey, as the door shut behind her.

"Don't listen to her, she's just a teenager with delusions of grandeur. Like we need a babysitter anyway," was Larissa's reply. The girl's remarks had stung her too.

Together they walked over to the door. Inside, they could hear a swift and anxious conversation taking place, in voices so low that even their shifter-hearing could not make out what was being said. Nate pushed open the door and held it for his sister.

Bailey had stopped just inside the Chamber. She had her eyes glued on the Dowager, and she seemed to be waiting for the older woman to acknowledge her. The twins entered the room, and Nate let the door shut quietly behind him. They walked into the room so that they were standing even with Bailey and yet as far as they could possibly be from her. The Dowager was sitting in a chair to the left of the panterite studded throne. She spoke in hushed whispers with a stout man whose only visible feature was close cropped curly brown hair.

Abruptly the conversation stopped and the Dowager flashed a glance in their direction. Concern was etched on every feature of her face, though she tried to smooth her countenance as she looked at the children.

"Bailey, why don't you take Nate and Larissa on a tour of the grounds. I should be done here by the time you return."

At her request, Bailey went rigid. Nate could almost feel her fury pouring off of her in waves.

"So now I am a tour guide," the girl muttered, turning away from the Dowager.

"Serves her right," Nate thought. Larissa smirked.

As they were turning to leave the Dowager called after them, "Make sure to stay within the Kula. And Bailey," the Dowager's voice was a purr. This time the girl stopped and looked over her shoulder at her leader. "I am sure that you will make a wonderful tour guide."

At that, the twins could not help but giggle out loud. They exited the Bastion's Chamber, a red-faced Bailey racing forward at breakneck pace, grumbling all the way.

For the next hour, Bailey guided them around the Kula, showing them all of the various buildings and detailing their uses. To her credit, once ordered to do so, the girl took her duties as tour guide quite seriously. The tour she gave was thorough and, this time, informative, though delivered with a decided lack of enthusiasm.

She started by showing them more of the Inner Kula, the rooms designated specifically for the Imperial Bastion, her family, and certain members of the Imperial Bastion's Guard, or IBG. Bailey, who was a member of the IBG, lived there, as did Marcus, the man that their grandmother had been talking to, and his wife.

The Inner Kula was mostly composed of sleeping chambers like the ones that the twins had spent the night in. Some were reserved for important guests, messengers and emissaries from the other Great Empires. Each empire had its own designated suite of rooms. Bailey explained some of the complicated etiquette surrounding those visits, but much of that went over the twins' heads. There was also a kitchen, a dining room for formal state dinners whenever a grand council meeting was called, and a small observatory at the highest level.

The observatory once served, she explained, as a look-out point. Though, she was quick to add, they had not needed to use it for that purpose for many years. The pronouncement struck Nate as odd. What had they been looking out for? It was another slight hint that things had not always been so idyllic in Panteria.

Now, the girl continued, with some measure of regret in her voice, it was simply the best place in the Kula to view the night sky. From her tone, it was more than obvious that she felt that the observatory should return to its original purpose.

According to Bailey, the skies of Panteria and the human world were the same, which didn't quite make sense to the twins. She gestured towards the telescopes that were placed here and there for daytime and nighttime viewing.

She then led them out of the Inner Kula and into the Kula proper. First up on the tour was the courtyard. This time, the gathering place was far less crowded than it had been when they arrived the day before. The twins had more time to look around unmolested, as Bailey led them through the plaza.

Along the perimeter were dozens of little open-air shops,

none of which seemed to be open yet. They all sold a variety of things, though most of them seemed to primarily stock the Panterian tunic in all of the shades of the green rainbow.

In one open window, Nate saw body suits hanging from some hidden mechanism. The bodysuits were in all colors, ranging from the palest beige to the tawniest gold—so dark, it was almost red. Though he saw none in the midnight shade that he and Larissa required, it dawned on him that this must have been where his parents got their P. E. suits. He had always known that the suits were special-made by some secret tailor or something. Apparently, they were even more special-order than he had thought.

Bailey walked them briskly through the courtyard, paying scant attention to any of the shops, until she came to one. There she stopped so suddenly that Larissa almost crashed into her back. In the window, if it might be called that since there was no glass to speak of, were weapons, the likes of which Nate had never seen before and most of which he could not even begin to imagine how to use. For a long moment, Bailey just stood there, staring covetously at one weapon that looked something like brass-knuckles with wicked looking white metal claws extending from them. To Nate, the girl looked like she was about to drool.

All of the weapons, though made at their base with the same golden colored metal that he had seen throughout Panteria, were silver in color. Nate marveled at them, wondering what the metals were and knowing that the weapons could not actually be made of gold. If it were real, he reasoned, it would not have lasted a second here, unguarded, in the open display area that separated the shop from the rest of the courtyard. He reached out to touch one of the ornately carved swords, laying his hand on it before Bailey could yell out and stop him.

It stung. His whole palm felt like it was on fire. He pulled his hand back and saw the faint red welt that had risen on his hand, even from that briefest touch. It was silver.

Almost simultaneously, he felt a surge of cooling, tingling energy enter his body—piercing through the soles of his shoes and coursing up through his limbs. Amazed, he watched as the welt began to fade and sink back into his flesh. At the same time, he felt his shoulders being yanked back, as Bailey pulled them away from the shop.

She led them away from the store and back towards the great domed building that was near the back of the courtyard. As it turned out, the building was a town hall of sorts, big enough for all of Panteria's residents. As she walked them past it, pointing out the various features, Nate realized that something was happening inside.

People were making their way slowly to the building in groups. Adults mostly. As they were walking by the open doors, they saw Marcus walking into the front door.

"What's going on," Nate ventured to ask, already knowing what the response would be.

"Don't worry about it," Bailey snapped, not disappointing at all. She hustled them along before they had a chance to see anymore.

Next, she led them to the school rooms, which were in use. Classroom after classroom, five in all, were filled with students. Unlike their classes at Greendale, the students in these classrooms did not appear to be the same age. In any one room, there were kids that looked as young as seven to teenagers about Bailey's age.

There, the girl explained, they learned about Panterian history, the science and biological systems that were unique to the land, and Panterian art and literature. There was some overlap with the human curriculum. Math, she explained, was the same in all of the worlds, and they often read and studied the human masters alongside their own literature and art. The classes were taught in multiple languages, including Panterian and Spanish, to prepare the anakulan for the outside world. Some of them were even taught in English.

For those Panterians who wanted to go on to college in the human world, there was an intensive two year study program after graduation to get them up to speed on all of the human knowledge that they would need to have.

"Though," she concluded with a voice that was at the same time weary and scathing, "I can't imagine why anyone would ever want to live in the human world."

At the final classroom, Bailey allowed them to pause for a moment to watch the instruction. The lesson seemed to be history. On the board was filled with a bunch of numbers and explanations that, despite the fact that they were written in English, were confusing nonetheless.

> P142—Lion and Tiger altercations escalate.
> P143—Emissaries from Leonin and Tigeri arrive in Panteria
> P146—The Tiglion/Liger Treaty is signed.

The instructor, who was also speaking English, was in the midst of an explanation of the material.

"Of course, if you ever find yourself discussing this matter with a lion, it's the Liger treaty. For a Tiger, it's Tiglion." A few of the older students tittered, while the younger ones looked just slightly less lost than the twins felt.

Ever curious, Larissa could not resist turning to Bailey and asking what it all meant. She thought that she had spoken softly, but apparently she had not been quiet enough. One of the students nearest the door overheard and turned in their direction. Seeing the twins, she tapped her desk-mate. It was like a domino effect. One by one, the students tapped each other, and in a ripple, they turned to the back of the classroom.

The teacher's voice trailed off as he realized that he no longer had a captive audience. Suddenly, the twins found themselves in the increasingly familiar position of being stared at by fifty pairs of eyes.

Searching for a safe place to look, Larissa found herself staring at yellow-flecked eyes so blue that they were almost purple. Laughter danced in those eyes and a smile played on his lips.

The boy flicked his ears, and it was only then that Larissa noticed the spotted leopard ears that rose from beneath his shaggy golden hair. Her mouth dropped open. The boy smiled, and Larissa blushed. Then the boy laughed, and that set the whole class off. Flushing to her roots and rumbling about loud mouth brats, Bailey hustled them away from the door.

From there, they practically raced through the rest of the tour. Bailey showed them the public library, which was several times larger than the library behind then Bastion's Chamber, its shelves stacked high with books filled with histories of Panteria, the human world, and the three other Great Empires

She pointed out the storehouses for food, the gymnasium, with a basketball court and other equipment, and the theater, for plays and music, Bailey explained. Were-leopards, it seemed, made for particularly fine musicians. It had something to do with their well-honed sense of hearing.

This made an odd kind of sense to the twins. They both had a sophisticated appreciation of music for their age. Much of what their friends listened to, the twins could not stomach. The shrill, off-key warbling of some of the most popular pop acts was grating to their shifter-hearing.

There was also a small museum, which held artistic treasures that dated back to the origins of Panteria. Bailey allowed them to peek inside, but just for moment. The paintings that hung on the walls appeared unremarkable at first, until Bailey instructed them to use their shifter-sight to view them.

Initially, Nate was confused. He had never used shifter-sight while in human form. Then, his mind went back to the day of the graduation, and a flash of an idea entered his mind. Grasping on to the thought, he concentrated on one of the paintings.

As he stared, Nate felt his eyes change. This time he was completely aware as the iris bled outward to fill his eye socket. Amazingly as his eyes changed, the paintings came alive, vibrating with a color spectrum too sensitive for human eyes to behold. He had never been one for art, but there was something breathtaking about those paintings.

Bailey dragged them away far too soon, leading them back out into the courtyard, which was beginning to fill with life and noise. The shops were opening and crowds of people hustled here and there. As with the day before, everywhere they went they drew stares. And as they passed, inevitably the whispers would begin. Nate found himself growing quickly weary of it all.

More and more people seemed to be moving toward the Great Hall, and Nate wondered anew what was happening there.

"We have to find out what is going on in the town hall." Larissa's words were an urgent whisper in his mind. *"I feel like it might have something to do with Mom and Dad."*

Nate responded by nodding his head imperceptibly. But Bailey led them quickly away from the action and back into the tower that led to the Inner Kula.

As they made their way back up the stairs, the twins learned that there was no electricity in Panteria and there never had been. Bailey pointed to the lamps that decorated the walls and explained that they were powered by some sort of advanced version of solar power.

The green leaf-looking panels that covered the tops of many of the buildings were actually solar energy collectors that powered any machinery in the Kula, including the lights. Not that there was much of that. Panteria seemed to have missed out on the Industrial Revolution. There were no televisions, no radios, no computers. None of the modern electronics that were so commonplace in the human world.

Just as she finished that explanation, they made it to the top of the stairs. With haste, she led them to the Bastion's Chamber, clearly wanting nothing more than to be rid of them and on to more important things.

CHAPTER 21

THE WORST KIND OF TRAITOR

When they entered the chamber and discovered that the Dowager was still indisposed, the twins saw their opportunity. Without much difficulty, they convinced Bailey escort them back to their rooms. The girl, having carried out the Dowager's orders, did just that and was half way down the hall before the twins could thank her.

Ten minutes after Bailey left him standing just inside the entry to his bedroom, Nate met Larissa her door and they quickly made their way down to the courtyard. Once again, the courtyard had emptied. With the exception of a few shopkeepers, who were fussing over their wares, all of the leopards in Panteria seemed to be at the Great Hall. Nate and Larissa crept into the courtyard, trying hard not to attract any attention as they made their way toward the building. That in itself was a task, because the courtyard was a wide open space and there were essentially no places to hide.

The twins darted and ducked between buildings as they tried to get closer to the Great Hall. Finally, they stood directly across from the building. Nate stepped forward and peered around the courtyard. The way was clear. He motioned for Larissa to follow and then sprinted out into the open, running towards the building. He reached the building, pressing himself against the side and trying to shrink into the shadow it cast.

He turned back to look for Larissa. She was still standing in the shadows of one of the shops. He gestured for her to come and she hesitated just a moment longer before breaking into a full-speed run towards him. And then, just as suddenly, she stopped. Right out in the open.

Nate stared at his sister, wondering if she had lost her mind. But she just stood there, frozen in the middle of the courtyard, for all to see.

"What is it," he thought to her.

"Behind you," she thought back.

Nate inched a little further around the building and saw what had stopped her. There stood Bailey. She was talking to the owner of the weapons shop. While she was not completely looking in Larissa's direction, Nate had no doubt that the older girl would be able to see his sister in her peripheral vision.

"What should I do," Larissa asked. Nate's mind worked. Part of him wanted to tell her to keep going. At the same time, if Bailey saw her, then their chance to finally get some actual answers would be ruined. He tried to figure out how to create a distraction without giving himself away at the same time.

Just then, there was a blur of legs and arms in front of him. The blur sped past and came to a halt right in front of Bailey.

"Bailey," the boy hollered and Nate recognized him from the classroom earlier. He grabbed the girl around the shoulders, turning her slightly away from the courtyard, even as it was clear that she did not want him bothering her. When Bailey was distracted, the boy reached behind his back, waving at Larissa, signaling for her to run. At the same time, Nate waved Larissa forward and the girl sprinted to his side. As she paused next to him, Nate notice a curious flush on her cheeks that seemed to have nothing to do with the exertion of her run.

The meeting in the town hall was switching into full gear, and they crept around the building looking for a place where they could both hear what was going on inside and hide from curious onlookers if necessary.

The first task was less of a problem, as the people inside seemed to be taking no particular care to be quiet or secretive. They could hear voices quite clearly as they circled around to the front of the building. Finding an unassuming location from which to listen, however, proved slightly more difficult. The town hall was smack dab in the center of the courtyard and exposed on all sides. There was no place to hide.

Sneaking in was out of the question too. The twins knew that inside the Great Hall, there was no way that their presence would go unnoticed. They moved toward the rear of the building, away from the crowds that stood just inside the front doors. Deciding that it would be best for them to separate, Larissa headed in one direction, circling around the dome, and Nate took the other.

When he was far enough from the front of the Great Hall and the eyes of those arriving to attend the meeting, Nate stopped and leaned, in what he hoped was a casual manner, against the building, pressing himself once more into the shadows as he tried to hide his conspicuous emerald green tunic.

"*Bro.*" He heard the word in his mind and realized that Larissa had come back into telepathic range.

"*Yeah.*"

"*Stay where I can hear you.*" Nate agreed and then trained his mind back on the conversations happening inside the hall.

The conversations had quieted and a deep male voice reached his ears. As the voice went on Nate realized, to his dismay, that he could not understand a word of what was being said. The man was speaking the same foreign language that he had heard since arriving in Panteria; Panterian Bailey called it. Nate heard a rumbling of voices as the crowd inside began to discuss the announcement. It was obviously an important one, and he could understand—at all—what it was.

He almost kicked the wall with frustration. Another dead end. Just then, a voice rang out clearly, cutting through the confusion of muffled voices, and this person, amazingly, spoke in English.

"Why should we?" The anxious mumble of the crowd was silenced by the shocking question. "Why should we," the voice continued, sounding both nasal and yet strangely compelling to Nate's ears, "risk ourselves for an Imperial Bastion who doesn't even deign to live with her people?"

For a long moment, the crowd was silent and then the murmuring began again. To his horror, Nate very clearly heard several people voicing their agreement.

"James has a point," one voice called out, also in English.

"It's true," another agreed.

Nate's blood began to boil. Who was this James, to talk about his mother like that? She was the kindest, most thoughtful…. His thoughts trailed off as James spoke again, his voice more confident this time.

"Ask yourselves this," the man, cried in clear, strident tones. "Would we even be in this mess if we had a Bastion who valued her duty to her people more than her own selfish whims?"

This time there were more and more rumbles of agreement.

"Thank you, James," Marcus's deep voice interrupted the ever-growing rumble.

"No," James retorted. "I'm not finished."

"We have heard enough," Marcus replied, his voice darkly insistent.

"I will not be silenced," James rejoined. "You must let me speak. It is the way of the Kula."

Grumbles of support came from the audience, growing louder each moment. Then a woman's voice, cool and tinged with resignation, broke in.

"He's right," she said. "He must be allowed to continue."

"For far too long," James began again, warming to both his subject matter and the crowd, "we have suffered the caprice of this Bastion at the risk of the safety of Panteria. Look! Just look around Panteria, and you will see where that has gotten us. And now she is captured because of her own carelessness, and we are asked to save her. She, who is supposed to be protecting us!"

The utter disdain in the man's voice cut Nate to the quick. Against his own volition, he began moving to the front of the building. Regardless of the trouble, someone had to speak for his mother. Someone had to defend her against this James's attacks. And it was becoming obvious that no one inside would.

Almost without realizing it, he found himself standing at the doors of the town hall, which had been thrown wide open to reveal its interior. Stopping, he stared down the long center aisle that ended in front of a dais, not unlike the Bastion's Chamber of the Inner Kula. Ten feet in front of him started rows of benches that lined the aisle and spanned the length of the building. Every last square inch of those benches was occupied with Panterians.

On the dais were Marcus, a woman with long black waves, and a ginger-colored man with ginger-colored hair. Bailey stood off to the side, a look of smoldering rage on her face. It was not any of these people who spoke, however. Rather, in front of the dais stood a large pale man, facing the gathered crowd. Nate's entrance went unnoticed as the man concluded his speech.

"Well, I don't know about you," James said, "but I refuse. I am not going to risk life and limb for Anna Pantera. Too long has the Pantera family taken its obligations and our allegiance for granted. Too long have they just expected our obedience. This mess is their fault, and they should figure out how to get us out of it themselves. Isn't that, after all, their duty?"

This time there were more than just a few shouts of agreement. Almost half the crowd was standing and shouting their support of the man. With each passing second, it seemed like more people stood, casting their lot with James.

"And," James said finally, as the crowd quieted, "if she is not found, we will elect a new Bastion." Abruptly, the crowd was silent, and James's last words were little more than a fervent whisper. "It's what we should have done thirty years ago."

With those words, a cheer erupted in the hall. Though a good portion of the crowd was noticeably silent, a healthy contingent seemed to be in support of the idea. Even with his very brief time in Panteria, Nate understood the seriousness of what James proposed. He was shocked that so many in the crowd were agreeing to what amounted to a coup.

He looked at the people on the dais, wondering why they did nothing to silence the man. Marcus looked angry, but resigned. The black haired woman was serene and unreadable. Curiously, the ginger man's expression was tinged with something like excitement.

Bailey, alone, looked infuriated. Her teeth were bared, showing canines that were slightly larger than they should have been for a human. She looked like she wanted to attack James right then and there. Nate liked the girl just slightly more in that moment.

The pale haired man stood before the crowd, a smirk on his face and a triumphant gleam in his light brown eyes. A flicker of recognition ran through Nate. There was something very familiar about this man, though, try as he might, he could not place it.

"But what about our mother?" The voice was soft, but somehow it broke through the increasingly raucous noise of the crowd. Nate whipped around in surprise. Larissa was standing right next to him, and he had not even sensed her approach. That had never happened before. Larissa's voice, calm but plaintive, silenced the crowd as they all turned to stare at the twins who now stood side by side, just inside the doors of the town hall.

For a moment, in the complete silence, Nate saw looks of guilt cross the faces of several who just seconds before had been cheering at the idea of a new Bastion. And then, the man, this James, spoke again.

"Yes," he almost sneered the word, "What about your mother? What has she ever done to deserve our loyalty or our help?" The man had abandoned all pretense of diplomatic concern. He was pure malevolence now. Nate could hear Larissa's mind working as she searched for a response.

"That's not fair!" The words burst from Nate's mouth in an angry shout before Larissa could reply. And it was true. It was an unfair question. Until yesterday, neither Larissa nor he had even known about the existence of this place. They knew nothing of their mother's time as Bastion. They knew nothing of whether she had or had not fallen short with regards to her duty to the people of Panteria.

"What's not fair?" James responded. "I only asked a question that any true Panterian already knows the answer to. Oh, but that's right. You two, like your mother, are not really

Panterians. Are you?" He smirked, a mean gleam making his tea colored eyes glitter.

Nate clenched his fists at his sides, his anger threatening to overwhelm him. It was not just James who enraged him, but the entire silent crowd. None of them would speak for his mother. Not one even tried. He had never felt so angry and yet so powerless. Except that he had, once before.

Larissa spoke, interrupting Nate's thoughts. The words she said were the only truth that she knew. "I don't know," was her soft reply. With her words, James beamed his triumph, but Larissa was not done. "I don't know what my mother has done to make her deserving or undeserving of your help." She paused for a moment and an ugly smile bloomed on James' face. "But I do know that my grandmother has served Panteria proudly all of her life, and her mother before her, and her mother before her. Doesn't that deserve something?"

The crowd seemed to consider her words. They began to whisper to each other again. What had been a near mutinous rumbling had quieted but did not subside. Then, abruptly, all of the noise in the building ceased entirely, and Nate realized that the people in the town hall were no longer looking at his sister, but behind her. Tearing his gaze from the cowardly people before him, he turned to follow their stares and saw what had stopped their chatter.

There, in the doorway, stood the Dowager. Though Nate only knew that because of her emerald green tunic and the thin gold diadem filled with glowing green stones that circled her forehead. Beyond that, she was completely unrecognizable.

In that moment, the Dowager looked more panther than human. Her face was absolutely feline, with no traces of the human woman that he had come to know. Her impossibly broad cheekbones narrowed to nose and chin that were at once delicate and strong. Her hair was longer, curling down over her shoulders in blue black waves. And her eyes. Her eyes, when he finally looked at them, were not human at all. They were cat eyes, glowing emerald green even in the shadowy town hall, and her pupils were narrowed into angry slits. She looked like some sort of scarily distorted version of their mother.

Power radiated off of her in waves that Nate could actually see swirling around her feet. At first, he thought it was a trick of lighting, but with each step that the Dowager took, not only could he see the power that writhed around her, but he could feel it too.

The strange energy that had plagued him throughout the journey to the Kula had not bothered him since the day before, all but disappearing when he shifted at the gates. Now, he could feel it again. Though this time it was moving away from him as a gentle but insistent tug drew the power to the Dowager. The stones of the crown shone brighter each time her foot touched the ground. And, when she opened her mouth to speak, she had fangs.

"That's enough." Her voice was a purr of quiet authority and she spoke not only to the twins, but to James and all of the others gathered in the town hall.

Nate couldn't help it. His mouth dropped open. He should have been afraid but all he felt was amazement at the powerful creature that stood before him. Nate began to wonder which of the creatures they had met was the true Dowager. The exotic, feline woman that had greeted them yesterday, the matronly grandmother that she had transformed into, or this ferocious cat woman that stood before them now. It made him begin to wonder about himself too. If she could be all of these beings, what was he?

Larissa seemed less impressed by the Dowager's entrance. She began to protest, but the Dowager held up a finger from which a vicious looking claw extended. The sight of that was enough to silence even Larissa, and her protest died in her throat.

"You have done well," the Dowager continued softly, with something like pride in her voice. She looked first at Larissa and then at Nate. "But this is not your place and this is not your fight. Not yet. Return to the Inner Kula." The last was a gentle command that, at the same time, brooked no argument. Nate, though, was past being reasoned with.

"These are our parents," Nate said, grinding his words out through his anger, which was reappearing now that his awe had begun to subside. "Don't we get to have a say?" The Dowager shook her head, her strange face sympathetic even as she motioned for someone to escort the twins from the hall. Nate and Larissa saw the two men approaching them and he watched Larissa's shoulders slump in defeat as he turned away from his grandmother and the crowd.

"Come on." He whispered the words in Larissa's mind, feeling dejected and defeated. It was clear that they weren't needed or wanted there. Larissa turned to him surprise.

"You're going to give up that easily?"

"JUST COME ON!" His anger caught him completely off-guard. It welled up in him suddenly like lava in a volcano that was about to erupt. And when he shouted at Larissa, he felt it pour out of him into her in one hot rush. The girl actually took a step back, her eyes full of reproach. Still, she was too shocked to do anything other than obey. As he began walking toward the door, one of the men reached for his arm. Shrugging his shoulder, he threw the man's hands aside and stormed out of the hall. He didn't stop until he was standing near the front gates of the Kula.

He turned back towards the Great Hall and almost ran into Larissa, who stormed up right behind him. She swept past him without saying a word.

When she turned back to Nate, her eyes blazed with a fury that almost matched the anger that boiled inside of him.

"Ris, I didn't mean to…" he began, thinking that she was angry with him for what had just happened. She waved her hand, cutting off his apology.

"Can you believe that guy?" Her voice was low and furious as she paced agitatedly back and forth.

"That guy," Nate recovered, his anger cutting a broader swath. "What about the rest of them? Not one of them said anything. Not one of them. What happened to all of that loyalty stuff the Dowager was talking about."

"And she wants us to go and, what, twiddle our thumbs?" Larissa's rage now turned to the Dowager. "Does she really think that we can do that?"

It was strange to see Larissa so enraged. He was usually the one that she had to calm down. Now the shoe was on the other foot, and he couldn't, or wouldn't try to sooth her. He was tired of waiting around for someone else to find his parents. From the looks of things, half of the people of Panteria didn't care if they were ever found. They would just as soon elect a new Bastion and move on as though nothing had ever happened.

"If she isn't going to let us help, we are going to have to do it ourselves." Nate said, mumbling almost to himself. With those words, he ran towards the gates. To Nate's surprise, no one ran to stop him. He looked around the courtyard and realized that it was entirely empty. No one would try to stop them. Within seconds, he was at the gate, shifting as he ran, his tunic and pants sliding off and falling away. The gates remained firmly shut, so instead he ran to a tree that grew near the wall, neatly scaled it, and leapt from one branch to the top of the wall.

Then he heard Larissa's voice in his mind. "Nate! Wait!" He turned back to Larissa expecting her to try and talk him out of leaving the Kula. Instead, as he watched, she shifted and began to scale the tree.

Not wanting to waste another moment, he ran across the wall and climbed down the wall on the other side. Before he reached the fountain, Larissa had caught up to him. Together, they bounded across the grasslands towards the jungle.

Chapter 22

Saved By a Tail

The pair climbed back up the steep hill that they had descended just the day before. Every few moments, Nate glanced behind them, expecting to see a pack of leopards chasing after them. Each time, however, he was surprised to find that there was no one on their trail.

Soon, they were at the top of the cliff. Together, they ran through the jungle, heading due north, towards home. Instinctively, they were making their way towards the place that they had seen the night before. The place of empty darkness.

They left the dense jungle, running back across the plains that bordered the Lake of Falcons. As they entered the jungle on the other side, Larissa abruptly stopped. She glanced around at the woods with no idea where to go next. Nate pawed the ground, feeling the electric shocks of energy course up his body. The sensation gave him an idea.

"Give me a second," he thought to his sister.

As Larissa watched, he walked in a large semi-circle, testing the ground with each footfall. He did not know if it would work, but perhaps the land could tell them which way to go. With each slow step, Nate listened to the energy from the land, searching for any hint of a change in the tune of the power. He walked in a slow semi-circle around Larissa.

Then, he felt it. As he set his paw down, he felt a tingle of energy that was both like and unlike the energy that he had felt just a moment before. The melody was recognizable but slightly off key, kind of like a song played on a piano that needed to be tuned. Keeping one paw firmly on the ground, he pivoted in the direction from which that energy seemed to flow, peering into the dark, nearly impenetrable depths beneath the trees. Then he looked over at Larissa, who watched him intently.

"I think it's this way," he thought to her, motioning with his head towards the dark, thick growth that stretched out before them. He took a tentative step in that direction and Larissa followed.

They moved slowly at first, walking side by side. Nate paid special attention to the feel of the ground beneath his paws, searching for clues that might lead them towards that mysterious patch of emptiness that they had spotted the night before and, ultimately he hoped, to their parents. With each step, the energy that emanated from the ground became slightly more discordant, jarring his body. But Nate did not slow or hesitate. The stranger the energy felt, the more confident he grew that they were moving in the right direction.

For a long time, nothing changed as they traveled. The lush green plants and trees ahead of them were virtually indistinguishable from the lush green plants and trees that they had just trekked through. The energy that entered his body played the same off key melody. Vaguely discordant.

Then, abruptly, the trees began to thin out ahead of them. Where there had been almost impenetrable jungle growth, so dense that it had practically blocked out the sky, there were now visible and wide patches of cerulean. The ground around them was changing as well. The dense lush undergrowth through which they had passed for the last hour was rapidly thinning, showing the dark earth beneath. Soon, even the earth itself began to look damaged. It became dry and cracked, scratching and digging into their paws as they moved forward.

Nate noticed too, as they ran, that the strength and unending energy that had coursed through his body ever since entering Panteria, seemed to be waning. As it drained away, his stomach began to churn, making him feel like he was going to be sick. The further they went, the more pronounced the feeling became until each step was agony, sending nauseating waves of energy jolting through his body. Soon he slowed to a walk, dragging his feet along, each step sending his stomach rolling. Then, feeling like he could not move another step forward, he stopped and leaned his suddenly weary body against a tree.

Larissa, who had been following behind him, stopped next to him. *"You okay,"* she asked.

Nate was about to respond when he heard it. A crackling noise that he couldn't identify at first.

"Did you hear that," he asked his sister. Both of the twins went still, their ears perking up. They heard it again. The crackling noise of rustling leaves. Something large was moving through the underbrush, and it was very close.

"I think that it's coming this way," Larissa said. Nate nodded. She was right. It was loud and clumsy, taking no care to hide its approach. Something told Nate that it was not another leopard, because even he and Larissa, who had been trained for years not to be like shifters, didn't make as much noise as that. Then they heard the voices.

"Why are we even out here," one voice said. "He said they are all going to be at that meeting anyway."

"Look," another, gruffer voice replied. "The boss says patrol, we patrol. No questions. Now be quiet. I think that I saw something over there. You know how well they can hear."

The sounds came more quickly, as though whoever they were, they were running.

"Nate, we have to get out of here," Larissa said. *"Quick."*

Nate knew she was right. At the same time, he was having difficulty moving. He tried several times to push himself away from the tree trunk, but he didn't seem to have the strength. Instead, he felt like he was going to faint.

Meanwhile, the sounds were getting closer and closer. Larissa panicked and grabbed Nate by the tail, pulling him away from the sound. Nate stumbled away from the tree using the momentum from his sister's tugging. From there, with Larissa half pushing and half pulling him, they ran from the men who sounded like they were right behind them.

"There! Did you hear that?" It was the gruff voice again. "I told you I saw something."

Larissa realized that there was no way that they were going to be able to move quickly enough to escape their pursuers. The only thing that they could do was hide. She looked around, trying to figure out where. When she moved again, rather than running forward, she began pushing Nate toward a nearby tree. With her help, Nate got up into the tree, digging his claws into the trunk and straining in the effort to pull himself away from the poisonous ground. The higher he got, the easier he found climbing on his own. The nausea and weakness began to fade and soon he had reached the cover of the leafy branches. When Nate was hidden among the branches of the tree, Larissa followed him, reaching the sheltering leaves just as the men chasing them came into view.

The men clambered noisily into sight, crashing through the underbrush just beneath the branches where the twins crouched. The twins ducked, hugging the tree branch and trying to hide their bodies among the leaves. They held themselves motionless, their breath caught in their throats, as the men stopped to look around.

The two in the clearing were obviously human. They were too nervous, too anxious, to be anything else. Nate could hear their harsh breathing and, beneath that, the pounding of their hearts in their chest. He could smell the acrid aroma of their sweat.

They carried weapons with them. Large, dangerous looking arms, which they held expertly in their hands. They looked around, crouching to look beneath the mossy, upturned roots of the trees and using the tips of their weapons to move aside the thick bushes that covered the floor. The men circled around and around, and for some reason even though they found nothing, they would not move on.

As they lingered beneath the clump of trees in which the twins hid, Nate and Larissa began to wonder if they had indeed been spotted, and the men were just trying to trick them into revealing themselves. Soon, however, it became clear that that was not the case. The men, it seemed, were just stumped.

Then one of them, the one with curly blond hair, placed a hand over his eyes and turned his face to the branches. He swiveled in a slow circle scanning the trees. Any moment, his eyes would be on the tree in which they hid. Though they were fairly high in the branches, they could not stay hidden under such careful scrutiny. They would be seen.

Just as the man was about to turn in their direction, there was a rustling noise. The sound echoed through the silent jungle like a clap of thunder, and the men below froze. Nate's eyes shot to his twin, but Larissa had not moved a muscle and the sound was coming from farther away than that. Instantly, the man scanning the trees turned in the direction of the noise.

Nate tried to look around without moving. Larissa was doing the same, and she was looking in the opposite direction. He couldn't see anything, but he could sense eyes on them. Slowly and carefully, he raised his head and turned in the direction of the sound. In a tree, just a few yards from the tree where they hid, there was a honey-colored leopard, and it was looking directly into his eyes.

Nate's heart seemed to stop in his chest as the leopard gazed at him. He froze, waiting to see what the creature would do. What happened next could not have been more of a surprise. The leopard slowly winked at him, and a wide grin spread across its cat face. Then the creature turned and, making as much noise as it could, bounded off, soaring through the tree branches. The leopard was trying to lead the men away, Nate realized with excitement. And it was working!

"There! There it goes!" A frantic voice rang out from down below.

"I can't see anything," the other man said, training his weapon towards the trees.

"You can hear it can't you?! Follow it! Follow it!" The men started, getting a firm grip on their weapons and running in the direction of noise.

Nate and Larissa watched in amazement as the leopard ran across the tree branches leading the men away. As they ran from the clearing, the men kept trying to take aim at the cat, but they could not get a clear shot through all of the branches. Soon, both the leopard and the men had disappeared.

For several long moments, the twins stayed in the tree. Better safe than sorry. Finally, when it was clear that the men were long gone, they climbed down to the jungle floor.

"We have to go quickly," Larissa said as they reached the ground. *"They could come back this way at any moment."*

Nate nodded. "They were coming from that direction," he said, motioning towards the direction in which they had been traveling. *"I think we are getting close to something. Let's go."*

CHAPTER 23

THE PRICE OF WEALTH

THEY HEADED QUICKLY IN the direction from which they had so recently fled, though Nate feared the return of the nausea and weakness. This time, prepared, he tried to steel himself against it, but soon he noticed the tell-tale signs creeping up his limbs and growing stronger with each step. Soon they were back at the tree where he had stopped to rest before. It was then that Nate noticed that the ground just a few yards ahead of them was completely barren.

There was nothing. No trees. No shrubs. No plants of any kind. Nothing but a wide open stretch of dry, cracked, arid earth that looked as though it had baked too long in the too hot sun. The very earth looked as sick as he felt. Nate studied the ground that stretched out before them like some sort of horrible scar, a blight on the gorgeous, lush landscape that surrounded it. He stopped, knowing instinctively that he could not and, more importantly, should not set foot on that ground.

"Is that it?" Larissa asked. "Is that what we saw last night?" She took a few tentative steps forward, but Nate stayed where he was, his stomach rolling.

Larissa continued to advance, stepping unaware out on to

the cracked barren ground. It was several seconds before she noticed that Nate was no longer by her side. She stopped and looked back at him.

"*What is it,*" she questioned, her face a mask of feline concern and curiosity. Amazed that his sister could not feel how wrong the land felt, he tried to explain.

"*The ground. The energy. There is something very messed up about this place.*" His voice was a mere whisper in her mind, each word forced out through the pain that was constantly building. He gave up trying to explain as another wave of nausea swept over him. "*Jeez. Can't you feel that?*"

Larissa looked at her brother, whose face was contorted with unspoken pain. His knees shook and he fought to lock them so that he would not fall to the ground. Something seemed to be attacking him, something that she could neither see nor feel. She had no idea how to help him.

"*Okay. Just stay there,*" she thought back to him, even though his ability to move any further was non-existent. She turned away, taking another tentative step forward. They didn't have much time before the men would return, and she wanted to find out as much as she could before they had to leave.

Taking another cautious step, she caught her first glimpse of the gaping pit that was the mine, and she could not help but gasp. The land was in utter ruin. The hole stretched out before her, several hundred yards wide, and the land had been ripped, gouged, and stripped until there was nothing left but grayish, brittle earth.

She walked right up to the edge of the cliff, which sloped precipitously downward. The basin of the mine was empty, but she could see where miners had dug deep into the core of land, creating a huge shadowy cavern in the side of the cliff.

Still, there was nothing to suggest that their parents were being held there. In fact, the mine was completely deserted.

Confused, Larissa turned back and began walking towards her brother. With each step, she ground her feet into the earth, still searching for some hint of what Nate felt. But with each step, all she felt was the dry cracked earth, scrapping the pads of her paws.

"There's nothing here," she called out to her brother as she got closer. Nate looked at her confused. He shook his head at her. She was wrong; there had to be something.

"Look Nate, there's nothing. In fact, there's no one," she stopped abruptly, as a curious tingle tickled her paws. She stopped moving, digging her feet into the ground, certain that she had just imagined it. But, no, it was there. She felt it again, like little shocks in her feet. Her paws began to tingle as though they had fallen asleep.

Her breath caught in her throat at the queer sensation that swiftly enveloped her entire body. Then suddenly her ears popped and her paws felt like they were being suctioned to the earth and secured there. Suddenly, she was immobilized.

Without warning, the shocks of energy intensified. What had started as a tingling swiftly changed into waves of energy. But instead of coursing into her body, the energy seemed to be leaving her body, through her paws, and draining out into the land beneath her feet. All of a sudden, she felt extremely tired and wanted nothing more than to lie down. The longer she stood, the stronger the sensation became until she felt as though her very soul was being siphoned out through the pads of her paws.

"What? Do you feel it?" Nate whispered the question softly in her mind. There was a tinge of excitement in his voice, as though he was glad that she finally understood what he was going through. But it wasn't the same. Larissa's cat features twisted into an expression of confusion as she tried to explain.

"It's like my energy…is being…sucked out of me." She said

the words slowly, describing the strange sensation that had overtaken her body.

Larissa tried to lift her paws. If she could break the connection with the earth, maybe she could stop the sucking and draining that was making her feel weaker by the moment. Frantically, she tried again to lift her feet. She found, however, that she could not move her paws at all. In fact, the more she struggled, the more firmly she seemed to be stuck to the ground.

"*Nate.*" Larissa called to him, really frightened now. "*Nate, I don't think that I can move.*" She looked up at him, the black pupils of her eyes wide with fear and pain.

Nate, ignoring his own pain, shoved himself away from the tree and moved to help her. He had only taken two steps before something else happened.

It was as if some invisible switch had been flipped. Suddenly, the tingling energy from the ground was not merely coursing throughout his body; it was being pulled through him, entering into his paws, racing through his body and then shooting out from all over. When Larissa's expression changed from utter fear to surprise, her mouth dropping open, Nate knew that the energy was somehow flowing out of him and into her.

"*What is going on?*"

Nate could not answer. But whatever it was, it was growing stronger by the second. Wave after wave of energy rose from the earth, channeled through him, and pulsed into Larissa. Both of them were held frozen in place by the phenomenon. But it did not stop there.

The change was subtle, almost unnoticeable, at first. The ground beneath Larissa's paws grew darker and darker. No longer dry and cracked, the soil looked rich and fertile once again. The dark earth spilled out from beneath Larissa's paws and spread like a puddle of water, creeping slowly towards Nate.

"*Look at that,*" Nate whispered, awed and fearful. Larissa followed his gaze to the plants that were sprouting up all around her.

Stunned, Nate watched as green plants shot up around Larissa's feet. The halo of green grew around her, expanding outwards in ever widening circles. In seconds the plants grew from tiny green shoots to fully blossoming bushes that brushed around Larissa's legs. Within moments, she was standing in a patch of plants and bushes that should have taken months to grow. The land was healing itself.

"*Nate! What is going on?!*" Larissa was not at all awed. She was utterly terrified. Her fur stood on end and the green of her eyes disappeared entirely behind the black of her pupils. She struggled to move again, growing more frantic with each passing moment.

Nate shook his head. He had no idea how to explain it, and only one idea of how to stop it. "*I think one of us needs to start moving. Otherwise, I don't think it is going to stop.*"

Both of the twins fought to move but found their paws affixed inexplicably, and seemingly permanently, to the ground. Meanwhile, the cycling of power grew in both speed and intensity. Almost as soon as the energy entered Nate, it shot over to Larissa and poured back into the land, a never-ending chain.

The force of the coursing energy made every inch of fur on Nate's body stand on end. He looked as though his tail had been stuck in an electrical socket, which was also how he felt. Larissa's fur, on the other hand, was flattened to her body, as though the energy was pounding her both inside and out.

Wave after wave of energy funneled through the girl, entering into every fiber of her body and then pouring in molten waves out of her paws back into the ground. The strength of it brought her to her knees. Then, unable to stop herself, Larissa tumbled to the ground.

As soon as her body came into contact with the earth, the searing energy held her immobile as it pulsed through her and into the land wherever her body touched the ground. Green plants burst forth from the ground more quickly, rippling out in ever broadening rings, almost completely covering the space between the twins. At the center, Larissa writhed in pain at the invisible force that held her there, pinned to the ground.

"*I can't stop it Nate.*" Larissa's voice was little more than a whimper. He could tell that she was crying though he could not see her face. He redoubled his efforts, trying again to move even one paw to halt the agony that she endured. Even the smallest movement, he was sure, would break the cycle. But nothing. No matter how he struggled, he could not get his paws to budge one single inch.

Then, Nate had a hunch. He remembered that the energy had not bothered him so much while he was human. At least in not the same way that he felt it when he shifted. In fact, he had barely been able to feel it at all, while he was human. Maybe if he could shift, he could stop whatever this was that was happening to them.

"*Hold on Ris,*" he thought to his sister, "*I think that I have an idea.*" Clamping his jaws together, heedless of the way that his fangs sliced into his gums, he focused all of his energy on shifting. He imagined himself in his P. E. suit, pushing away the image of the panther with all of the force that he could muster. His panther fought him as it had the day before, but slowly Nate felt tell-tale signs of the shift. He could feel his fur retracting, hair by hair. His bones shortened in some places and lengthened in others. Moments later, Nate opened his eyes and saw human fingers rather than feline claws gripping the dark black earth.

He was on his hands and knees in the same spot. The energy, which only moments before had electrified every atom in his body, was suddenly cut off. Glancing over at his sister, he saw that she lay still in a bed of waxy-leafed foliage, no longer twisting under the weight of that invisible force. He had been so focused on shifting that he had completely blocked her out of his mind.

"Ris," he called to her, using his voice and not his mind this time. She did not respond. Not even a twitch of her tail to let him know that she heard him. Slowly, he got to his feet. Every muscle ached, and his body protested with each movement.

As quickly as he could manage, Nate crossed the distance between them, calling her name softly with each step. She was still in panther form, which for some reason surprised Nate. She did not reply either audibly or telepathically. He could not feel her thoughts, even as he reached out to her with his mind. There was nothing but darkness. With each step, he grew more afraid. He knelt beside her, gently touching her sleek black fur.

"Ris," he gently shook her paw. "Ris," he shook her more roughly, panic starting to outweigh shock as he tried to rouse her. But she showed no signs of awakening. He had to get her some help.

Resolutely, Nate slid his arms underneath her body and lifted her gently from the ground into his arms. Though she weighed more as a panther, he was able to lift her easily. As he adjusted her body in his arms, he heard the echo of a far off roar. Glancing around, he saw nothing, but he knew that he had to get Ris back to the safety of the Kula.

Steeling himself against all of the emotions that warred inside, the boy turned and started running back in the direction of the Kula, being as careful as he could with his sister, who lay unconscious in his arms.

CHAPTER 24

GRRRLLL!

LESS THAN TWENTY YARDS away, Anna and Robert watched it all, powerless to help the twins. Anna strained towards her children, ignoring the way that the silver-laced metal bars singed the flesh beneath her fur wherever she touched them. She and Robert called out to Nate and Larissa over and over again, but the twins gave no sign that they heard. Finally, they watched Nate carry Larissa off into the forest and Anna let out a roar of grief and rage.

This was not the first time that this had happened. Since Anna had been captured, several search parties had passed by, not fifteen feet from where she was suspended in her cage. No matter how loudly she roared, often to the delight of her mocking captors, the search parties continued on, never realizing that she was right beneath their noses or above their heads, as it were.

She had noticed, also immediately, that her captors took no care to hide themselves or the camp, even from the search parties. That fact had initially struck her as odd, because the camp was so close to a known mining area and likely to be the first place that her mother would look for her. As the days passed, however, it became clear that there was no reason for them to conceal themselves. They could see out but, for some reason, no one could see in.

Though she could not tap the *fuerza* to confirm her suspicion, Anna knew some strange yet familiar magic was at work here. That explained, in part at least, how the humans were getting into Panteria. Somehow, their adversary had figured out a way to manipulate the shields that concealed and separated Panteria from the human world, and seemingly, they had figured out how to create a prison within Panteria using those same shields.

All of this amounted to very bad news. Anna was beginning to fear that they would never be found.

Chapter 25

Revelations

It was hours before Nate reached the Kula and well after dark. The jungle was, as Windy had warned, extremely difficult to navigate in human form. Shifting was not an option, however. Larissa was still unconscious, and he had to carry her all the way back in his arms. Plus, he had taken a different, longer route back, trying to avoid the men that had chased them before.

As he stood at the top of the cliff, wondering how he would get himself and his sister down in one piece, Nate was thankful to see a familiar form coming towards him. Within seconds, the bird had alighted on his shoulder and was peering down curiously at Larissa.

"The Bastion is furious with you for your disobedience." Windy trilled. Then, in the same breath, "What has happened?"

Nate tried several times to explain, but each time he had to stop because of the lump in his throat. "Windy, I can't. I just can't." His voice cracked with exhaustion and something else. He looked down at his sister, smoothing her black fur, his throat working furiously. "I need help. Can you find someone to help me? Please." With the request, a pleading note entered his voice.

In a flash, the bird was flying back towards the Kula, and mere minutes later a contingent of three leopards loped across the plain.

Before he knew it, Nate found himself being ushered through the courtyard of the Kula toward the tower that led to the Bastion's Chamber. Beside him walked a guard carrying Larissa's still motionless form. In front of him walked Bailey looking rather grim-faced. Every few moments, she would cast a look of disgust in his general direction.

Though there were fewer shifters out in the wee hours of the morning, their party created an immediate sensation, just as it had when they had first arrived. But now, the other shifters didn't even try to hide their curiosity. People stopped, turned, and stared as the motley crew made its way through the courtyard. Conversations dropped off and it was like moving through a wall of silence.

Suddenly a voice called out, "What happened?"

Nate had kept his eyes stonily to the ground, refusing even to glance at these people who would leave his mother to rot. At the question, though, his eyes shot up and he saw a lanky blond-haired boy running towards them. When Nate saw the tips of leopard ears peeking from beneath the mop of hair, he realized that it was the kid from earlier that day. The one who had helped distract Bailey.

"What happened," the kid yelled again, even as a woman reached out and grabbed him, holding him back. "I thought I had gotten them off of your trail. I did the best I could," the boy called.

At that, Nate stopped and turned to stare at the boy. So he had been their mysterious savior not once, but twice that day. The boy looked frantically back and forth between Nate and Larissa. There was some wild emotion in his eyes that Nate could not identify.

"Avery, hush," said the woman who held him. Nate realized that she must have been some sort of relation, because the two shared the same mop of honey-colored hair.

At the same time, Nate felt a tug on his arm and looked up to see that Bailey had taken a firm grasp on his arm. Her message was clear. There were to be no detours and the Dowager would not be kept waiting. Nate shot the boy a glance of gratitude and then turned and marched on. When they reached the tower, Nate could hardly climb the stairs, but he refused to give Bailey the satisfaction of seeing him falter either.

When Nate entered the Bastion's Chamber, they were all waiting there. The Dowager, Marcus, and another man with long black hair streaked with white and almond-shaped brown eyes. A new face. The Dowager sat upon the dais in one of the smallest chairs, and the two men stood off to the side. Nate walked into the room, feeling as though he had been called before the judge to be sentenced. Indeed, the Dowager glared down at Nate as he came to a halt just a few yards from where she sat. Her face was almost feral with rage. It was a look that should have terrified him, but Nate was too numb even to be afraid.

The Dowager was just about to speak when the guard entered the chamber carrying Larissa. Nate heard the sharp gasp, and the look on the Dowager's face morphed from rage to fear. Suddenly the room was a flurry of motion. Nate felt a hand on his shoulder and followed along as Marcus ushered him behind the dais to his grandmother's antechamber. The guard followed just behind him, laying Larissa on one of the lounge chairs.

As soon as the guard stepped away, Nate sank to the floor next to Larissa, forgetting the other shifters in the room, and stroked the fur of her neck.

"Please be all right," he thought fiercely. *"Please be all right."*

He repeated the thought over and over again as he buried his face in the cushion next to his sister's head. There was only silence in the room as Nate stroked his sister's neck and looked for signs of life. At first, the sound was so soft that he was not sure that he actually heard it. It sounded like the faintest of groans. Nate's entire body froze.

"*Ris,*" he called to her, and then held himself still.

There! There it was again. A faint moan. It wasn't words, but it was something. "*Ris,*" he called again, and this time, her eyelids fluttered. She expelled a soft breath and then groaned again. Nate felt relief pour through his body. She was alive!

Then, to his chagrin, he started to cry. Embarrassed, he buried his face again in the cushion, but he could not hide his shaking shoulders.

The Dowager watched him, her rage melting away. She brought her hand to her mouth as tears stung her own eyes. What must those two have been through?

At that moment, the long-haired man stepped forward. He gently shooed Nate away and knelt to examine Larissa. Wiping his tears with the back of his hand, Nate drew away, and found himself standing beside the Dowager, who reached up to put her arm around his shoulder. Though he still wasn't sure how he felt about the woman, Nate allowed her to hug him close, feeling less afraid and alone for the first time since Larissa had collapsed in the jungle. The leopards were tense and hushed as they all watched the Healer do his work.

After a while, he looked up and pronounced, "She is suffering from acute exhaustion and shock. She is coming back around, though, and will be fine after several days of rest." He took a few medicines out of the bag that he had carried with him and began to treat Larissa with them.

Around the room, the shifters breathed a collective sigh of relief, and Nate found himself being hugged by the Dowager, his grandmother. Before Nate could even respond, the Dowager pushed him away. Still holding him by the shoulders, she forced him to meet her gaze.

"You must tell us everything that happened out there," she

said. "Everything."

In quick order, the Dowager cleared the room. Bailey left, bearing Larissa in her arms and grumbling audaciously all the way. Marcus followed soon after with orders to secure the Inner Kula and continue organizing the massive search party, which would leave as soon as it was assembled. Finally, there were only four left in the library, Nate, the Dowager, Windy, and the Healer. Nate squirmed under the weight of the inquisitive gazes that fell on him. Looking from the Dowager to the Healer to Windy, he began to tell the story.

Nate took his time, explaining everything the best that he could. He told the Dowager about their anger over the meeting and their decision to look for their parents themselves. He told her about the space of emptiness and their feeling about their parents' whereabouts. Then, even though he did not quite understand it himself, he told her about the strange power that had affected both him and Larissa.

"The *fuerza*," the Bastion murmured, interrupting him. Nate looked over at her for explanation. Before answering him, she looked across the room at the Healer, who was also her oldest and closest friend Li. He already knew of and guarded carefully the Pantera family secret. She could speak candidly before him.

"*Terra Fuerza*, earth power," his grandmother continued. "All of the Bastions of the Pantera line have possessed this power. This connection to the earth." She paused and Nate held his breath waiting for her to continue. "It is a power that we do not even fully comprehend ourselves. We do not know its source or why we seem to be the only family that possesses it. But it gives us a strength that you have yet to understand. You will have to be trained to use it and control it." She paused again, giving Nate a significant glance.

After a moment of silence, a look of consternation crossed the Dowager's face. "But this other thing, this exchange between you and Larissa, is something that I have never heard of before."

"I didn't tell you the strangest thing," Nate said, cutting her off. They all turned expectantly towards him, wondering what might be stranger than the story that he had told them so far. Nate looked around the room, finally resting his gaze on his Dowager. "When we were connected, Ris and I, grass and plants grew from the ground." At her baffled look, Nate struggled to explain again. "The plants just seemed to spring up around her feet. Like she was making them grow."

The Dowager took a startled breath. She stared at her grandson as though he were a stranger; more than just a stranger, some extraordinary alien creature the likes of which she had never seen before. Nate shifted uncomfortably under the weight of her gaze before finally looking away. Scanning the room, he found that the Healer wore a similar expression and even Windy's face was the picture of bird-like wonder. The silence was deafening.

Abruptly, the Dowager broke the strange spell. Using the cord to summon Bailey to the chamber, she sent Nate off to his room under the girl's care, promising him that he would see his sister as soon as he awoke. Then only she, the Healer, and Windy remained.

"What do you make of it?" she asked.

"Sounds miraculous," Li replied.

"We must find out whether there is any record of such a power."

"I will begin the research immediately," he replied.

"Thank you, old friend," she whispered as he exited the chamber.

CHAPTER 26

ONCE UPON A TIME...

NATE LOOKED AT THE shelves stacked high with books before him. He was back in the Bastion's library. He had wandered up there after going to see his sister earlier that morning. Ris had been asleep when he entered the room and she had not awakened the whole time that he was there.

She did seem better though. For one thing, she was no longer a panther. When he entered the room, he was relieved to see her tousled black curls peeking out from beneath the sheets. Also, her breathing had been almost normal. Today, she seemed as though she were really just sleeping, not recovering from some great shock that had almost.... He could not even finish the thought.

Everywhere he went that morning, he felt like he was being watched. Even though he did not see anyone watching when he looked around, he felt eyes on him all the time. From the looks of it, his grandmother was taking no chances that he might slip out again, and just when he itched to return to that place in the jungle. There was something off about that place, he just knew it. He just needed more time to figure out what. But he could not even get out of the Inner Kula. There were now guards posted at every exit. This room was the only place where he could escape the surveillance.

For a while, he lounged on the chaise, replaying the events of the previous day in his mind. Over and over, he watched the events unfold, trying to figure out exactly what had happened.

At a loss, he turned his eyes to the book stacks. Among the volumes, many of which were written in multiple languages, including a strange one that looked like so many jagged claw marks, there were a few that written in English with such curiosity-piquing titles as *Plants of Panteria: A Guide to Panterian Herbology. The Four Great Kingdoms, Bastions of Panteria: A Compendium, 7th Edition.* There were other titles too. Titles with the names of people that he did not recognize, such as *Natalia the Restorer* and *Gretchen the Wise,* and the more ominous *Margot the Deceitful,* and *Virginia the Pitiless,* alongside more ancient-looking and familiar volumes like *The Complete Works of Shakespeare* and *The Divine Comedy.*

He got up from the chaise and went over to the shelf and pulled down *Bastions of Panteria.* Taking the book, which was actually quite large and heavy, over to the eight-sided table, he set it down and then took a seat. Opening the book, Nate scanned the table of contents. Instead of chapters, the sections were listed by the name of a person followed by a set of years. Some of the names matched those on the covers of other books on the shelves. He flipped through a few pages. Each section seemed to be a brief but detailed account of the reign of a Bastion.

Nate turned back to the Table of Contents. Upon closer consideration, he discovered that the book was partitioned off according to family last names. There were Levharts, Beos, Parducs, Nahtepas, Macans, and dozens of others. He turned the page and suddenly he saw his own last name written in ornate script.

Pantera

Underneath, there was a list of five names, first and middle, Juliana Ines, Teresa Iliana, Natalia Yoana, Veronica Adriana, ending with Marisol Larosa (P137-178). Curious, he flipped to the history of the Dowager's years and began to scan it. Much of it did not make sense, but he did manage to understand a bit.

According to the history, Panteria had enjoyed great peace during his grandmother's reign. Called Marisol the Peacemaker, a big portion of the history was about her role as mediator between two of the other three kingdoms, the were-lions and the were-tigers, whose people had been having increasing clashes in the human world. Suddenly, the history lesson from the day before made a lot more sense.

He turned back to the beginning of his family's section of the history. From the looks of it, Panteras had been leading Panteria for almost 200 years. He flipped the pages slowly, reading lines here and there. As he scanned through the section about Natalia Yoana (P62-97), his great, great grandmother, one word caught his eyes. Twins.

Nate's hand froze. He lowered the page slowly and started reading from the beginning of the section.

> Natalia Yoana, the Restorer, led Panteria for thirty-five years. By all accounts, her reign was an unusual one. First and foremost because Natalia was a twin.
>
> As is well known, twins are quite unusual among the leopard people; they are more common among the lions. Statistical data shows that there is

> only one twin birth per every 50,000 births among were-leopards. Given the rather small size of the were-leopard population, that amounts to one set of twins every century or so. Natalia the Restorer and Rafael were the first known set of twins among the Pantera clan. They were also the first set of twins born to a reigning Bastion.

Nate paused for a moment in wonder. Though he and Larissa had been the only pair at Greendale Middle, it had never occurred to him that being a twin might be such a rare thing. He continued to read.

> Initially, there had been widespread speculation about who would become the next Bastion. The people were greatly loyal to the Panteras because of the stability that Juliana the Peacemaker had brought to Panteria after years of in-fighting among some of the Kulan's most prominent families. They wanted the Panteras to continue on as guardians of the Kulan and the land. But which Pantera?

> Indeed, though the Bastion had always been a female, there was no formal edict stating that it must be so. The people of Panteria wondered whether Natalia might face opposition from her own brother, who, by the laws

of Panteria at least, had as much claim to the Seat as she.

Such a challenge never emerged, however. Rafael seemed content to let his sister Ascend to the Seat, disappearing almost completely from Panterian life soon after her installation as Bastion.

The Bastions of the Pantera clan had proved themselves to be particularly adept leaders in the sixty-one years that preceded Natalia's ascension. Natalia, however, far outstripped even her forebears. Despite several amazing challenges during Natalia's time as leader, Panteria enjoyed its greatest prosperity ever.

Nate read the rest of the chapter about Natalia with equal parts confusion and awe. It was during Natalia's reign that Panteria had experienced its most pressing threat of exposure to the human world in recent history. Some Panterians, living in the human world, had grown careless about concealing their true nature from humans. Several, it seemed, were actually deliberately revealing their secrets to humans and in doing so were also threatening the secrets of Panteria. With the new technologies like cameras, humans had begun to accumulate irrefutable evidence of shifters. Photographs, and even moving pictures, had been made that documented the shift.

Natalia had helped to rein in the rogues, found and destroyed the harmful evidence, and even drafted something called the "Articles of Expatriation" that laid out both a code of conduct for leopards who chose to live in the human world and a system of punishment for those that posed a threat to the security of Panteria. Throughout the history though, there was no further mention of the brother, Rafael or his role, if any, in Natalia's reign.

Nate's head swam with the new found information as he returned the book to shelf. Suddenly, the names on the books began to make a lot more sense. Many of them were named for the Bastions that had appeared in the book that he had just shelved. Gretchen was a Bastion, not a Pantera, but a member of one of the other families. The books probably contained longer biographies of the different Bastions. He looked again at the titles and found his grandmother's volume, Marisol the Peacekeeper, alongside the others.

Searching the bookcase, he located Natalia's biography on one of the shelves closer to the top. He went over to the table and pulled one of the eight chairs out from beneath it. As he wrapped his hand around the top to drag it across the room, he felt the smooth face that was carved into the top slat. He stopped for a moment and tilted the chair back to examine the carving.

He expected to see another leopard carving like the ones that were found throughout the Kula. Instead, he saw the wild-maned visage of a lion staring up at him. The image was rendered expertly almost entirely out of the dark wood of the chair. The only exception were the eyes, which were made of a honey-colored stone with a sliver of black material in the center. The stone was faceted so that the eyes looked very realistic, and the honey-colored stone sparkled so intensely that Nate had the curious sensation that he was actually staring into another pair of eyes.

Momentarily sidetracked by curiosity, he left the chair and

returned to the table to examine the others. There was another chair carved with a lion sitting right next to the empty space left by the other chair. Next to those were two chairs carved with spotted leopard visages, their eyes made of emerald green panterite. He touched the stones and was amazed to discover that they felt warm to his touch.

Then came a pair of chairs carved with the fierce, striped countenance of the Tiger, with eyes made of an orangey-red stone. On the last pair of chairs were carvings that at first Nate thought were more leopards. Upon closer examination, however, he saw that the face was broader and the spots looked slightly different from the carvings on the other chair. The eyes were different too. The stone that made them was not the rich, emerald green of panterite, but a softer yellow-green. Again, the eyes on this chair were so realistic that Nate was struck by a curious sense of staring into a real set of eyes. Nate pondered the collection, his curiosity getting the better of him for just a moment before he remembered what he had been about to do.

He walked back to the other chair, grabbed it, and dragged it across the floor to the bookshelf. Standing on it, he reached up and pulled down Natalia's biography, hoping that the book would have information about Rafael. Maybe there would be something in the biography that would help him understand more about the peculiar connection between himself and his twin. Perhaps Natalia and Rafael had shared a similar bond.

Even as he took the book from the shelf, he had to chuckle. Who would have thought that he could ever willingly spend a day of his summer vacation in a library? Of the two of them, Ris was definitely more of a bookworm. The chuckle abruptly turned to a frown as his mind turned to his sister, lying injured in her bed downstairs. It seemed that he would have to do the research for both of them this time. Flipping through the pages, he walked back over to the chaise and settled in for an extended study session.

The book turned out to be a complete disappointment. It was long and boring and there was not much more information about Rafael than there had been in the *Compendium*. Nate closed the book and slumped down in his seat. He had spent the last several hours alternating between reading and scanning its dense passages. While there had been some tales about the twins in their childhood, their early mischief-making, and their favorite haunts around the Kula and throughout Panteria, there was nothing that would really be useful.

As the history of Natalia's reign had moved into her teen years, there was less and less about Rafael and the book focused more on Natalia and her preparation for Ascension and Installation. As close as Nate could tell, Ascension was where Natalia was designated the Bastion Imminent, the next Bastion of Panteria. Installation was when she became Bastion for keeps. If nothing else, he certainly had a better understanding of Panterian politics than when he had begun.

But there was nothing that even began to explain the phenomenon from the day before. If his great, great grandmother and her brother had shared the same connection as he and Ris, the book had not hinted at it at all.

Putting the book back on the shelf, he sighed in disappointment. He searched the shelves again, looking for any other books that looked like they might have some useful information. He saw nothing. As he glanced out of the window, he realized that it was nearly nightfall. He hurried from the library and down to Ris's room to see if she were any better.

When he reached her room, Ris was sitting up. He couldn't help the deep sigh of relief that he expelled in a great rush of air. He wanted to jump on her bed and give her a huge hug. Though he knew that she could read his mind, Nate hung back, leaning against the door still a little afraid.

Although she was sitting up, she still looked very fragile. There were huge dark circles beneath her eyes, and Nate could see her hands tremble as she lifted a cup of something to her lips. When she spoke, her voice was hoarse, as though it had been weeks rather than just one day since she had last used it.

"Bro." Her smile was wan. He returned it and walked over to the bed, sitting down gently on the far corner.

"How ya feeling?" he asked. Both of them were using their voices. Communicating telepathically took a fair bit of concentration and energy, and she was not up for the strain yet.

She chuckled quietly before responding. "Probably about as good as I look," she replied, and they both laughed together. There were several moments of silence as she sipped from the white bowl-like cup.

She carefully set the cup down on a wooden tray next to her, and gave her brother a thoughtful glance. Then she asked the question that she had been thinking since she had awakened earlier that afternoon. "What happened?" The last thing that she remembered was feeling stuck to the ground out in the jungle.

Nate took a deep breath and told her the entire story, beginning with his return to the Kula the night before and ending with what he had learned that day in the library.

"Avery," Larissa whispered, a faint smile curving on her lips as he told her about the boy who had been their ally in the jungle. "What a funny name." Nate wasn't sure, but he thought he saw a rush of color flood Larissa's still pale cheeks.

"*Terra Fuerza*," Larissa uttered, when he finished the story, her voice tinged with awe. "And another set of twins?" Nate nodded to both. He could tell from the look on his sister's face that her brain was working over all of the information that he had just shared.

Finally, Larissa let out a soft sigh. "Wow, you miss a little, you miss a lot here, hunh?" Nate chuckled and nodded. "And no one could explain what caused this?" She gestured towards herself and her condition. Nate shook his head.

"In fact, it was like they had never heard of such a thing. I swear they stared at me like I had sprouted another head."

Larissa giggled. "And there was nothing in any of the books?"

Nate shook his head again. "Not that I could tell."

Larissa gave him a dubious look.

"I looked," he protested. "I really did."

When she asked for news about their parents, Nate had to shake his head in frustration, again. The day had yielded no answers, and it seemed to Nate as though they were wasting valuable time.

Larissa took another trembling sip from the round white bowl-like cup, which Nate could now see contained some sort of liquid, dark brown and thick with leaves floating around at the top. From his perch at the end of the bed, Nate could also smell the concoction. It smelled like fried liver.

"What is that," he asked, screwing his face up in disgust as Larissa took another sip.

Larissa grimaced with him, even as she raised the cup to her lips again. "I don't know. Some tea that Li, that guy with the black and white hair, left. It's gross, but whatever it is, it feels like it's working." As Larissa slowly finished her medicine, they fell into silence, while each pondered the seemingly indecipherable puzzle that their lives had become.

Chapter 27

Disappointing News

Marisol heard the sounds of his footsteps before he entered the room. She could tell by the echo and length between footfalls which of her two expected visitors it would be. Li walked into the room and in less than a second he stood next to the table where she sat almost buried in papers.

She had not been idle while he had been searching for information about the strange events that her grandson had described just the day before. She too had been scouring her own documents, caches of family letters, a few old diaries, looking for any mention of such a power.

Oddly, she had not remembered, until she had come across some brief mention of it in her mother's journals, that her grandmother had been a twin. Though perhaps it was not so strange, since she had never even met her great-uncle.

After reading the entry from her mother's diary, a memory had come flashing back. Her mother, Veronica, had only mentioned her uncle once, and that was just to say that she had never met him either. Marisol, a child at the time, had thought it strange that her mother did not know her uncle. Being a child, though, her curiosity about the matter had been fleeting. Of course, now, the fact seemed of the utmost importance. She had scoured her grandmother's journals, diaries, and letters for more information, but there wasn't much.

To begin with, the records from Natalia's time as Bastion were relatively sparse, especially when compared to the stacks of journals that her own mother had left. Natalia had journaled occasionally during her youth, but by the time she became Bastion, she was writing in her diary once a month. If that.

This didn't surprise Marisol. Her grandmother had been a great storyteller, but she had always preferred to weave her tales before a live audience rather than to record them in solitude. Though she had loved to sit at her grandmother's knee and hear the woman's stories of her childhood, at that moment Marisol could not help but wish that Natalia had picked up a pen just a bit more frequently. Especially now that her own memory was growing fuzzy. From what she could remember though, Rafael had not stayed in Panteria long after his sister had Ascended to the Seat. He had chosen, instead, to live in the human world, never returning to Panteria.

"What have you discovered?" The Dowager asked without glancing up from her reading to look at Li.

Silence followed her inquiry and, as the silence stretched on, the Dowager was forced to look up from the papers that were spread before her. When she saw Li's face, her shoulders slumped. The look on his face made it clear that he had found nothing new, or at least nothing illuminating.

He briefed her on what he had found. There was some small bit of information about Rafael's doings while he lived among the humans. Apparently, he had settled in the American south after leaving Panteria.

The Dowager shook her head in wonder at that bit of information. Why, of all places, would he choose to settle there? She remembered her time in the human world. She had visited the Americas briefly, including its notorious south. That had been nearly sixty years after her great uncle would have gone there and it was no piece of cake then. She could not imagine what things had been like during her great uncle's time. That was the only new information that Li was able to report. It wasn't much, but it was a start.

"Keep looking," she said, dismissing him to turn back to her own reading. She heard him turn to go, knowing that her friend would forgive her abruptness in this moment of crisis.

As Li exited the room, Marcus entered. He stopped just inside the door, waiting for the Dowager to address him before he gave his report. Immediately, the Dowager rose from the table, going over to the window. She did not want Marcus to see how hopeless she was beginning to feel. Outside, thunderheads loomed in the distance, and she could tell the rains would soon come. The storms would make the search even more difficult than it was already.

"What is your report?" Though her face was hidden, she was unable to disguise the weariness in her voice.

"No new information, Guardian," Marcus replied. "We have scoured the jungles, paying particular attention to the area described by your grandson, but there is nothing. No evidence of any sort." Marcus's voice rose slightly with his own frustration. "But what he reported was true, the area is completely deserted. The mining seems to have stopped for the time being, and the machinery is gone as well."

The Dowager's brow furrowed. They had abandoned the mines. What would make them do that? She looked again at the clouds. Perhaps the cessation was only temporary, until after the rains. Then, as though a light bulb had turned on in her mind, a plan started to formulate.

"There is no one?" She asked.

"Yes. The sites are completely abandoned."

She turned back to Marcus, a new spirit of resolve lighting her eyes. "Thank you Marcus," she said her voice echoing that determination. "Continue your search and make me aware of any changes." With that, Marcus was dismissed.

The Dowager turned back to the window, outside of which thunderheads filled the sky darkening it more with every passing moment, her plan taking shape in her mind. She would have to do it. She would have to leave the Kula and find her daughter.

Leaving the safety of the Kula walls was something that she had hesitated to do since her daughter's capture, and something that she felt would be most unwise once Robert had gone missing as well. With both Anna and Robert missing, she was the sole representative of Pantera leadership. And now that the children were there, someone had to ensure that they were protected. If she went missing too…. She did not even want to consider the consequences. Still, it was becoming increasingly clear that this was the only solution. There was no one else who would be able see the things that she would see and know the things that she would know just from walking the land. And if she ran into trouble, well she was more than equipped to face it down. Though with Anna's Ascension, she had relinquished some part of her control of the *fuerza*, she was still powerful enough to wield it as an effective weapon. She would be more than a match for any enemy that she might meet.

It was settled, but no one could know. No one could suspect even for a moment that Panteria had been left unguarded. Because, if her suspicion was correct, that was just the moment that these conspirators were waiting for.

Just as she turned from the window, there was a flash of light followed by a loud clap of thunder. She could almost feel the clouds ripping open to unleash torrents of rain that hit the ground just seconds later. As soon as the rains slacked, she would go. But first, there were provisions to be made.

CHAPTER 28

COVERT OPERATIONS

NATE WANDERED ALONE THROUGH the halls of the Inner Kula. His skin crawled with anxiety, and he felt as though he might literally climb the walls.

It had been three days since he and Larissa had ventured out into the Panterian jungles. Ris was still bed-bound, but she was doing better. Just that morning he had taken her an armload of books from the Bastion's Library. While he was glad that she was feeling well enough to do some research of her own, sitting there watching her read did not rank among the most exciting ways to spend the afternoon. It was right up there with watching paint dry.

The Inner Kula was still on lockdown with no way out. Not only was he trapped inside the Kula walls, but there was absolutely nothing to do. There was no television, no video games, no computers. He could not even call one of his friends. There was nothing to distract him from the fact that his parents were still missing and there was nothing that he could do about that. Their house arrest at home was suddenly looking like a walk in the park compared to the virtual prison that the Kula had become.

Not that there would have been anywhere to go even if he

had been able to sneak past the guards. It had been raining for the last two days. Actually, rain was too mild a word. Monsoon seemed more appropriate to describe the torrents that fell from the skies. There was nowhere for him to go unless he felt like going for a swim.

The rains, the Dowager had explained, were seasonal, crucial to sustaining the lushness of the Panterian landscape. To Nate, they were nothing more than another obstacle that stood in the way of his parents' rescue. The storms put all searches on hold, because in the first couple of days it was impossible to see more than five feet, even with shifter-sight. All of this added to Nate's frustration. He was beginning to absolutely despise the Kula and all of Panteria, for that matter. There was nothing that he could do but wander the halls of Kula searching for ways to distract himself from the helplessness that he felt.

As a result, he now knew the Inner Kula like the back of his hand. So well, in fact, that he could have navigated its labyrinth-like halls blindfolded. He had explored every room with an unlocked door and delved into every nook and cranny that there was to discover.

Coming to an intersection where two broad hallways crossed one another, he turned right, going down the hall that would lead him towards the chamber that he and his sister had found on their first night there. He knew now that the chamber belonged to the reigning Bastion and that their parents used the room whenever they were in Panteria for any extended period of time.

He reached the room, opened the door, and slipped inside. He sat on the edge of the round bed and sniffed hard. The scent of his parents grew fainter each day, but if he tried hard enough, he could still make out the mellow spiciness of cinnamon. He had spent quite a bit of time there over the past few days. Being in that room helped to soothe some of his anxiousness, as though he were closer to his parents somehow.

Falling backwards into the plush, cushiony mattress, he stared up at the domed ceiling of the room. The steady thrum of the rain on the dome roof was mesmerizing, and a cool breeze blew into the room beneath the wooden shutters that had been closed to keep the rains out. He felt his eyes drifting slowly shut.

Just as he was about to fall asleep, he heard her voice. It was his grandmother. She was talking to someone, and from the sound of the voices they were headed in that direction. His ears perked up, and he listened as the voices floated closer and closer.

Holding his body very still, paranoid that even with that, the shifters on the other side of the wall would hear his pounding heart, he tried to make out what was being said. For a moment, he could make out little more than changing and hurried tones. As the voices moved closer, he started to pick up snatches of sentences.

"Anna….Robert….necessary." If it were possible, Nate became even more alert. She was talking about his parents. Abruptly, the voices, which had during that time been floating closer and closer, stopped moving. Right in front of the door. Nate looked over and saw the knob begin to turn.

He scanned the room for a place to hide. But like all the other sleeping rooms, this one was completely devoid of any furniture besides the bed. Though the mattress was elevated far enough off the ground for him to squeeze underneath, that hiding place would not do. There was no hiding from the acute hearing of a shifter in close quarters. Not as long as he was breathing, at any rate.

He looked towards the terrace. Through the thin slats of the shutter, he saw the rain pouring down in sheets. He grimaced, but it was the only place that he might possibly hide. It was either that or be sent away yet again from an important conversation. Moving faster than he had ever moved in his life, and faster than he thought possible, Nate leapt from the bed and ran for the terrace.

He quickly opened one shutter a sliver and stepped outside. Instantly, he was drenched. It was like stepping out of the door into a swimming pool. The rain pounded against the gray stone of the terrace, drowning out almost every other sound. And it was cold. Nate shivered and was on the verge of rethinking his plan when he heard the door open.

The door shut and Nate heard his grandmother's voice. He could not see either occupant of the room, but the Dowager's commanding voice was unmistakable.

"I will leave as soon as the rains start to let up. That should be some time this evening. If I am not back by morning, I want you to take the children and leave the Kula." His grandmother's voice was hushed and urgent. Nate could just make out what she was saying over the steady drumbeat of the rain.

"Marisol, I wish you would reconsider," a male voice responded.

"What other option is there Li, I have considered them all. The guard has searched every square inch of Panteria and found nothing. That can only mean one of two things. Either they are not in Panteria or...." She trailed off, not wanting to admit the other possibility.

"Or," Li said, finishing the thought for her, "there is nothing to find." At his words, Nate felt like some sharp object had been plunged inside of him. He wanted to open the shutter to scream at the man, to make him take the words back. He could not imagine his world without his parents.

"I refuse to believe it" was his grandmother's vehement response, and Nate liked her that much more in that moment. "I know they are out there somewhere. I know. Who else can find them but me?" There was a long silence after that, which Nate interpreted as recognition of the truth in his grandmother's words. Or perhaps what followed was just drowned out by the rain, which was suddenly pouring down hard.

When he could hear them again, he caught the end of Li's question. "Go?" was the only word he heard.

"I will use the passage in the library. It is the only way out of the Kula other than the gates, and those are too public. It is imperative that no one knows that I have left." Her voice was urgent, but it also held a tinge of weariness.

"It is too dangerous Marisol. This adversary is turning out to be much more treacherous than any we have faced. Can't I convince you to take someone with you?"

His grandmother's words, when they came, were weighed down with a heavy sigh. "Who Li? Whom would I take? I know it is dangerous. But after James's outburst at the gathering, I don't know whom to trust. It seems that there are too many here who would relish the opportunity to do me and my family harm. You are the only one that I can trust completely. I know that you would never let anyone hurt Anna, and I need you here. I need you to promise that if I do not return, you will make sure that the children are safe. I fear that if I do not return, there is nowhere in Panteria where they will be safe." There was an anguish in his grandmother's voice that surprised Nate. She sounded tired, sad, and worried, so different from the stern woman that he had grown familiar with since meeting her.

"Of course, Marisol. I will watch over the children until you return."

In that moment the rain came down harder, the staccato beat of the droplets on stone drowning out any further conversation inside the room. Water pooled around Nate's feet, soaking through his gym shoes. He shivered, though he did not know whether it was because of the cold or because of what he had just heard. Still, he did not move as sheet after sheet of rain soaked him to his core. His mind worked furiously as he thought about everything that he had just learned and began to formulate a plan of his own.

When he turned his attention back to the interior of the room, it seemed to be empty. He listened carefully for any sound. There was none. His grandmother and Li had left. Even so, he waited for several more minutes to be safe and then he slipped back inside. Sopping wet, he sloshed across the room and paused at the door. Listening again, he searched for evidence of his grandmother and her companion in the hall. When he heard only silence, he slipped open the door and skidded out of the room, almost falling down in his haste to get to Larissa.

CHAPTER 29

DOWN THE HATCH

NATE SCANNED THE LIBRARY again, ready to give up. He was sure that he had heard his grandmother correctly, that she would leave through a passage located somewhere in this room. But he had been over every inch of the library and saw no sign of any way out other than the door that he had used to enter the room. Maybe she had meant the other library; the one that Bailey had pointed out on the tour.

He looked out the window. In the time that he had been searching, the rain had lessened from sheets of downpour to merely a hard rain. With every moment, it slackened just a bit more. He didn't have a lot of time if their plan was going to work. And, if the Dowager was leaving from the other library, he had already blown it.

At Larissa's suggestion, he had come immediately to the library to attempt to find the passageway. They figured that it would be easier for him to find the passageway now and wait for his grandmother on the other end than it would be for him to try and follow her through without being discovered. But it was looking like they would have to scrap that plan, because he had no idea what he was looking for.

Racking his brain, he thought about all of the movies

he had seen and the books that he had read. In the books and movies, secret passageways were revealed by saying a magic word to a painting, or tugging on the right candlestick, or pulling out the right book.

Nate looked at the hundreds of books that lined the shelves around the room and felt daunted. He was in trouble if he had to find the exact book to open a secret passage among these stacks. He glanced at the walls again. They were infuriatingly devoid of both paintings and candlesticks. Only the strange lamps that hung through the Kula decorated the walls. And he had already tugged on all of those. Twice.

He slumped defeated on to the plush green circular rug at the center of the room and put his chin in his hands. His face scrunched up in confusion and frustration.

Think Nate, he said to himself, *if you were a secret passage way, where would you be.* His mind was blank. He stared out before him, defeated, blinking away the sudden dampness in his eyes.

This place was so stupid. Here, he couldn't do anything right. Everything that he attempted turned out completely wrong. The dampness became more pronounced, blurring his vision so much that he almost missed what was right in front of his face.

It would have been easy to miss, too. It was only the smallest indentation in the carpet and it would have been invisible if he had been standing, especially since he had not known that it was there. He blinked several times, thinking that his eyes were playing tricks on him. But each time he opened his eyes, the raised area was still there.

He crawled towards it on his hands and knees. When he reached it, he touched the rectangle through the rug, feeling it give way slightly beneath the pressure. His heart soared even as a slightly harried giggle escaped. After all of that searching, it couldn't be this easy.

Turns out, it was exactly that easy.

"Not very high tech, is it?" Larissa murmured the words in a dour but amused tone. Nate shook his head wryly as they stood together considering the stone stairs that led down into a darkness that was finally impenetrable.

He had realized, after finding the door, that there was no way that his departure would remain a secret without her help. If his grandmother came into the room and saw the furniture in disarray and the rug pushed back, she would know that something was up. Someone had to be there to move all of the furniture back into place after he left.

Though Larissa was still quite weak, they had managed to make it back to the library swiftly and undetected. While Larissa watched, Nate moved all of the furniture and rolled back the rug. There, underneath, was a rectangular wooden hatch.

The tunnel beneath the hatch seemed to be just tall enough for a full grown leopard. It certainly wasn't designed to be traveled by humans. Glancing over at Larissa, Nate quickly took off the tunic and pants that he wore and handed them to her. For one indecisive moment he stood in his P. E. suit before darkened tunnel entrance. Then he shifted. He took a few tentative steps into the passage and then glanced back at Larissa, who looked at him nervously.

"*Don't worry,*" he thought to her and then he took a

few more steps into the tunnel until he was completely inside. Turning to Larissa again, he thought, *"Make sure that everything is perfect."*

Larissa's face screwed up into a scowl. *"I can at least do that,"* she replied, but there was humor in her voice. Then her face smoothed out. *"Be careful,"* she said, concerned. He nodded, turning away from her and walking deeper into the passage.

He stopped and waited, giving his eyes a chance to adjust to the darkness. After several moments, though, he could not see anything. The darkness, in fact, seemed to deepen. He realized then that Larissa had shut the hatch. After several more moments, he knew then that his eyes weren't going to adjust anymore to this impenetrable darkness, which meant that he was going blind. He took a deep breath, hearing Larissa's faint whisper of *"Good luck,"* in his mind as he turned to take his first steps into the darkness.

On the other side of the door, Larissa chewed her lip with worry. She was starting to have second, or perhaps third, thoughts about the plan. She had not been a hundred percent sure about it to begin with, but she had known better than to try and talk Nate out of it when she had seen the determined gleam in his eyes. She wished, again, that she were strong enough to go with him.

Pushing her worry aside and moving as quickly as she could, she rolled the rug back into place and started to readjust the furniture. Just as she was moving the last chair into place, she heard it. Footsteps echoed across the Bastion's Chamber coming closer and closer to the library at a supernatural pace. Hurriedly and with her last remaining strength, she lifted the chair and adjusted it to the right angle, shoving Nate's clothes underneath.

Huffing, she walked over to the book shelf and tried to calm her breathing as she pretended to look for a new title. When she heard the door close, she turned around, with what she hoped was a look of surprise, to see Bailey standing there, eyes narrowed and hands on her hips. As the older girl glared at her from across the room, Larissa felt nothing but fed up with her unyielding hostility.

"What are you doing up here," the girl asked suspiciously.

Larissa didn't bother to conceal her sigh of exasperation. She was too tired and too worried about Nate and her parents to care anymore about what this angry girl thought of her. She looked away from the glowering girl and glanced around the room.

"Well, it's a library," she answered, very slowly. "So, obviously, I'm fishing." She gave the girl a quick, bland smile, and steeled herself against the barrage that she knew was coming.

Bailey's face reddened. For a moment, she looked as though steam might pour out of her ears. Instead of responding, however, the girl turned and was gone from the room before Larissa could blink an eye. Larissa collapsed into a chair, all of her energy suddenly evaporating from her body. Then she heard it. It was so faint, that she was sure that she had imagined it.

She sat straight up and stared wonderingly at the door through which the girl had just departed. She held her breath and listened. Then it came again, and there was no mistaking it this time. It was a laugh. The wicked witch of the Kula was actually laughing.

Larissa fell back in her chair, amazed. It was a miracle. An honest-to-God miracle. Maybe everything would be okay after all.

Chapter 30

UNEXPECTED KIN

Nate stumbled again, sliding down a few more stone steps before regaining his footing. His heart pounded in his chest, and he fought to calm himself. It was the third time he had slipped, and each time he felt as though he were tumbling to his death.

The stairs were steep and narrow, just big enough for a cat's paw. That, plus the darkness, made them very difficult to navigate. The passage was still pitch-black, though he had been in the tunnel for at least ten minutes, and he couldn't see anything in front of him. There was no way to tell how far he had come or how much farther he had to go. He reached out into the darkness and placed his foot down on the next step. He traveled forward, each step tentative in the seemingly endless dark.

With his next step, he almost stumbled again. Tentatively, he reached a paw forward and felt around. There was only solid, flat ground as far as he could reach. It seemed that he had come to the bottom. Nate breathed a sigh of relief. At least there were no more stairs to fall down. Still, he walked forward slowly, just in case this was merely a landing. After a time, when he did not feel any more stairs, he picked up his pace, running forward at full speed.

Seconds later, he slammed into a wall. Nate stumbled

back, momentarily stunned by the impact. After recovering, he stepped forward again. When he felt a slight air current ruffle his fur, he realized that the tunnel veered to the left. Concentrating, he used the faint periodic bursts of air to navigate the tunnel. After another left, it continued in a straight line for a long time.

He smelled the end before he saw it. The dusty tunnel air, which had tickled his throat since he entered the passage, began to smell damp. The cool air, which had only trickled through the tunnel, became a steady breeze of rain-scented air. At the same time, the ground began to slant steeply upward. Even though the tunnel remained pitch-black, he knew that he was getting close. Only in the last few yards could he begin to see.

Gray light from somewhere stretched into the tunnel, illuminating the walls and floor, which appeared to be made of stone. To human eyes, there would have been no difference in the darkness at all, but his shifter-sight seized the thin strands of light and used them to see. He began to run, eager to leave behind the disorienting darkness of the passageway.

As he reached the end, Nate saw four more steps that went up instead of down. The stairs led up to a hatch that was essentially identical to the one that he had entered back in the library. Faint light filtered down through the slender gaps between the thin slats of wood that comprised the door.

The hatch, he found, as he climbed the stairs, opened easily enough. It was something like a doggy door—a thought that would have made him laugh under different circumstances—the mechanism sliding open as he pushed against it. He exited the tunnel, blinking his eyes against the bright gray-green light of the cloud-covered late afternoon, which was almost blindingly bright after the deep darkness of the tunnel. As he stood still to readjust to the light, he felt the familiar tingle of the *terra fuerza*.

He had come out in a small glade in the middle of the

jungle. All around him were the ever-present towering trees with huge leaves. He was surprised to find that the rains that were still drenching the grounds of the Kula were less severe on the jungle floor, becoming irregular droplets as the downpour worked its way through the dense vegetation that formed a natural umbrella.

As he stepped fully out of the tunnel, he heard the hatch fall back into place with a resounding click. Looking back at the door, he had noticed that it all but disappeared into the foliage on the jungle floor. He fiddled with the hatch with one paw. It didn't budge. He jiggled it again and it remained closed.

It was smart, he had to admit. Having the hatch inaccessible from this side meant that it could not be used to sneak into the Kula. It also meant, for better or worse, that he was stuck out there. Wherever there happened to be.

Turning away resolutely, he surveyed his surroundings for a hiding place. He decided that his best bet would be one of the trees that enclosed the small clearing. Finding a good one, with branches that were low to the ground, thick, concealing leaves, and an unobstructed view of the escape hatch, he hastily climbed it, his claws slicing easily through the damp bark of the tree trunk to grip its core. He hid himself as best he could among the leaves, trained his eyes on the hatch, and waited for his grandmother.

The Dowager rolled the rug back a little more with each piece of furniture that Li pulled away. She lifted the hatch door, and adrenaline raced through her as she considered the mission that lay before her. There was a very real chance that she would not return. At that thought, she turned to Li, her friend and her companion of these many years, and felt a bit reassured. He would make sure that the twins were okay. If it came to it, he would keep them safe.

With the hatch open and waiting like a hungry mouth, the Dowager shifted. She was as impressive as a panther as she was as a human. Even more so. Her black fur gleamed glossily, even in the dim light, its midnight darkness broken here and there by flecks of white and grey. Her yellow-flecked green eyes glinted both dangerously and purposefully. From her huge paws sprouted lethal looking claws that clicked on the hard stone floor as she moved towards the hatch.

"Be safe, Marisol," Li whispered as she stepped into the tunnel. With a low growl that rumbled in her chest, she turned and made her way into the darkness.

When she had gone a few steps and Li had closed the hatch, the Dowager stopped. Standing still and closing her eyes, she concentrated on the earth that lay many feet beneath the stone stairs, calling the *fuerza* to her. Soon she could feel the power as it began to rise through layer after layer of stone, and her body relaxed in anticipation. The power entered through her paws and soon filled her entirely.

When every inch of her body tingled with electric power, she concentrated and forced it outward into the stones of the wall. Instantly the walls began to glow green as the panterite slivers embedded in the stone responded to the *fuerza*. The tunnel, which had been shrouded in complete darkness, was now alight with a warm green glow. In the glowing light, the Dowager was easily able to navigate the stairs, loping quickly down the steps before sprinting through the maze of tunnels. It wasn't until she reached the end of the passageway that she caught the scent.

It was faint, muddled and almost washed away by the damp air, but it was unmistakable. She gave a low angry growl and charged the to the end of the tunnel. Bursting through the hatch, she shifted mid-leap, coming to a stop in the center of the small glade.

From above, Nate watched, taking just a moment to be amazed by his grandmother, even as he prepared to follow her. He was not at all expecting what happened next.

"Nathanial Arturo Pantera," she called. Her voice was a fierce whisper that echoed through the glade and up into the branches where Nate hid.

Nate stayed very still. He hadn't known what would happen once his grandmother came through the hatch, but he certainly had not expected her to know that he was there.

"You might as well come out," she said. "I know you are here somewhere. I can smell you."

Had he had one, Nate would have smacked his forehead with his hand. His scent. How could he have been so stupid? He rose from his hiding place and began to make his way carefully down the tree. In seconds, he was on the ground standing sheepishly in front of his grandmother.

"What," she asked, "do you think you are doing?" Her voice shook with both anger and concern. How long had the boy been out here? Didn't he know what danger he put himself in? She asked as much.

Nate was quiet for a moment, trying to figure out how to explain. "I heard you this afternoon," he began softly, staring down at ground. Then, with a flash of courage, he raised his head and met his grandmother's eyes defiantly. "I had to do something. They're my parents." He waited for her to yell at him, to order him back to the Kula. But all the Dowager did was nod.

"I suppose you did," she replied softly, catching Nate by surprise.

When the woman spoke again, exasperation, understanding, and urgency mingled in her voice. "Well, I guess you are coming with me," she said, surprising Nate again. The Dowager continued unheeding. "It's too late to take you back, and I dare not send you to find your own way." She stopped and sighed, regrouping.

"Stay close," she said, nearly barking the command. "Don't you dare fall behind. And do exactly what I tell you, when I tell you, without any questions." She crouched down to look at him. "Do you understand me," she asked again, grasping his shoulders and forcing him to meet her gaze.

Her green eyes glowed with a fire that was mesmerizing. Gazing into those depths, he swallowed and nodded. His grandmother stood back up, released his shoulders and stepped away.

Just then, they heard several shrill chirps. Looking past the Dowager's shoulder, Nate saw a colorful bundle of feathers flying full speed towards them. Windy landed, somewhat clumsily, between the Dowager and the boy and performed a rushed version of his usual ceremonial bow. Even in the midst of a crisis, that bird would not abandon protocol.

"My apologies, Guardian," the bird said, "but the Healer suggested, rather forcefully, that I join you."

The Dowager could not stop the small chuckle that escaped her. Li.

At her chuckle the small emissary bristled. "I don't see what's funny. That leopard threatened my life." Then both the boy and the old woman laughed, which just upset the bird all the more.

The Dowager was the first to smother her mirth. Quite suddenly, she began to shift, her human body dissolving away. In an instant, she stood before Nate, a majestic panther. She growled at Nate, and he obeyed and shifted. Then they were off, little cat following big one, loping into fast darkening night. The colorful bird, recovered, was not too far behind.

CHAPTER 31

WHAT'S WRONG WITH THIS PICTURE?

BEFORE NATE REALIZED IT, they were nearing the mine. They had run through the jungles immediately surrounding the Kula and slogged through the saturated grasslands around the Lake of Falcons, entering the jungle on the other side. Slowly, he could feel the land changing beneath his feet, and the closer they got the more he struggled to keep up with his grandmother as the now familiar weakness struck. Soon he was forced to halt. He stopped taking deep breaths to calm his rolling stomach. Immediately, his grandmother was by his side in human form, kneeling. Nate looked up at her fearfully.

She did not have to ask what was wrong. She felt it too, with every step. The land was sick, and because of the *fuerza*, Nate was getting sick too. This was a lesson that she had only learned recently about the power of the *fuerza*. One that they had been forced to learn because of the calamity that now threatened their home.

The *fuerza* not only gave them energy and strength, it apparently could make them weak as well. The former, they had known for many generations. The latter they had never even suspected, and, of course, until now the land had never been in such crisis.

Even so, the poisonous energy was not affecting her the way that it was affecting him, because she had been trained to use the *fuerza*. She knew how to call the power to her and how to send it back into the earth. She knew how to take only what she needed and leave the rest behind. Nate had not yet learned to flip that switch.

"I can feel it too," she told him as she rose. To teach him the trick that would help him to filter out the infected energy, unfortunately, would take time that they just did not have.

Instead, shifting back, the Dowager grabbed Nate by the scruff of his neck and began to climb the tree. Though he had not been carried that way since he turned four, Nate was too weak to protest. He let his grandmother carry him into the branches of the tree, feeling better almost as soon as his feet left the ground.

The effect was just shy of miraculous. As soon as the Dowager set him down among the leafy branches of the tree, he felt recovered. And not a moment too soon, because without warning, his grandmother was bounding across the branches and through the tree tops, making haste towards the mine. She ran across the branches as though they were solid ground. Within moments, she was so far away that he could only dimly make out her midnight black form.

"Stay close" Her stern command echoed in his mind. Collecting his wits, Nate hastened to follow her. He moved slowly, cautiously, at first, because he was fearful of falling to the ground a good fifty feet below, and then with more confidence as he realized that if the branches could support his grandmother, then he probably would not plummet to his death. He quickened his pace, bounding through the tree tops, mindless of the scores of tiny branches that bit into his face and ripped at his fur. Soon he was right behind his grandmother again.

Ahead, he could see the trees thinning, to reveal the green-gray storm clouds that hung low and menacing over the jungle. His grandmother had slowed, making her way carefully across the rapidly diminishing branches. Before he knew it, the Dowager was stopping and he came to a halt behind her. Within seconds, Windy had sailed down and settled on the branch as well. They stood above the mine and Nate saw what he had not been able to see from the jungle floor before.

It literally was a scar. A wound, deep, gaping, and black, ripped into the side of the hill. Rain had melted the earth around the cavernous tear in the soil, transforming it into some sort of ghastly and terrible lesion. Water, dark like blood, pooled at the bottom of the chasm created by the mining. The sight filled Nate with an all too familiar horror.

Just to the left of their perch, he saw the patch of new vegetation that had sprouted under Larissa's feet just a few days before. To his surprise, small trees were growing from the ground, surrounded by thick undergrowth that looked like it had been there for years.

He heard a rustle of movement and, as he turned his head, he saw his grandmother leap from the branch to the ground. For a split second, she seemed to be flying, suspended in the air between the tree and the earth. Then she landed silently on the damaged soil.

As Nate and Windy watched, the Dowager walked towards the mine, each step tentative and probing. Nate recognized his own instinctive movements in hers. She was testing the ground. Looking for something.

On the ground, the Dowager paced the earth, listening to the stories that it told. With deliberate care, she pushed away the energy that would weaken her and searched for the whispers that would lead her to her daughter. Even as she tried to filter out the infected energy, her stomach churned and all she could hear was the sound of the pain.

One continuous, jarring note screamed the suffering of the land. The discordant, disjointed song played along her body, irritating her like the sound of fingernails on a chalkboard.

She closed her eyes and focused her thoughts. Blocking out the sound of the earth's pain, she channeled the *fuerza* through her body and into her eyes. When she opened them again, her eyes glowed vibrant green with power that shone like a beacon in the fast dimming daylight. She looked down, and she could see the energy coursing through the earth beneath her feet like blood through the veins in a human body. Near the mines, the energy was the yellow-gray of bile. Dying. It was a color that was becoming all too familiar across the jungles and plains of Panteria.

As it neared the jungle, the energy slowly changed from yellow-gray to a more vibrant and healthy emerald green. But even there, the energies were at war, with the yellow-gray encroaching into the healthy green, spreading further with each falling leaf and each dying tree. Veins of yellow energy snaked into the green, seemingly weakening it from the inside out.

She turned around slowly, using her *fuerza*-augmented sight to scan the land. Her eyes fell on a patch of young vegetation that stood like an oasis in the middle of a desert of blight. This, she quickly surmised, must have been where Larissa had fallen. The patch glowed a bright emerald green. What was more, the yellow-bile energy that surrounded it seemed unable to penetrate it. Wondrous.

The energy beyond the new growth grew darker and darker, changing from the yellow-gray of bile to a deeper, almost orange color.

Then she saw something curious. Something that she had never seen before. Red. The energy that flowed within the earth was red, like it was bleeding. But it wasn't just running beneath the earth, it extended out of the ground creating a shimmering, transparent red wall that stretched upward as far as the she could see, a red miasma that distorted the image of the jungle beyond. Amazed, the Dowager walked towards the aberration.

Nate saw the Dowager turn away from the gaping pit that was the mine. She walked several paces in the direction of the patch of new growth that Larissa had created. Abruptly, she stopped and pawed the ground several times.

There was a sudden rustle from behind. Tearing his eyes from the Dowager, Nate scanned the jungle around him. There was no movement. Even the rain itself had tapered off. They were alone.

The Dowager's soft growl drew his attention back to her and, seconds later, he felt it. Something was happening below. Something so powerful and drastic that he could feel it even fifty feet above the earth.

The tingle of the *fuerza*, which had reached him faintly, even there on his perch, drained away without warning, as though the energy were being sucked up by some invisible vacuum. The abrupt absence shocked his system. He felt stripped bare somehow, and he shivered against the cold and damp that suddenly pierced through his fur. Though it no longer tingled through his body, he could still feel the *fuerza* gathering like a storm cloud that was difficult to ignore. And then, all at once, he could see it too.

It started like a wind that rippled through the grass and bushes, rolling over and under the ground, flattening grasses and plants and dislodging pebbles and dirt here and there. As he watched, the energy began to gather around his grandmother, who glowed like a nightlight in the halo of power that was suddenly visible to Nate.

Then the energy became a little cyclone, collecting in waves that stacked on top of each other, surging against one another. The very air around the Dowager swirled, the force of it flattening her fur against her body. In the middle of it all, she stood, her green eyes glowing with supernatural fire.

"What is she doing," Windy asked, reminding Nate that he was still there. Nate looked over at the creature, surprised by the question. At the look of confusion on the tiny fellow's face, Nate realized that Windy could not see what he saw. He had to shift to answer him.

"I'm not sure," he whispered to the bird when he could explain, "but I think that she found something."

Then, as he watched, his grandmother leaned back on her hind paws and with a roar that seemed to shake the trees, she slammed her front paws back down to the earth.

And then the world did shake. Literally. At least the world in front of his grandmother.

The trees and ground in front of the Dowager wavered like an image seen through water into which someone had thrown a stone. Starting at the ground, the ripples extended outward and upward as far as the eye could see. Then, for the briefest instant, he heard it. A roar that seemed the answer to the Dowager's call. Whipping his head up, he scanned the still rippling trees and air and caught a glimpse of green eyes and fur at eye level. His mother.

It was a mirage! He realized this abruptly. Just like the mirage that protected their home, this mirage had hidden his mother in plain view, and his grandmother was doing something that was weakening it.

"They're here!" He whispered fiercely to the bird that now sat on his shoulder. "Did you see that? They're here! I knew there was something about this place, as soon as I saw it!"

The Dowager reared back again, gathering all of the energy that ebbed and flowed around her and slammed her paws into the ground once more. This time, instead of rippling, the trees in front of her disappeared entirely, and the scene of his parents' captivity was laid bare for a mere second.

Nate saw his mother, caged and suspended from a tree at eye level. Below, Nate saw his father in a cage that rested on the ground. Around his father's cage, people scrambled and yelled frantically at one another. They looked surprised. Caught off guard. And they kept casting terrified glances at his grandmother. Just as quickly, the scene disappeared. Seconds later, it reappeared. It flickered in and out of view, like the picture on a television that was about to break.

His mother roared again before they disappeared. Galvanized by her command, Nate flew into action. "Windy," he instructed. "Go back to the Kula. I think we might need some help." The bird launched himself from Nate's shoulder and took off like a shot off in the opposite direction.

Nate immediately shifted, eased away from his perch, and began to make his way over to the branch from which his mother's cage was suspended. He crept carefully, quietly, instinctively hiding his presence from the people who fumbled below. Every couple of seconds, the rope reappeared, letting him know that he was getting closer. Finally he stood on the right branch, in the tree from which his mother was suspended. From there, he watched as his grandmother reared back a final time and slammed her paws into the ground.

Like a mirror, the mirage cracked and then shattered. Nate could almost hear the tinkling sound as the shield of energy collapsed under the weight of his grandmother's assault.

Down below, the men, there were only two now—the same two who had chased him and Larissa before—were shouting to each other. One dived into the makeshift shelter, reemerging with a weapon in his hand. The two men came together and began to advance on his grandmother, the armed man bracing his weapon against his shoulder.

The Dowager needed help. He had to do something. Right in front of Nate was the rope that held his mother's cage. This time however, it did not disappear. Running forward, he unsheathed his claws and sliced the rope. A few of the strands frayed, but the rope held strong. Nate saw the glint of metal woven into the rope, just as he felt the sting where his paw had touched it. Silver.

His grandmother roared, and, glancing away from his task, he saw the reason for her cry. Closing in on the panther were two humans, one with a weapon, and four leopards, one with fur so pale that it was almost white.

The leopards stalked slowly in an ever contracting circle around his grandmother, whose eyes moved quickly to follow their progress. They were looking for an opportunity to pounce, as the armed human kept his weapon trained on the Dowager. The *fuerza* still rippled around her, waiting to be used. Even with that, though, Nate knew that his grandmother was outnumbered. Luckily, her attackers had not spotted him yet.

Quickly, he turned back to the rope, sawing at it more furiously, ignoring the pain of the silver biting into his paws. His claws, however, were doing nothing against the rope, and the leopards were getting closer to his grandmother with each second that passed. He swiped more frantically, but nothing happened.

Come on, come on, he thought, willing the rope to break. *Come on!* With the thought, he felt something shift in the air around him.

Like lava in a volcano, the *fuerza* rushed up through the tree and exploded into his body, filling him from the tip of his tail to the tips of his ears. His blood boiled and his flesh burned. He felt like he was on fire. Every cell of his body was bursting with a power that he had to release before it ignited and consumed him.

Somehow he focused that energy into his paw, swiping again at the rope and this time the strands sliced like butter under a hot knife. Then the cage that held his mother was falling, and it hit the ground with a resounding crash. Amazingly, the cage remained intact, with his mother, who seemed to be unhurt, still trapped inside.

The noise startled the pack that was stalking his grandmother and they all turned towards the sound. Nate watched from the tree as his mother reached a claw up and sliced through the steel and silver bars of the cage like they were nothing more than Styrofoam. Chunks of metal fell outside of the cage and, with another swipe of her paws, the Bastion had created a hole large enough to escape the cage. Without a pause, she went to his father's cage and freed him.

Suddenly, the clearing was a din of shouting and roaring, as the men and leopards struggled to regroup. The Dowager had used the distraction to break away from the tight circle that the leopards had been forming to trap her. His parents had joined his grandmother, and all three faced down their attackers with fierce fang-exposing visages. No longer was it six on one. It was now six on three, and Nate had the sudden impression that the odds definitively favored the Panteras.

The armed man swiveled his weapon around as if unable to decide which of the panthers posed the biggest threat. The other man was wide-eyed and frightened, looking like he wanted nothing more than to turn and run. But where the humans were indecisive, the leopards prepared to pounce.

Before Nate could blink, his father sprang, claws unsheathed. He landed on the leopard with cream-colored fur. With unbridled fury, his father attacked the leopard, knocking it to the ground with his massive paws. The cat struggled, unsheathing claws and lashing out with lightning speed against his father.

The two cats rolled around on the ground and their ferocious growls echoed through the jungle. Moving with supernatural speed, they bit, clawed, and slashed at each other. After a minute that seemed like an eternity, his father began to overpower the other leopard. He raked claws across the creature's belly, and bright flashes of red bloomed on its stomach. As the leopard bellowed in pain, his father batted the cat in the head a few times and soon the creature lay still beneath him.

Simultaneously, the Dowager ran forward with a roar that echoed with blood-curdling rage. When she flung out her paw, Nate could feel and see the force of the *fuerza* as she knocked aside another of the leopards, throwing the cat into the unwitting human that held the weapon. The rifle flew out the man's hands as the big cat hit him, and both man and cat went sprawling.

His mother didn't move a muscle. Still, somehow, she knocked the other two leopards to the ground. One second, the cats were standing. In the next moment, they were on the ground on their sides looking dazedly and fearfully up at the Bastion. Only then did she move, leaping atop one of the downed cats and swatting it ferociously, just once, in the head. The leopard's eyes rolled back into its head and then closed.

All three below seemed to have momentarily forgotten about the final human. During the melee, he had picked up the weapon the other man had dropped. Now he raised the it, pointing it at his mother who now stood over the other cat, preparing to strike.

Nate tried to call out to them, but fear trapped his voice in his throat. He crept to the edge of the branch, looking at the jungle floor below. It was so far, at least twice as far as the distance from the deck to the ground at home. He glanced behind him at the tree trunk. That would take too long. He had to do something now.

Without another thought, Nate crouched and launched himself from the tree towards the human. This time there were no flailing arms or fear. Every thought was on stopping the man who seemed intent on hurting his mother.

He tried to aim himself at the man's back but he overshot, arcing over the man's head and landing on the ground between the man and his mother. The man started, shifting his gaze from Anna to Nate. Along with his gaze, he swiveled the gun too, and Nate found himself staring into the barrel of the weapon.

The next thing happened so fast that Nate barely had time to realize what was going on before it was over. He felt the *fuerza* surge again like hot lava into his body, filling him until he thought that he would explode. Just when he thought that he couldn't hold any more energy, it rushed out of his feet and back into the ground.

Nate felt the ground move beneath his feet. The earth shook and cracked beneath his feet and, splintering outward, exploded under the man and tossed him several feet into the air. The man flew backward, with a look of utter fear and surprise on his face. For what seemed like forever, he hung suspended in mid-air. Then, just as quickly, he fell on his back and was still.

Then the clearing was completely silent. The battle was over. All around lay their enemies in varying states of consciousness. Two humans and three leopards. Nate paused, confused. That wasn't right. He did a recount. His eyes had not deceived him. The fourth leopard had indeed disappeared.

Abruptly, Nate felt the heavy weight of his parents' and

grandmother's gaze on him. At the same time, a heavy wave of nausea hit him as the sick energy from the ground beneath his feet overwhelmed him. He could only take one stumbling step toward the man before collapsing to the ground.

When he opened his eyes again, all three of the adults stood over him in human form. They had moved him. Instead of lying on the cracked and dry earth, he was now surrounded by verdant, green blooms. He felt the *fuerza* seeping into his body, and with every moment he felt himself growing stronger.

"Are you okay," his mother asked kneeling down beside him. Nate opened his mouth to speak and all that came out was a growl. He realized he was still in panther form. Concentrating, he willed his body to shift. Luckily, this time his panther was too weary to fight him. Then he stood on wobbly knees with his mother's help.

"I think so," he finally replied when he was standing. His mother grabbed him, squeezing his arms and legs and then touching his face as though looking for injuries. But all Nate felt was amazement.

"I'm fine, Mom," he insisted again, pulling away from her and taking another halting step towards the man, who was still unconscious on the ground. Even from where he stood, Nate could see the huge, bright red knot that was rapidly forming on one side of the man's forehead.

"Did I do that?" he questioned.

Anna glanced at the man and then back at her son. "I think that you did," she whispered in wonder.

"How?" Nate asked, equally awed.

Anna and the Dowager exchanged a significant glance, and then a flurry of movement interrupted any further conversation. The reinforcements had arrived.

Anna turned away from her son and walked over to the first leopard. She knelt next to the cat and placed one hand on its chest and the other on the ground. Nate saw her mouth move and then watched, bewildered, as the leopard's fur began to retract to reveal her human form, a dark woman with short curly hair. She repeated the same with the other two leopards, one a short, burly man with shoulder length brown hair and the other a tall, slender man.

By the time she had finished, the guard had arrived in the clearing. They all shifted into human form and Nate was not surprised to see the familiar faces of Bailey and Marcus among the group. The girl, however, was almost unrecognizable. Tears glimmered in her eyes as she ran across the clearing and threw her arms around his mother. Anna hugged the girl long and hard in return, before pulling away to give instructions to the four other guards that had entered the clearing. At her order, the guards bound the three leopards and two humans. For the first time in several generations, the Panteria dungeons would be filled.

Standing with his grandmother, he watched as the guards began to carry the prisoners away.

"What about the other one?" he asked, looking up at the woman.

"There will be time for him later," she answered, her face grim. Though she could not be certain, she had a good idea who the fourth leopard had been. Time would reveal whether or not her suspicions were correct.

The two stood silently together as they watched Nate's mother and father confer with Marcus and Bailey, who had stayed behind to get further instructions.

"Grandmother," Nate said, tentatively, the word feeling strange on his tongue. The woman standing at his side looked down at him at last, her heart curiously light at the sound of that particular title.

"Yes," she asked.

"That thing I did with the *fuerza*, will I be able to learn how to control it one day?"

"Yes," she answered with a smile.

Nate grinned, surprised that he could smile after all that he had been through. "Where do I sign up?"

She smiled more broadly, wrapping her arm around his shoulder. "All in good time. And Nate," she paused, waiting for the child to meet her eyes, "call me Mimi."

Chapter 32

Too Little May Be Too Late

Nate was completely unprepared for the crowd and the cheers that greeted them as they entered the Kula's gates. The whole of Panteria, it seemed, had gathered there to celebrate the Bastion's return, and the courtyard was filled with smiling, joyful faces.

His mother waved to the people who shouted her name as she passed. She smiled gratefully as they tossed flowers in her path.

Nate marched resolutely through the crowd, which parted before their band, looking neither right nor left. With each cheer, his lip curled in something akin to derision.

These were the very same people who, just a few days ago, had almost decided to let his mother rot out in the jungle. They were the same people who could not find anything to say in his mother's defense when she needed them the most. And now they wanted to cheer? There was something so wrong about that.

The group, which consisted of Nate, the Dowager,

the Bastion, and Robert, made their way through the courtyard to the stairs that led to the Inner Kula. There his mother led them to the Bastion's Chamber. While Robert and Marisol continued onward, through the small door to the Bastion's library, Anna walked to the front of the room and stood for long moments before the Seat of the Bastion.

Nate silently watched his mother, who was slightly skinnier, but otherwise no worse for wear from her imprisonment, as some unreadable emotion worked on her face. Finally, she stepped up onto the dais and collapsed wearily into her Seat. It was then that she looked over at her son and gestured to the chair at her right.

Nate hesitated, feeling somehow intrusive, but then he walked forward. He stepped onto the dais and immediately felt the surge of power enter his body. The energy both soothed and refreshed him, and suddenly the exhaustion from their battle began to fade away. He looked wonderingly down at the gray slab of stone that was the dais. Though he could not see anything unusual about the stone, the power of the *fuerza* was unmistakable, and the stone was filled with it.

He moved forward and sat down in the chair next to his mother. That chair, too, sang with the energy of the *fuerza*. It coursed through him, relaxing his tense muscles and calming his still churning stomach. Both he and his mother were silent for long moments, as the energy flowed through them, healing them. Finally, Nate spoke.

"Why didn't you tell us?" His words, even though they were spoken softly, echoed through the empty chamber in the silence that followed his question. He leaned forward in the chair, turning to face his mother, who at once looked all the more tired. Minutes later, she sighed and spoke.

"I never wanted this," she confessed, shaking her head. "I never wanted to be Bastion…. And I wanted Larissa to have the choice that I did not have."

She paused and then looked at Nate with astonishment in her eyes. "I didn't want you," she corrected herself, "to feel that this life was forced on you…the way that I always did."

The weight of the confession seemed to sap all of her remaining energy. She stopped speaking and leaned her head against the back of the chair, her eyes closed. The stones above her head glowed intensely, like little green beacons.

Nate leaned back too, turning her words over and over in his mind even as he basked in the rejuvenating energy that flowed through him. Even with that revelation, he knew there was so much of the story that he still did not know.

He glanced over at his mother. Her hands lay across the armrests and her head leaned to one side as though she had fallen asleep. She looked utterly exhausted. Now was not the time to press for more answers. After another long moment, he spoke.

"You have to be more honest with us, Mom," he said. "I just wish you would tell us what is going on from now on. Ris and I aren't kids anymore. We can handle it."

At his words, Anna opened her eyes and turned toward him. He met her gaze intently and earnestly.

"Okay sweetheart," she promised. I'll try, she added to herself.

CHAPTER 33

HOMECOMING

"ARE WE READY?" THE question came from Mimi, who was seated at the head of the table in the place of honor. Before her was spread a lavish meal of roast beef, roast lamb, broiled salmon, mashed potatoes, and steak tartar. It was a meal fit for a king, or something of a queen as the case seemed to be. Of course, the only thing that the Dowager would eat was the steak tartar. She adamantly refused to eat cooked meat.

Prepared over a long day of cooking, the meal had an air of celebration. It was their first since they had come from Panteria late the night before, returning to the human world and all of its familiar comforts.

"Just about," Anna called from the stove, where she was dishing up the last of the meal.

"Really, Anna," his grandmother said. "Making us wait over some stringy green plant. We're leopards for land's sakes." Nate chuckled at Mimi's words. He was beginning to like her more and more.

His mother turned from the stove, walked to the table, and placed the dish in the center. Green beans. He could not stop himself from rolling his eyes, even as a broad smile played on his lips. His mother, always trying to feed vegetables to cats.... It was good to be home. For Nate, at least, their return had been too long in coming.

In the week that had passed since they had captured the five prisoners, he and Larissa had barely seen their parents or their grandmother, all of whom were leading the interrogations. Despite his mother's promise, his parents remained customarily tight-lipped about the questioning, which frustrated Nate more and more with each passing day, even as he tried to give them the benefit of the doubt.

For the last week or so, almost all of their information had come from a most surprising source. Bailey, who had treated the twins with a new air of grudging respect since the prisoners had been captured and the Bastion had returned, was willing to tell them the things that their parents would not. From her, they learned that the humans had been easy to intimidate, but they knew nothing. They didn't know who was behind the mines or even about what happened to the rough once it left Panteria. They were simply following orders from the leopards.

The leopards, on the other hand, had posed some difficulties for the interrogators. They had been harder to break. How difficult it was and what had been done to get them to talk, Bailey would not say. But when they did start talking, it turned out that they had not known much more than the humans. James had been the one in charge, or so they all claimed.

As the Dowager had suspected, the fourth leopard turned out to be James. When no one had seen or heard from him for more than two days after the battle near the mine, they reached the conclusion that he was in hiding in the human world. No one in Panteria seemed to know much about what James did or the places that he frequented though. The IBG was contemplating mounting a full-fledged search. Such a task would be daunting.

The only upside to the whole thing was that the mining seemed to have stopped entirely. Scouts had been patrolling the area constantly since the rains stopped, and there was no sign of renewed activity. Also, his mother and the Dowager managed to locate the portal through which the interlopers had entered Panteria. Bailey could not say anything more specific than that it had been located and destroyed.

The next step was a trial for the leopards, which their mother, as Bastion, would preside over. The leopards, Bailey said, had committed crimes that amounted to treason against all Panterians. The punishment for their crimes was the most extreme in all of Panterian law. Expatriation. Nate still wasn't quite sure what that meant, but he could tell that it was something serious from the way the girl whispered the word.

The trials would begin in a few weeks. So here they were, home at last.

As soon as the last dish was on the table, the family began to dig in, all eating to their hearts' content. Anna and Robert scooped serving after serving onto their plates as though still trying to make up for all of the meals that they had lost while in captivity. Larissa, too, ate more than usual, which Nate was glad to see. Her appetite had taken a long time to return after her recovery.

The conversation was happy, though halting. The twins were slowly learning more about their grandmother, whom they were getting more and more used to calling Mimi. They were also very excited to be home. Nate would have never thought that he could be so happy to see a television, and Larissa could hardly wait to hang out with Miko and Kayla. It had been almost a month since she had talked to or seen them. That was like ten years in girl time.

At Larissa's mention of her friends, Nate suddenly remembered Ray. Ray, who had been waiting weeks for an explanation. He would have to do something about Ray very soon. Finally, all five pushed away from the table, sated and content.

He and Larissa stood to clear the table, but Anna gestured for them to return to their seats. Her face was suddenly strained and serious. Nate and Larissa looked at each other confused, and slowly lowered themselves back into their chairs.

"I am going to have to be in Panteria for the trials." There was hesitation in her voice. The twins nodded. Bailey had warned them to expect that.

"I will probably be gone for a while," their mother continued. "Maybe until the end of the summer. Possibly longer." This part of the announcement caught the twins completely off guard. There were still more than six weeks left in the summer. They had not thought that the trials would take so long. Larissa said as much.

"Panterian trials are long. Thorough," their mother explained. "The proposed punishment, expatriation, is the harshest in all of Panterian law and it is irrevocable. I want to make sure that all get a fair hearing."

Nate couldn't believe his ears. He did not understand why, after all that they had done, his mother was so intent on making sure that the prisoners had their say. If he had been in charge, he would have thrown the book at them before they had a chance to open their mouths.

"I have to be there until we get to the bottom of things," she continued, with a bit of resignation. "I didn't want this," she said, pausing to look at her own mother with both an apology and a small bit of defiance mingled in her expression. "I didn't want this," she repeated "but being the Bastion is my duty. For the last thirteen years, I have made this family my priority—in ways that have been unfair to the rest of the Kulan. Panteria needs me now, and as their Bastion, I have to be there."

"When do you have to go," Larissa asked, breaking the silence which had stretched on after that pronouncement. She sounded far more understanding than Nate felt.

"Tomorrow or day the after," was the soft reply.

That was the final straw for Nate. He glared down at his empty plate, his knife and fork clinched in one hand. Here she was again, springing something on them at the very last moment. So much for being upfront and honest. He couldn't tell if anything else was being said, he could only hear the refrain, you promised, that echoed through his mind again and again.

"How long have you known," he asked when he could finally manage to speak.

He looked up just in time to see his mother flash a guilty glance at his father. He shook his head in disbelief and asked again.

"For a while now," Anna admitted.

The two stared at each other, tension crackling between them. The other three at the table were silent.

"You promised," he said aloud, his voice more strident than he meant it to be. He flashed his eyes to Larissa, who studiously gazed at the table cloth. She wasn't going to be any help here.

"I know I did sweetheart," his mother began gently, but he wouldn't let her finish.

"No 'buts', Mom," he interrupted. "You promised. I really thought things were finally changing, but it's just going to be more of the same isn't it?"

"That's enough Nathanial," Anna said, breaking off further protestations.

Nate, who had been about to say more, snapped his mouth

shut. After everything that had happened, nothing had really changed. His parents would still keep their secrets, and the CKC zone was still very much in effect. Perhaps it would never change.

"So you are just going to leave again to go and protect a bunch of people who would have left you to rot in the jungle," he muttered bitterly, crossing his arms over his chest.

Larissa glanced up. She did not have to think or say anything. Her look was all reproach.

What? It's true. Nate thought to his sister, dismissing her reproving gaze.

"They are my people honey. I am their leader, and it's high time I started acting like it."

"But they don't care about you Mom," he said earnestly. "None of them would defend you when James was saying all of that horrible stuff. They were going to just elect a new leader. Like it was nothing. Why do you have to protect them? Why do you have to care, when they didn't?"

Anna rose from her seat and went to stand next to her son, laying her hand on his shoulder. He flinched away from her, as though her touch caused him pain. Anna stepped back, with a sharp intake of breath. Because he would not look at her, Nate missed the tears that sparkled in her eyes.

"This is my duty. Nate, you must understand. I have to go." There was a pause, and then Anna continued. "And I want you to go with me."

"What?!" Nate and Larissa yelled simultaneously.

"I said that I want you to come with me. Back to Panteria," Anna answered, turning to her daughter.

"Forever," was Larissa's shocked and breathless reply.

"Not forever," their mother said, smiling. "But I was thinking maybe for the rest of the summer. You can get to know more about Panteria. More about what I do."

Larissa's eyes lit up. His mother had used the magic words where Larissa was concerned. There was nothing that his sister loved more than a new adventure and something new to learn. Her curiosity was piqued. Nate knew then that she would go.

"I'm in," she said a few seconds later, proving him right.

Nate narrowed his eyes at his sister. *"Traitor,"* he thought. She raised her eyebrows and shrugged slightly as if to say, what's a girl to do. Then his mother turned expectant eyes on him. His shoulders tensed under the weight of her gaze, and he opened his mouth to speak.

"Think about it before you make up your mind." Anna said, holding up her hand to stop his words. "There is so much that you, both of you," she paused looking intently at Nate, "need to learn."

Nate looked back and forth between his mother and sister. Unable to take the hopefulness that shone in their near identical eyes, he turned to his grandmother. Her face was mercifully blank, but looking at her reminded him of that day in the jungle when he had used the *fuerza* to disarm one of his mother's captors. The adrenaline and the triumph of that moment washed over him in a rush. It was true, there was so much that he still had to learn not only about Panteria but about who and what he was.

Yet when he looked back to his mother again, he felt nothing but anger and disappointment. Anger at her for keeping so many secrets for so long; for keeping the truth about them from him and Larissa. The anger bubbled up, spilling over onto Panteria, the place that was at the roots of all of the secrets. He began shaking his head, before he spoke.

"Nate, they're your people too," Anna added then, a last ditch effort. "You don't understand how important you will be to them one day." But it did not work. In fact, it had the opposite effect.

"No," Nate said, rejecting her words as his anger flared once again. "I don't want to be anything to them."

Anna took a step back, and a hurt look passed fleetingly over her face. "Nate, I don't want to force you...."

It was his turn to stop her.

"You can't force me Mom," he said quietly, staring down at the table. Out of the corner of his eye, he saw Larissa's face fall. He felt his first shred of guilt. Still, try as he might, he couldn't muster an inkling of desire to return to that place. Not even for her. Nevertheless, he said, "I will think about it."

There was a long silence. Though no one spoke, Nate could feel the weight of their disappointment, and, suddenly, he had to get out of that room. He pushed his chair back from the table, heedless of the jarring, scraping noise that it made against the wood floors and was halfway up the steps before anyone could say a word.

At that, the tears that Anna had held back for too long began to trickle down her face. Robert went to his wife, wrapping his arms around her. "He will come around," he whispered, hugging her.

"Will he?" Anna replied. She wasn't so sure.

CHAPTER 34

PROMISES KEPT

Two nights later, Nate stood at his window and watched the rest of his family who had gathered together at the woods' edge. The four stood in the moonlight saying their goodbyes. Over the past few days, Larissa and his father, even Mimi, had tried to convince him to change his mind, but he had refused. His mind was made up. He couldn't return to that place. Not now, and maybe not ever.

So Ris was going without him. It would be the first time in their lives that they would be separated. Even the thought of not seeing Ris was not enough to change his mind. He could not even bring himself to go down there and bid them goodbye.

As he watched, his mother hugged his father and then shifted. The sequence was repeated twice more and then three panthers, two large and one medium, stood on the lawn next to the man. Nate watched as first his mother and then his grandmother walked through the garden and disappeared into the woods. Finally, Ris walked forward.

Suddenly she stopped, turned, and looked up at his window. Green eyes locked with green eyes and he wondered what she was thinking. The distance was too great to tell. Finally, Nate let the shade drop and walked away from the window.

He picked up the phone and went and sat down on the edge

of his bed. For a long time he didn't do anything but stare at the numbers. At last, taking a deep breath, he dialed.

"Can you meet me in thirty minutes. Near the swings at the park around the corner from your house?" Seconds later, he hung up the phone and put on his shoes.

As Nate sat on the swing waiting for Ray to arrive, he pondered what he was about to do. The playground was at the center of the park, far away from any streets and passing cars. At that time of night, the park was also completely deserted. If he actually was going to go through with his plan, it was the perfect place.

He still wasn't sure that it was the right thing. He did know that there would be no turning back once it was done. His stomach twisted in knots and he rose from the swing to pace a few indecisive steps. There was still time to leave.

Nate heard a rustle of movement and smelled the faintest whiff of coffee floating on the breeze. Ray was in the park, but he wasn't in eyesight yet. He didn't have much time to change his mind now.

What he was contemplating would be a serious breach of Pantera Family Laws and he could only begin to guess what his parents would say if they knew. He felt a sudden rush of anger and kicked the ground. It didn't matter what his parents would say. He was tired of the Pantera Family Laws.

For his entire life he had listened to them, trusted them, and followed them without question, and what had that gotten him. If there was anything that he had learned in the last few weeks, it was that those rules seemed to cause more problems than they solved. Maybe it was time for some new rules, starting with tonight.

Besides, Ray's questions were not going away.

"What's up?" Ray asked warily, walking out of the shadows and up to the playground. He walked as far as the slide and then he stopped, not coming any closer.

Nate's palms began to sweat. He was suddenly quite nervous. The silence stretched on between the two boys while Nate worked up his courage. Finally, he spoke.

"I promised I would explain," he said quietly.

"Yeah," Ray responded. He moved forward a couple of steps and sat down at the bottom of the slide. He was slightly less wary now that his interest was piqued.

"But first you have to promise that you will never say anything about what I tell you tonight. If you can't promise me that, I can't tell you anything."

Ray considered Nate's words, and then Nate added, "Take your time and decide, because it is a promise that I can and will make you keep."

Ray gave him a glance that was both intense and measuring. Then, slowly, he nodded his head. "Okay."

"Okay," Nate replied, as a flood of nervous energy entered his body. When he spoke again, his words came out in a hurried breath. "Well, my explanation kind of has to happen in person. It's something that you have to see to believe." Then he stopped and a silence enveloped the playground.

"And..." Ray pressed after a few moments. Instead of answering, Nate ducked behind the jungle gym. When he stepped back out, all that he wore was his P. E. suit.

Ray gaped at him, clearly trying to figure out Nate's strange attire. "Does this have something to do with it," he finally asked, wholly confused.

Nate ignored his question saying instead, "There is a reason that my eyes looked weird that day." With that, Nate closed his eyes and called to his panther. The beast came quickly this time, eager to be free.

"Nate," he heard Ray call his name. "Nate, what's going on?" It was over in seconds and when he opened his eyes, Ray was staring at him, his mouth wide open. "Nate?" This time his name was a question. Nate nodded his head yes.

"No way," came Ray's response. Nate closed his eyes again, pushed the panther away, and shifted back. In moments, he stood before Ray in his human form.

"I'm a shape-shifter Ray. That is why I am as strong as I am. That's why I can do the things that I do. Now you know the truth. And now you know why no one else can find out."

Epilogue

"The others are to stand trial," James reported to the woman who sat behind the desk. His arm rested on his stomach, which still had not quite healed from the battle. "And I have been compromised. It is no longer safe for me to return to Panteria."

She rose and walked over to the window, her long skirts swishing across the hardwood and churning curiously around her feet. James's news was unexpected. This was not how she had planned it. She had known that the mining would eventually be stopped, but she had hoped to have a while longer to sow the necessary seeds for the final stage of the plan.

On the other hand, the news from the meeting of the Kulan had been promising. Maybe there was not as much work to be done as she had once thought. Still, it was imperative to keep the discord alive, in order to achieve the end goal. That would be especially hard to do now that the Bastion had returned to Panteria. For some reason, she had not anticipated that turn of events.

Turning from the window, she hobbled over to the mirror. Its gilded frame was studded with panterite stones that glowed softly as she neared them. Looking in the mirror, she raised a hand to smooth her straight blue-black hair. Hers was a perfect face, almost as perfect as her lower half was warped. Shaking away the thought and the ire that it always raised, she turned her mind to the Bastion.

Maybe what they needed was a distraction. Something to draw the Bastion out of Panteria and away from her duties for good. Staring past her reflection, she caught James' gaze.

"We're moving to phase three," she said.

James considered her words. "Do you think that is wise," he asked. "This is far sooner than you had planned. Are you sure that we have enough rough?" His queries were quelled by the anger that began to smolder in her yellow-flecked green eyes.

"Do we have a problem James," she asked raising an eyebrow.

"No, mistress," James answered hurriedly. "I will instruct the others to initiate phase three." With that, James was dismissed.

The woman left the study and made her way up the stairs to the bedrooms on the second floor. Though the stairs were really quite difficult for her, she wanted only the best for her Charlie. Opening the door to the first room at the top of the stairs, she looked in on the girl who lay sleeping in the bed.

Like her, the child had straight black hair and peaches and cream complexion. Like her, the girl's eyes, which were now closed, were green, flecked with yellow. Unlike her, her daughter was absolutely perfect in every way. She gazed lovingly at the child that she had worked so hard for. She was the reason for everything.

Stooping down, she picked up a pair of sweatpants that lay on the floor. She shook out the bottoms of the Greendale High gym uniform and folded them neatly, placing them on the desk that sat near the door.

She closed the door quietly and continued down the hall to her room. Her daughter would be the next Bastion of the wereleopards, even if she had to destroy Panteria to make it so.